AF426958

THE FALL OF VALDEK

PETER NEALEN

aethonbooks.com

[1]

"THE DATA FROM THE FIRST SCANS IS COMING IN, CENTURION," Captain Brecan Mor reported over the *Dauntless*'s intercom. "The yeheri 'task force' is in orbit above the second moon of Iabreton, as expected. Initial assessments have tentatively identified two battle-cruisers, two frigates, and what appears to be a heavy transport."

Centurion Erekan Scalas was strapped into his acceleration couch aboard the *Dauntless*'s lead dropship, roughly amidships and several decks below the command deck where Captain Mor was watching the starship's holo-tank from a not dissimilar position. Every Caractacan Brother aboard the starship was armored, sealed, and strapped in. Anything else would be tantamount to suicide. They were about to go into combat.

He did some quick math in his head. That many ships could mean that there was as much as a regiment of yeheri fighters on the ground. After all, they'd already had some time to deploy.

"How far out are we?" he asked.

"Still sixty-two light-minutes," Mor replied. Which meant that the information was likely outdated. The *Dauntless* was still fully inertialess, though the Bergenholm fields had been turned down to the point that she was no longer tachyonic. The drive was pointed toward the gas giant Iabreton, the system's sole major body, firing just hard enough to gradually slow the ship. None of the Brotherhood aboard could feel it; they would have to go fully inert for the acceleration to register, and that wouldn't happen until they were far closer to their target.

Scalas looked around the interior of the dropship. The First Squad of Century XXXII of the Caractacan Brotherhood, twenty consummate soldiers encased in the best armor that human ingenuity could produce, was strapped into the cramped circle of the hold. They were faceless behind their helmets' vision slits, looking like little more than gray-green automatons, dull, matte armor festooned with ammunition packs, comm antennas, and other specialized gear. Weapons were secured in racks alongside their acceleration couches.

"Two battlecruisers, two frigates, and possibly one heavy transport," he relayed to the rest of the squad, and to the squad sergeants in their separate dropships, with the rest of the century. "That means we could be facing up to a regiment in strength on the ground."

There were no complaints, no exclamations, no chest-thumping displays of bravado. There were some nods of faceless helmets. Scalas was not a man given to much emotion, but he felt a surge of pride and satisfaction at the calm way his hundred men received the news that they would probably be terribly outnumbered. He might not be able to see their faces, but he knew every Brother in that compartment by sight, even in armor. They were Caractacan Brothers. They were *supposed* to be outnumbered.

"We will engage the ships on the first pass, and if conditions merit, deploy you and your century before returning to mop up," Mor continued.

"Understood," Scalas replied. Behind his visor, he allowed himself a half-grin. "Are you certain you're not biting off too much for only one pass?"

"The yeheri are not known for the quality of their so-called 'battlecruisers,'" Mor replied tartly. "Nor for their skill at space combat.

You worry about the ground deployment, Centurion. Leave the orbitals to me."

There was a general chuckle around the dropship's troop compartment; the exchange had been on the century's open comm circuit. Scalas smiled as he flexed his shoulders and settled himself a bit more comfortably in his acceleration couch. "Brace yourselves, gentlemen," he said. "Captain Mor's admitted mastery notwithstanding, this could get a little bumpy."

Captain Mor was not quite as stoic as his friend Erekan Scalas. He was grinning tightly behind his sealed helmet visor as the exchange ended. It was rare, usually only in the tense moments before combat, that he could get Erekan to come far enough out of his shell to actually banter with him. The man was usually as quiet and dour as a cloistered monk. Granted, such temperament and deportment were encouraged in the Caractacan Brotherhood, but it sometimes seemed as if Scalas took his bearing as a Brother slightly *too* seriously.

Mor turned his attention fully to the task at hand. The distances and timeframes of space battle were deceptive. A moment's lapse in concentration could mean instant death for all aboard.

The *Dauntless* had already executed her synchronization maneuver, going fully inert just outside the system and matching her base velocity to Iabreton's star. At the same time, the attack vector had been laid in. The maneuvers had been done far enough out that the yeheri would not detect the drive plume for another ninety-seven minutes. That time to detection would steadily decrease as the ship plummeted closer to Iabreton, but for the moment, they were still in the "blind spot" of the enemy's light cone.

Iabreton swelled steadily in the command deck's holo-tank. The command crew's couches were bolted to the deck in a circle around the tank, granting each officer a clear view of the overall situation in addition to their more specialized displays projected on plates in front of them. Controls were close by their hands, allowing for every function of the ship to be handled even when under high gees.

"Now," Mor snapped.

The *Dauntless*'s Bergenholm fields shut down. All the inertia set in during the synchronization maneuver returned, and she hurtled toward the gas giant's second moon at hundreds of kilometers per second.

As soon as the inertialess field was off, the starship's weapons constellation began to deploy. Hatches along the outer hull opened, and a string of egg-shaped X-ray laser pods drifted outward, propelled by tiny gas charges. At the same time, canisters in the starship's nose cone fired, sending clouds of pellets and reflective chaff ahead, drifting a few hundred meters per second faster than the ship. Point-defense lasers were unshrouded, powergun turrets rose from the hull on long, telescoping booms, and missiles drifted out of their launch cells, stabilizing a few dozen meters from the hull. The missiles didn't need to be nearly as far away as the bomb-pumped X-ray laser pods.

Iabreton loomed large, a massive, roiling, green-and-orange crescent of storms and exotic gasses. The dark side flickered with lightnings the size of planets. The second moon was currently a tiny point of light, just over the limb of the gas giant, but was quickly growing larger.

As the *Dauntless* closed, the moon grew to a reddish, rocky ball, with the faint flickers of drive flares in space above it. The yeheri had clearly noticed the starship plummeting toward them, and they were now maneuvering to meet the coming attack.

"Focus on the battlecruisers first," Mor instructed. "We can clean up the frigates later, if need be."

He watched the tank closely, counting down in his head even as the weapons officers worked out their firing solutions. The X-ray lasers would fire line-straight and light-swift, but even then, at that distance their targeting could only project probability cones for enemy positions. The missiles and powergun bolts would be even trickier.

Mor didn't concern himself with the firing solutions. His command crew was just as skilled and finely honed as Scalas' armored ground pounders, ensconced in their dropships below. His responsibility was timing and strategy. Engaging any farther out than a light-minute was generally folly; there were too many variables that couldn't be accounted for based on information that old. And yet, waiting too long to engage could give the enemy a chance to get in a kill shot first.

It was jousting, just like armored knights on long-lost Terra, thousands of years before. Only with energy weapons, guided kinetic kill munitions, and high explosives, at velocities that a man on horseback could never have imagined.

"Open fire."

The first wave of missiles ignited their drives and streaked away at fifty gees. Moments later, actinic flashes out in the dark on the ship's flanks announced the deaths of X-ray laser pods as the weapons immolated themselves with the nuclear explosions that drove the powerful directed energy weapons. They were one-shot devices, just like the missiles.

A moment later, the powergun batteries opened fire, pulsing blue-white streaks toward the reddish orb of Iabreton II. At these distances, the relativistic packets of copper plasma actually appeared as discrete bolts.

A ravening storm of high-energy destruction blazed toward the enemy ships in orbit over Iabreton's second moon.

The yeheri battlecruisers were ugly, *ad hoc* constructs, with mushroom-shaped forward hulls kept far away from temperamental reactors and drives by long, slender booms. And they were about as high-tech as they looked. As a race, the yeheri were relative newcomers to the galaxy at large. They didn't have centuries of starship design behind them.

This particular band was also led by a fat, slovenly, careless lout who had been far more focused on cracking the last of the Quarisian resistance in the main mining settlement than in maintaining security for his "task force." As a result, the self-styled warlord had detected the *Dauntless*'s drive flare only minutes before. So now his ships were relatively low in the gravity well, barely maintaining orbital velocity—which wasn't high, given Iabreton II's gravity—and with half their weapons not yet ready to deploy.

For the flagship, there would not be time to remedy that mistake. The battlecruiser suddenly flared with incandescent brilliance as the boom took a direct hit from one of the *Dauntless*'s X-ray lasers. Alloy flared to plasma in a fraction of a second, and the energy dump shattered the rest of the boom with the force of a small nuclear weapon. The battlecruiser detonated silently with a titanic flash, only a fraction of a second after the laser touched it. The four missiles, two more laser beams, and salvos of powergun fire were wasted in the atomized debris.

The second battlecruiser fared rather better. That ship's captain was somewhat more conscientious than their leader—which of course meant that the warlord kept her on an extremely short leash. As soon as the *Dauntless*'s drive plume had been detected, the second battlecruiser's captain had disregarded orders and started accelerating out of the gravity well while deploying the first of her ship's countermeasures. That was why the first salvo of X-ray laser beams missed. Mostly. One struck the chaff cloud deployed above the climbing starship, spending most of its energy in a coruscating display of brilliance all but drowned out by the titanic flash of the flagship's demise. Radiation scoured away the top layers of the surviving battlecruiser's hull, melting sensors and weapons emplacements.

Then the powergun salvo arrived.

White-hot, coherent packets of copper ions flashed around the starship. Several missed, either tearing off into space where they would continue for nearly a light-year before becoming too attenuated to do much damage to anything, or else spending their fury against the thin atmosphere and crust of Iabreton II. Three struck home, detonating through hull and decks, venting entire compartments to space at the same time that the sheer thermal and kinetic energy release turned the crew inside into scorched debris. A fourth struck the reactor. The battlecruiser turned into a small sun, bringing a third dawn to the surface below.

Then the *Dauntless* was overhead, whipping past the moon at well over escape velocity, her drive plume a blinding dagger of blue-white fire ahead of her, dropships spilling from her hatches as her powerguns hammered at the two frigates that were either just rising above the moon's horizon or beginning to dip below it. A glancing hit on one killed a dozen yeheri in a fraction of a second. The other managed to get enough chaff in the way that the hull held when the remains of the plasma bolt got through. Then the Caractacan starship was gone, dwindling into the distance toward the dark limb of the gas giant even as the dropships decelerated savagely, falling toward the reddish surface below.

Scalas endured the gees as the dropship fell atop a thundering pillar of fire. The Brothers were trained to endure prolonged entries at up to six gees, and this was only five. Furthermore, his armor was designed to keep its weight off his chest under acceleration. Still, it was difficult to breathe. For a man to suddenly weigh half a metric ton is not easy on the human body, no matter how well-trained and honed that body is.

A holographic representation of the descent was being projected on his eyeslit. The five truncated cones of the century's dropships were beginning to glow and shake from the increasing friction of the moon's meager atmosphere. Still, this was nothing compared to the fiery blaze of atmospheric entry on a larger world. Besides, the drive plumes were also carving their way through the upper atmosphere, lessening the air resistance on the ships themselves.

"Five minutes!" came the warning from the cockpit.

The acceleration didn't lessen; if anything, the pressure seemed to increase. The pilot was throttling up, trying to dump as much velocity as possible before slamming into the ground below. Scalas's vision darkened, but he forced himself to stay conscious. The minutes ticked away with agonizing slowness. The shaking intensified, then started to smooth out.

"Thirty seconds!"

The pressure eased as the pilot throttled back. They were now descending at only one gee, and the Brothers quickly unclasped their weapons and prepared to deploy.

It was not a gentle landing. The dropship hit hard, the pistons in the landing legs compressing fully to absorb some of the shock of the multi-ton lander's impact. Every armored form in the troop compartment was hammered deeper into his acceleration couch.

Then the dropship doors were falling open. Scalas punched the release on his harness and rolled out of his couch, heaving himself to his feet and charging down the still-descending ramp, sprinting for the nearest cover. In four-fifths of a gee, it was more a series of long bounds than a proper sprint, but in seconds, he was down on a knee behind a rise, his powergun in his shoulder, scanning the broken ground around them.

The dropships had landed some distance away from the enemy emplacements, the pilot having picked the drop zone on the fly as he observed the visible enemy dispositions from above. All the information had been relayed to the ground troops via holo display on the descent, so they all knew where they were, as well as where the enemy was.

Scalas found himself and his century deployed on the bottom of what might have been a meteorite crater. The crater rim rose slowly above them and fell away to the west, where it had collapsed at some distant time in the past. The dusty ground underfoot was reddish, though there was plenty of iron-gray mixed in. There was no sign of vegetation. If there ever had been any on this moon, it was long since dead, killed by a waning atmosphere, or perhaps by the radiation sleeting from nearby Iabreton. The Brothers' armor would shield them from the radiation, at least until the job was done.

Scalas's own armor was already starting to shift to the same reddish hue as the dust. At least, in most places. The armor's chameleonic surfacing was always the first victim of wear and tear, impact, and in many cases, battle damage. Many of the Caractacan Brotherhood bore their armor's scars as badges of honor, often to the armorers' exasperation. Scalas's was as scarred as anyone's, but where the coating was still intact, it would soon be a perfectly camouflaged dusty red.

He looked left and right. The four tactical squads deployed quickly, spreading out and finding cover, setting security around the drop zone and watching for an enemy counterattack. There had been no way to miss the detonations in the sky, let alone the meteoric descent of the dropships. The yeheri pirates knew they were coming.

Fifth Squad was acting as the heavy weapons squad, and was already lugging the rocket mortar batteries out of their dropship and deploying the bulky weapons in the center of the drop zone. They wouldn't have much to shoot at until the tactical squads got eyes on the enemy positions, but the fire support would be welcome when the time came.

Satisfied that the landing had gone according to plan and that his men were oriented as they should be, Scalas rose and started jogging toward the crater rim.

The slope turned out to be steeper than it looked, and by the time he was halfway up, with most of First Squad spread out in a loose wedge behind him, he was down to a slog, even in the relatively light gravity. His armor's articulation ensured that its weight was well-supported and distributed, and thanks to the oxygen tank in his sustainment pack, he wasn't even breathing hard, but the footing was difficult and treacherous. The crater wall had had centuries to erode, and sand and dust constantly threatened to slip out from under his boots.

He slowed even further as he neared the lip of the crater rim. It appeared to be the highest point of the surrounding terrain, and while the Caractacan Brotherhood had a well-deserved reputation for aggressiveness on the battlefield, none of them were stupid. There would be no screaming charge here. He got close to the edge, dropped to a knee, and crept up to peer down the slope beyond.

The Quarisian mining camp was a scattershot collection of squared-off prefabs—about what Scalas had expected. Quarisia was a poor world and couldn't afford much more, which only made the yeheri attack that much more indefensible. At least three of the prefabs near the open-pit mine had already been destroyed.

The Quarisian defenders had dug in along the edge of the pit and were trading fire across relatively open ground with the yeheri troops, who were centered on a group of mushroom-shaped landers that squatted haphazardly on the plain between the Brotherhood and the Quarisian camp. Some of these forces, including a collection of blocky, balloon-tired, armored fighting vehicles, were attempting to reorient to face the incoming Caractacans. Scalas's eyes narrowed behind his vision slit as he watched. Mor had spoken disparagingly of the yeheri's reputation as space fighters. This band didn't appear to be much better on the ground.

He brought his powergun to his shoulder and found the holographic sight with his eye. The yeheri combatants were still a good distance off, and even though the powerguns fired their bolts very nearly line-straight at a substantial fraction of the speed of light, a small target is still a small target, and the plasma packets tended to attenuate more in atmosphere. Scalas had little doubt that he *could* hit at this distance… but it was always better to be sure.

He took his finger away from the trigger and got ready to move.

Searching for the next bit of cover, he went up over the lip of the crater rim, dashed down the slope, and dropped to a low knee behind a boulder. The rest of the squad followed, bounding forward in short dashes, either finding rocks to take cover behind or cracks in the ground, or even simply dropping prone when no better cover presented itself. Fire discipline held; just like their centurion, the Brothers would open fire when they were sure of kill shots, not before.

Scalas paused just before a landslide, where part of the outer crater wall had sloughed away, and checked distances and azimuths before relaying them to the heavy weapons squad back in the crater. He got a terse acknowledgment, and a moment later, the noise muted by the thin atmosphere, the rocket mortars were coughing skyward, each warhead aimed precisely, sight unseen.

The camouflaged Caractacan Brothers were practically invisible, dusty-red figures against a dusty-red backdrop, popping up for only a few seconds before dropping behind cover or out of sight altogether. That did not stop the yeheri from opening fire anyway.

A ragged fusillade of lasers, powergun bolts, and solid bullets ripped out from the equally ragged yeheri formation, blasting pits in the dirt and rocks around the advancing Caractacans. Many of the bullets were falling short, but the lasers, sometimes dimly visible in the drifting dust, and the brilliant powergun bolts, were getting much closer.

The Caractacan Brothers usually preferred precise, accurate fire, but there were times when volume counted for a lot. The squad support gunners began returning fire with their MT-41 heavy power-guns, sending sheets of brilliant discharges across the open ground and forcing the yeheri back into cover. The rate of incoming fire slowed significantly, but it did not die out altogether. Some of the yeheri were crouched behind cover and shooting blind.

Blind fire is rarely effective, but sometimes luck turns strangely.

Scalas dove into the dirt a moment before a powergun bolt slammed overhead, slapping him with the thunderclap shockwave of the plasma's passage and searing the surface of his armor with its heat. The Brother who tried to bound past him, Korvan, was not so lucky. The next bolt caught him in the faceplate. His helmet exploded, taking most of his head with it, and his armored body fell to the dirt, rolling another two meters downhill before coming to a stop in a cloud of grit.

There are few defenses against a direct hit from a powergun bolt. And as good as it was, even Caractacan armor couldn't stand up to that kind of firepower.

It was about that point when the rocket mortars reached the top of their trajectory, turned over, and ignited their secondary engines, plunging toward the ground at twenty gees. The rounds that hit landers and vehicles were moving fast enough to punch through most of the thin armor. After that, the molecular explosives did the rest. The leading edge of the yeheri company that was moving to engage the Caractacan skirmish line disappeared in a cloud of smoke, dust, and debris. The shockwaves slammed through the thin atmosphere, washing over the Caractacan warriors and shaking the very ground beneath their feet. Landers and vehicles exploded, belching billowing fireballs and clouds of dust and smoke as they died.

Scalas was on his feet and moving forward before the dust had even begun to settle. The rest of his squad wasn't far behind. The yeheri fire had died away to almost nothing in the wake of the bombardment. This was the time.

He plunged into the murk left behind by burning vehicles and airborne dust that was slowly starting to settle back toward the surface. The dust was going to shorten the range of his powergun, but that was a small price to pay.

With Maldon, Brunuk, and Squad Sergeant Kahane close behind him, he advanced on the nearest yeheri lander.

A dazed yeheri, its long tail and hammerhead distinctive even in the haze and hardly disguised by a wildly impractical spiked battle-suit, staggered out from behind the shattered wreckage of a crawler. The vehicle was burning, but the flames were guttering, strangled by the dust and the low oxygen content of the atmosphere.

The yeheri must have spotted some movement, because it turned toward the advancing Caractacans and froze. With a faint yawp, the staggering alien lifted its stubby weapon, at which point four powergun bolts thundered through the dust and smoke to blast its head completely off with a cataclysmic flash. The smoking remains of the corpse collapsed to the dirt.

The line of armored figures continued their advance through the destruction.

[2]

THE PALL OF DUST AND SMOKE FORMED A MASSIVE PILLAR IN THE sky, only slowly dissipating under the assault of Iabreton II's weak, languid winds. In a dispersed crescent, the Caractacans closed in on the wrecked landers and burning vehicles. They still moved cautiously, from cover to cover, careful to avoid exposing themselves for too long.

A man in a Quarisian spacesuit—a bulky, ribbed construct of orange composite that might have been built a century before—ran toward the wrecked lander where Scalas crouched with his squad sergeants. He carried a blocky PS-19 caseless rifle that looked even older than the spacesuit.

He was also trying to move too far without taking cover, and a powergun bolt nearly took his head off. He sprawled on his face in the dust before the Caractacans leaned out of cover and replied to the shot with a crackling fusillade of fire that at least temporarily silenced the yeheri shooter while simultaneously blasting more of the remaining yeheri lander's plating into superheated, glowing scrap.

The man in the spacesuit scrambled back to his feet and sprinted the last few meters to cover. Squad Sergeant Cobb grabbed him and propelled him farther back behind the wreckage. If Cobb perhaps put a bit more force behind the shove than necessary, Scalas didn't bother to say anything about it.

About fifteen more armed Quarisians were huddled in a knot at the edge of the half-ruined settlement, mostly crouched behind wrecked vehicles and in folds in the ground. Their generally orange spacesuits actually served as halfway decent camouflage against the reddish dirt, though the white fittings stood out a bit more. They made for a motley assortment, especially since they weren't all the same shape. Quarisia had been founded as a joint colony after humans and ekuz arrived there at nearly the same time, and the hexapodal ekuz looked wildly different from the humans. An observer would need to know something of their history to understand that both races together were Quarisians.

Scalas took note of the local militia even as he kept his attention on the remaining yeheri lander. He knew he could not discount the Quarisians entirely; in a way, they were as much a danger to his men as the yeheri, especially since these miners had their blood up after enduring days of assaults from the pirates. He certainly understood their mindset. But he also knew just how dangerous it could be.

The yeheri were now cornered and cut off. There had been at least one more flare in the sky, dimly visible through the dust and smoke, doubtlessly heralding the death of another of the yeheri frigates, and the Caractacans on the ground had carved through the assault force relentlessly, one hundred men reaping far higher numbers through a combination of discipline, fire, maneuver, and use of cover. The yeheri survivors were likely on the ragged edge of panic by now, and with nowhere left to run, Scalas expected they'd be willing to sell themselves dearly.

He wasn't willing to sacrifice Brotherhood lives to finish them off. Not at this point. But if the Quarisians tried to assault the lander, the Caractacans would likely *have* to go in, just to keep both sides from getting slaughtered for nothing.

"Leave this last one to us!" the man in the orange spacesuit exclaimed in Trade Cant. He was breathing heavily, his breath rasping through his exterior speaker. "We can take it ourselves!" While his face was disguised by the helmet's faceplate, his thirst for vengeance was impossible to miss.

Scalas didn't turn to look at him, but only held one gauntleted hand up to forestall him. "No," he said, in the same language.

"Maybe we should let them," Squad Sergeant Volscius suggested, in Brotherhood Latin. "If they want to die in a blaze of glory for their own colony, why should we interfere? At least the rest of the miners will be secure."

"No," Scalas repeated. "And that's final. This battle is over. The yeheri know it and we know it. I will not stand by and let the people we came here to protect be slaughtered trying to continue a fight that is already finished."

He continued to watch the last semi-intact yeheri lander. There was some movement around the still-open boarding ramp, which appeared to have been disabled by gunfire, but none of the hammer-headed aliens were showing themselves. Which was wise of them, after the response to that last potshot.

He touched a control on his gauntlet, and his voice boomed from his external speaker. "I am calling any yeheri survivors," he bellowed in Trade Cant. He couldn't be certain that the surviving pirates understood it, but it was the closest thing to an interstellar *lingua franca* there was. "I am Centurion Erekan Scalas of the Caractacan Brotherhood. Your ships have been disabled or destroyed. The rest of your force is dead or dying. If you surrender now, there is a chance that you might be shown leniency. If my Brothers and I have to come in and take that lander by force, no one will survive. I am offering you a chance to surrender."

The yeheri might not have been sure of the identity of their armored attackers before now, but the confirmation that they had just been steamrolled by the Caractacan Brotherhood had to give them pause. Of all the military brotherhoods in the galaxy, it was safe to say that the Caractacans were the most feared and respected, and justly so.

His words were met with silence. For now. But they weren't immediately greeted by a powergun bolt either, and that was a good sign.

"Do you really think they'll accept?" Cobb asked quietly in Latin. "They must know the usual penalty for piracy."

"And that is why I only said there was a *possibility* of leniency," Scalas replied. He and Cobb had served their novitiate together, and if any of his squad sergeants deserved his own century, it was Cobb. "It's a chance. They're cornered, and they know it. To give an enemy a perceived way out is usually a wise move in such circumstances."

Cobb nodded. He understood the logic. He only doubted whether it would work. Scalas doubted as well, but he had to try. It was part of the Brotherhood's Code. They were, ultimately, protectors and defenders. To avoid wholesale slaughter where possible and reasonable was expected of a Caractacan Brother.

There was movement at the ramp. Around Scalas, powerguns lifted fractionally. The Brothers might hope for a surrender, but none of them were going to let their guard down. Certainly not when a moment's inattentiveness could mean instant death.

Half-shrouded in the dark shadows of the lander's hold, a yeheri was standing at the top of the ramp. He still held his weapon in his hands, though he wasn't pointing it at anyone.

Unfortunately, the Quarisians saw him too. There was a yell, barely audible through the thin air, and then the Quarisian militia opened fire.

A hail of bullets, flechettes, lasers, and a couple of powergun bolts thundered at the lander. The yeheri at the top of the ramp toppled backward with a spray of orange fluids, its faceplate shattered by a laser pulse. Then the rest of the surviving yeheri were shooting back, ducking around the edges of the hatchway to return fire.

Scalas cursed. This was exactly what he'd been afraid of.

Leave it to amateurs.

Now they had no choice. They had to finish this.

He pointed at the lander. "Covering fire!" he snapped, then turned and looked for the two armored forms with their distinctive bulky weapons. "Torgan! Rostov!" he bellowed over the sudden ripping thunder of at least a dozen powerguns opening fire on the lander. "Turn that lander's bay into scrap!"

The two men dashed out into the open, lugging the heavy tubes of their launchers. They each took care to make sure their backs and their lines of fire were clear; HV missile shockwaves could easily pulp a man in armor, never mind the lighter Quarisian spacesuits.

With shrieking roars that drowned out even the lightning-bolt crash of the powergun fire, the two HV missiles slammed into the lander's open hatchway.

While the missiles traveled at considerably slower velocities than a powergun bolt, to the naked eye there was little difference, particularly at that range. Almost instantaneously the lander belched white-hot sheets of flame, the shockwaves blasting dust and smoke away, knocking nearby wreckage askew and nearly flattening the men themselves.

Everything was quiet in the aftermath, almost as if the entire world had stopped at that cataclysmic blast. But as soon as the shockwave had washed over him, Scalas was up on his feet, driving toward the wreckage with his powergun's buttstock solidly against the rest on his pauldron, the sight just below his eye.

The lander was beginning to lean hard to one side; the double explosion had crumpled one of the landing legs. The hatchway was wider than it had been, a jagged wound in the side of the mushroom-shaped craft. The odds that any of the yeheri in the troop compartment had survived were slim to none, but there might still be one or two still alive in the cockpit above.

The footing on the ravaged ramp was treacherous, but long training and conditioning kept Scalas balanced and moving quickly. Fortunately, the impacts of the HV missiles had been enough of a shock that the Quarisian militia had ceased their own fire.

He intended to demand punishment for the man who had opened fire first. This could have been ended quietly.

His vision slit adjusted as he entered the troop compartment, the integral night vision brightening the scene before him. There were massive gouges in the hull, open to the outside, where the overpressure had split the metal and composite like a bursting balloon. Everything was scorched, and only the faintest nubs remained of acceleration couches, weapons racks, and equipment cases.

Some of the shadows on the hull were likely all that remained of the shooters who had been in the troop compartment. The HV missiles' molecular explosive warheads were capable of awe-inspiring destruction.

The ladder leading up to the cockpit was a twisted, mangled mess where it hadn't been completely flayed away by the blast. Scalas realized as he studied the wreckage that the ladder had originally been encased in a hollow shaft, evidently blasted away by the HV missile warheads. That probably accounted for why some twisting remains of the ladder had survived. Still, getting up there was going to be difficult. Fortunately, Caractacan Brothers always dropped prepared for all sorts of eventualities.

Dravot and Powell stepped forward, understanding what needed to be done. Dravot took a knee and Powell stood behind him, reaching up and clamping an armored fist around the warped remains of the ladder. Dravot braced himself against Powell's back and nodded.

Scalas put a boot on Dravot's thigh and hitched himself up, grabbing the ladder above Powell with one hand as he lifted his other leg to put his foot on Dravot's pauldron. Once again, the armor's articulation would take most of the weight off the men themselves.

Scalas hauled himself up, raised his powergun, and pushed the overhead hatch open with his still-warm muzzle. The hatch fell open with a dull *clunk*, and he put his other foot on the remains of the ladder and heaved himself up to where he could grab the lip with one hand, keeping his powergun ready in the other. It took some scrambling, but then he was up and through, into the cockpit.

He lowered his powergun. He wouldn't need it.

The cockpit had fared less well from the blasts than he had expected. It was a wreck. The acceleration couches had been torn from their mounts and thrown against the overhead. The deck was perforated where shrapnel had sleeted through it from the HV missile warheads.

Three of the four yeheri in the cockpit were clearly dead, their mangled corpses leaking orange blood onto the consoles and the shattered deck. One had a gaping exit wound at the top of his head; it seemed that a fragment had been propelled up through his body from below. The jagged chunk of metal was embedded in the overhead, dripping blood.

The fourth yeheri was still alive, but badly wounded.

"Dravot!" Scalas called down the hatch. "Tell Forster to be ready. We have a prisoner, but he's in a bad way."

As Scalas stepped closer, keeping his powergun ready, he saw that the yeheri was actually a female. That was not unknown among the yeheri. Many of the pirate bands were essentially roving packs of exiles, clans and families cast out into the dark. Some were more organized and professional, and even received some sponsorship and support from various yeheri worlds and organizations; in fact, some of the "pirate bands" were actually fighting units from yeheri worlds. These did not appear to be the latter, however. Just outcasts, greedy or proud enough to take what they wanted by force. Though sometimes their attacks were motivated by need. None of their equipment seemed to be in the greatest of repair.

Yet any sympathy Scalas might have felt for their poverty had been wiped away when they turned pirate.

He looked down at the bleeding yeheri woman, looking for traps or weapons. When he was satisfied, he slung his powergun, lifted her from the buckled deck, and lowered her to the Brothers below.

———

Forster, the medic, was identifiable by the dark red cross on his pauldron as well as the medical bag he carried. He worked on the yeheri woman on the deck of the destroyed troop compartment by the light of two powerful handheld lights that he had clipped to his shoulders. He wouldn't have much in the way of medical supplies for a yeheri in that pack—most medical devices were constructed for specific physiologies, and it was simply impossible to have supplies on hand for every race that might be encountered in even one small sector of the galaxy—but some things, like bandages and direct pressure, translated across species, and he was doing his best to patch her up.

Still, she appeared to be catatonic, though she occasionally moaned when pressure was put on one or another of her wounds, and even without Forster's grim prognosis, Scalas could see that she probably didn't have long. Part of the problem was that Iabreton II's atmosphere was as inimical to yeheri physiology as it was to human or ekuz, and though the woman's suit was compromised, Forster had explained that her helmet was still feeding her enough oxygen to stay alive—which meant that he couldn't remove it without killing her then and there.

The shapes of humans and ekuz appeared in the hatchway. Half a dozen or so Quarisian militiamen stood there, weapons in their hands. Scalas turned to face them.

"So, there izz one left," said one of the ekuz, scuttling forward, a coilgun in his hands. "That will be eazzy enough to remedy."

Scalas stepped forward and blocked the Quarisian's way. "No," he said.

The Quarisian looked up at him in surprise. "It'zz a pirate," he said reasonably. "Why are you protecting it?"

"Because she is wounded and likely to die," Scalas rumbled. He stood nearly half a head taller than the ekuz, and his armored bulk was intimidating even without the powergun in his hands. "Are you the magistrate?"

"No," the Quarisian replied, a note of puzzlement in his voice. "Magizztrate Hozzkinzz wazz killed in the initial attack. We have not elected a new one yet."

"Then you do not have the authority to execute this woman," Scalas said. "The battle is over; this is no longer a matter of warfare. It is a matter of law." He stepped closer, looming over the Quarisian militiaman. "Even summary executions must be carried out by lawful authority," he growled. "If anyone here has that authority, it is me. Were I to let you kill her, it would be murder." He let a bit of dark amusement creep into his voice. "And then I would be obligated to take steps against you."

"You can't do this," a human protested from the hatchway. It might have been the same man who had nearly gotten himself killed running across the open ground to the Brothers' position overlooking this very lander. "This isn't your world. They didn't attack you."

"Which is utterly immaterial," Cobb snapped, stepping up beside his centurion. "We are bound by the Code, and the Code says that we protect the weak and defenseless. And if not for us, you would be dead or groveling at the feet of a yeheri slave trader right now." Acid dripped from his voice. "Besides, how do you propose to take her away from us?"

"Who do you think you are?" the ekuz demanded.

"Who are *we*?" Scalas thundered. "We are the Caractacan Brotherhood! We are the men who came to your rescue without regard for reward. We sacrificed nine of our Brothers to save your colony from these pirates. And now you dare to question our Code, and get angry at *us* because we will not step aside and let you take needless revenge on a helpless, wounded prisoner?"

The ekuz stepped back nervously. The Brothers in the troop compartment, as well as those outside, stood at the ready, powerguns in their hands.

"By all means," Scalas continued, lowering his voice, "find a magistrate to render judgment. But do not expect me to stand aside for a mob."

"A magistrate would be too late anyway," Forster announced, rising to his feet. "She's gone."

Scalas did not move, but continued to stare at the ekuz in front of him. His expression was invisible behind his visor, but he knew the narrow vision slit in his otherwise faceless visor was far more intimidating than any scowl. The chameleonic coating had shifted to a mottled, scarred gray and black inside the wreckage of the lander, making him a towering, broad-shouldered specter with a still-warm powergun in his gauntleted hands.

"Stand down, you idiots," another voice called, amplified by an external speaker.

A man in ancient space armor, though still painted in the same orange and white as the rest of the Quarisian militia's spacesuits, stalked up the ramp, shoving a few of the militiamen out of his way. He stopped in front of the ekuz and faced him, turning his back on Scalas.

"Po'ulu, I know you're not stupid enough to try to go toe to toe with a Caractacan, even if they hadn't just pulled us out of the fire. I trained you better than that." His face was hidden by his helmet, but he made it clear that he was looking around at the rest of the assembled Quarisians. "I trained *all* of you better than that. Now get your butts back to the staging area and report to Sergeant Traynor. We've got a lot of cleanup to do, and we've still got people missing."

The man continued to stand there, his hands on his hips, giving every indication that he was glaring at his subordinates, as the militiamen reluctantly turned and headed down the ramp. Only once they were gone did the man turn to face Scalas.

He was armed with a coilgun that looked like it had been built in a local machine shop. It was wired with a thick cable to a jury-rigged power pack on top of his sustainment pack; the attachable power packs must have run out at some point, if the coilgun had even been built to take them.

"My apologies, Centurion," he said, in Trade Cant. "It's been a rough few days. The men are… rather ragged."

"Apology accepted," Scalas said. "I trust we can expect no further such incidents?"

"Of course," the man replied. "I will make sure of it. The loss of Magistrate Hoskins has been a shock, but we are getting things back together, and I assure you that there will be no more such breaches in discipline. I am Captain Agalan Voss, acting commander of the Iabreton II Militia. I would like to formally thank you." He turned slightly toward the plain outside. "I wish that we could offer you something more tangible in the way of gratitude, but we have a great deal of rebuilding to do before we could even begin to repay you."

"Repayment is neither necessary nor desired, Captain," Scalas said. "As I said, we are the Caractacan Brotherhood. We only followed the Code. The only thing we ask is a place to bury our fallen Brothers."

Voss nodded. "You will have it. And when we are able, I promise that there will be a monument erected there. A monument that will last a thousand years."

"If you so desire," Scalas said. As he began to walk down the twisted wreckage of the lander's ramp, he glanced upward and saw the drive flare of the *Dauntless* making its orbital insertion burn. The last of the yeheri ships had either fled or been destroyed. "We shall conduct the burials and be on our way."

[3]

The Brotherhood's Avar Sector Keep was built into a
mountain on the fourth moon of Kaletonan, a super-Jovian gas giant
and the third planet in the Tokanan system, twelve parsecs from
Iabreton. Unlike Iabreton II, Kaletonan IV had a breathable
atmosphere and its own ecosystem.

As the *Dauntless* descended toward the massive landing pads that
had been cleared out of the red-orange vegetation on a pillar of blue-
white fire, her massive landing struts were already stretching out to
her flanks. In the distance, a herd of the local quadrupeds dashed
away through the waving, chest-high grasses, fleeing the thunder of
the descending starship, even as that thunder dwindled away to a dull
rumble and finally faded away altogether as the *Dauntless* came to
rest on her jacks. Steam billowed from the landing pad as the cooling
systems desperately tried to dissipate the drive plume's heat. For a
brief time, the area around the starship's base was uninhabitable by
anything not heavily shielded.

Scalas stood with Mor and the rest of his squad sergeants in the
antechamber above the descent pod. Grounded at the Sector Keep,
they were no longer in armor; instead they wore their white tunics
and black trousers, the badge of the Brotherhood pinned at each

man's left shoulder, a sidearm in an impeccably shined leather holster at each man's hip. These holsters might appear decorative at first glance, but closer inspection would reveal the telltale signs of wear that comes from hard use.

Even without his armor and helmet, Scalas cut an impressive figure. Not a millimeter below two meters tall, he had an angular face, burned dark brown by many suns, and a short, neatly pointed beard ever so slightly darker than the close-cropped shock of reddish hair on his head. His eyes, half-hidden behind a semi-permanent squint and a mass of fine crow's-feet, were black—a black that could quickly turn to icy-cold obsidian when he was angered.

Cobb stood next to him, slightly taller, significantly heavier, and considerably darker—except for his eyes, which were a pale blue so light that they made him look like a madman, and his hair, which was blond almost to the point of being white.

On the other side of Cobb stood Kahane, nearly as wide as he was tall, his skin nearly as pale as his tunic. He was rocking a little on the balls of his feet; "low" gravity—meaning gravity that was comfortable to most of his comrades—tended to make the young squad sergeant fidgety.

When the pad's cooling system had brought the pad and the surrounding atmosphere down to survivable temperatures, the indicator above the hatch turned green, and the small leadership contingent of the *Dauntless* and Century XXXII entered the car that would take them down to the surface. The outer hatch then irised open, and the car slid onto its descent rail, humming slightly as it moved along, its armored transparencies revealing the full glory of the moon's surface in the early morning.

The sun, a yellow dwarf edging toward orange, was rising over the shoulder of the mountain where the Avar Sector Keep was ensconced. Its rays gleamed off three more towering, tapered starships sitting on their tails on more distant pads, as well as off the shining pinnacle of the Keep itself. Mingled with the light of the sun was the reddish-purple reflection of Kaletonan, looming over the opposite horizon, filling nearly a third of the sky.

Two hoversleds approached rapidly from the direction of the Keep, the howl of their fans audible even through the descent car's armor. These weren't heavy cavalry sleds; they were sleeker, lighter, civilian models: Juaran Ibexes shipped from Otaiho, nearly two parsecs away. They were expensive, but the Brotherhood had no civilian vehicle manufacturing of its own. The Caractacan Brotherhood had only one business.

That business was war.

The car came to a slow, smooth stop at the bottom of the rail, the starship's massive drive bells looming and smoking overhead. The car was designed to descend as fast as a dropship if needed—but here at the Keep, that was unnecessary. Scalas led the way out, with Mor following immediately behind. Mor was actually the senior officer by nearly a year, but he was a starship captain; here on the ground, the centurion took precedence.

The two hoversleds stopped at the edge of the pad, and their doors opened. Two young men in gray novice tunics stepped out. Both had to be nearing the end of their five-year novitiate; only senior novices were assigned honor guard duties. The rest were deep in study and training, learning the arts of war and the philosophy of the Code as finely as possible before they would be allowed to don the tunic and armor of a full-fledged Caractacan Brother.

The first novice saluted stiffly, raising his immaculate BR-18 to present-arms. "Welcome back, Centurion," he said, his voice slightly raspy. The man's scars suggested that he had seen heavy action in whatever planetary defense force he had come from before joining the Brotherhood. Few men joined the Brotherhood without experience. "Legate Kranjick is awaiting your report in the Keep."

Scalas returned the novice's salute gravely, lifting his sidearm in front of his face. He well remembered his own novitiate, and not only did he refuse to condescend to the less-experienced soldiers, he strictly forbade his men from doing so either. Volscius often skated the ragged edge of disobeying that mandate, but Volscius was a problem for other reasons.

When the Brotherhood officers had climbed aboard, the two sleds rose fractionally off the pavement, spun about on roaring air cushions, and sped toward the distant Keep. The pads were situated far from the habitation sections of the Keep and its environs for good reason. The dissipating cloud of steam and faintly radioactive gasses floating downwind were all the illustration that was needed. Scalas sat in his seat, his arms folded, watching the plains speed by out his window. Much of this part of the moon was grassland, fading to forest on the flanks of the inert volcano where the Keep stood, high above the treeline. It could have been built down on the surface, but the forest was far too dense and the vegetation too iron-hard to clear efficiently without using a starship's drive to do it, and that had been considered not worth the effort.

Nevertheless, a path had been cleared for the road, although even that needed nearly constant upkeep. The tangled mass of the red-and-orange forest didn't grow quickly, but it constantly buckled and strained the ground beneath it. Some said that the entire forest shared a single root system—that it was basically a single tree draped around the flanks of the mountain. Scalas didn't know. Someday he might have the time to indulge his curiosity and investigate the matter. There were surely scholars living in the Keep who had studied the forest enough to know.

He listened with mostly detached attention to the low conversation behind him in the hoversled's main passenger compartment. Kahane and Solanus were debating some new sport that was coming from Wesalia. Scalas wasn't familiar with it, but it seemed to involve a combination of racing, sparring, and goal-scoring.

"Dershod's certainly got the endurance," Kahane was saying, "but he's never going to be able to go as long as Ikkaa."

"Of course he won't," Solanus replied, sounding exasperated. Solanus was the youngest squad sergeant in the century, and as such was usually reluctant to speak his mind. Sports, however, seemed to be the one subject on which he felt it was safe to venture an unqualified opinion. That was probably why Kahane had started in on it. "A human will never be able to match a tehud for staying power. It's a matter of two legs versus four. No one's disputing that. But Dershod's more agile. He can get around obstacles faster."

"Maybe." Kahane didn't sound convinced. "What do you think, Kunn?"

Kunn, the third squad sergeant in the sled, said nothing.

Scalas glanced in the rearview mirror on his side and saw Kunn sitting behind him, his narrow face the slight gray that was characteristic of Nostrics, sitting stiffly in his seat, his curiously blank, deep-blue eyes fixed on nothing. Kunn was an excellent soldier—he would never have reached the rank of squad sergeant otherwise—but there had always been something vaguely *off* about him. Scalas couldn't help but feel his hackles rise a bit every time he looked in the man's eyes, and he often found himself wondering just what was going on behind that blank, enigmatic stare. True, Kunn had never acted inappropriately for his rank or his position, but he did make his comrades wonder. No man could really be that… robotic.

"Come on, Kunn," Kahane pressed. "You've got to have *some* opinion."

"I have never watched the sport," Kunn said, in his usual dead monotone.

Kahane sighed. "What *do* you do during your personal time, Kunn? You don't watch sports, you don't hunt, you don't mingle with the other squad sergeants… Don't tell me you just sit in your cell and stare at the walls."

"I study." Kunn turned away to stare vacantly out the window.

Scalas did not comment, even as Kahane harrumphed in annoyance. Kunn might be strange, but he wasn't a problem. Not yet. Until he became one, Scalas wouldn't be too concerned with his oddity.

They passed under the eaves of the forest, bringing the sleds into deep shadows beneath the thick, intertwined canopy of branches and spatulate leaves overhead. The road turned ahead, the first of a series of switchbacks that would allow them to work their way up the mountain without straining the engines climbing the nearly sheer slope ahead. Every now and then an occasional ray of golden sunlight or reflected reddish Kaletonan-glow would break through and strike the windows, but for the most part they rode through a deep twilight.

And then at last the sleds broke out of the trees before the gates of the Keep.

The Avar Sector Keep was fairly typical of such Brotherhood fortresses across the Spinward Reaches. Tightly clustered around a central spire stood four squat, cylindrical towers, their domed peaks housing powerful ground-to-space defensive batteries. Those batteries would only be unmasked as a last resort, and would hopefully be made unnecessary by the powerguns and heavy laser batteries emplaced at strategic points in concentric rings around the fortress. No attacker would find the skies above a Brotherhood Keep uncontested. The Avar Sector Keep had never needed to employ these defenses, but in almost eight centuries of existence, the Brotherhood had made no shortage of enemies, and having strong defenses around their headquarters was simply common sense.

As the sleds sped forward, the gates swung open silently on well-oiled mag tracks, then closed again as soon as the sleds had passed. Keeping the gates shut at all times was one more aspect of Brotherhood discipline on display.

Not far into the shadowed courtyard, the two vehicles glided to a halt, the pitch of their fans changing as they braked. Golden lights, not far off the spectrum of the sun, blazed down on them from atop the towers. A massive figure in the red tunic of a Brotherhood legate stood at the top of the steps leading into the main spire. Even from a distance, there was no mistaking the man.

Brother Legate Michael Kranjick.

Kranjick stood well over two meters tall, barrel-chested, with arms bigger around than most men's legs. In fact, everything about the old Brother Legate seemed weighty—not just his size and presence, but his very manner, his faintly brutish, battered features, his slow, ponderous speech, his look of perpetual boredom. Yet any Brother who crossed his path was quickly disabused of the notion that his slowness was indicative of dullness of intelligence.

Scalas climbed out of the sled and mounted the steps, halting just below the Brother Legate to render his salute. Kranjick returned it gravely with his well-worn, ancient KT-5 pistol, much as Scalas had returned the novice's salute. As was fitting—Scalas had learned to be a Brother and a leader under then-Centurion Kranjick's command.

"Report, Centurion," Kranjick rumbled. He holstered his sidearm, turned about, and began to plod back inside the spire, motioning for Scalas to walk with him.

"The mining outpost is secure again, Brother Legate," Scalas said, accompanying Kranjick into the Great Hall. The gothic arches were hung with battle banners from nearly eight hundred years' worth of engagements across the Spinward Reach. "The yeheri pirate band has been wiped out. A few survivors of the ground fighting might have surrendered, but the local militia opened fire on them."

Kranjick nodded solemnly. "We cannot always expect the local forces to act with honor. Which is why we must always be on our guard. I take it you did not allow their actions to lead you to violate the Code?"

"Of course not, Brother Legate. Though matters grew tense with some of the militia toward the end. There was a single survivor. A pilot, I believe. The militia wished to execute her."

"And, of course, you prevented them," said a familiar voice.

They were nearing the knot of Brothers waiting in the center of the hall, but Centurion Joachim Dunstan was standing closest to the door, his hands resting on the impeccably polished pistol belt around his equally impeccably tailored and filigreed tunic. As always, Dunstan's uniform was slightly flashier than anyone else's in the room, including Brother Legate Kranjick's. And unlike most of the Brothers, he wore a thin mustache beneath his narrow beak of a nose.

"And what if they had insisted?" Dunstan continued. "Would you truly have been willing to sacrifice Caractacan Brothers' lives for the sake of a pirate?"

Kranjick halted, but said nothing. He simply watched and listened, like a massive, observant, sapient mountain.

Scalas looked Dunstan in the eye. "Yes, I was willing to do precisely that. The battle was over. She was wounded and unable to defend herself. The Code is fairly clear on such matters."

"And yet she was a pirate," Dunstan countered. "Condemned to be executed regardless." He peered behind Scalas as if looking for something. "I do not see this yeheri prisoner."

"That is because she died of her wounds before we had even cleared the battlefield," Scalas said levelly, knowing what was coming next.

"Well." Dunstan raised his voice so that his words echoed from the walls of the Great Hall. "I suppose it is a blessing that no shots were fired in defense of a pirate who was doomed to die anyway. Certainly not for a pointless display of 'honor.'"

"I should be careful speaking so lightly of points of honor, Centurion," Kranjick said grimly. He did not raise his voice, yet his words traveled nonetheless. "The Code is what makes the Brotherhood, after all."

"And yet how many Brothers were lost on Pontakus IX because of points of honor, Brother Legate?" Dunstan asked. "We might hold dearly to the Code, but our enemies surely will not. Disaster was averted this time, but by how close a margin? And what honor is there in defending a captured *pirate* who deserves nothing but summary execution in the first place? What was the point?"

Scalas's eyes narrowed. Dunstan was not speaking extemporaneously; this was a prepared speech. Scalas wondered just what had prompted the other centurion, who was known to be one of the most outspoken of the New School, the so-called "pragmatists," in the Legio X, to think that he would have the opportunity to use it at this particular time and place.

"If you really don't see the point," Kahane shot back from behind Scalas, "I wonder how you ever pinned on Centurion."

Dunstan fixed Kahane with a glare. "Your superiors are talking, Squad Sergeant," he said coldly.

The thickset high-grav worlder stepped up beside Scalas and folded his massive arms across his chest. "No," he replied, just as coldly. "Only those who outrank me, apparently by virtue only of time in service."

Dunstan's lips went white, and he too took a step forward, one hand dropping reflexively to the sidearm at his side. Instantly the atmosphere in the Great Hall crackled with tension. Brothers did not threaten to draw weapons on Brothers.

Scalas and Kahane stood motionless, staring Dunstan down. Kranjick stayed aloof, saying nothing, only watching. Dunstan was shaking with rage.

And then the man looked around, as if only then realizing that all eyes in the hall were on him—and none of them particularly friendly. His lips formed a thin line beneath his mustache, and he abruptly turned on his heel and stalked away.

"Centurion Dunstan," Kranjick rumbled. Dunstan looked for a moment like he was going to keep walking, but then stopped and stiffly turned back around.

"I suggest that you study Volume II of Donagan's *History of the Caractacans* tonight, Centurion," Kranjick said, still managing to look and sound bored, though there was a note of steel in his voice. "You seem to have forgotten some things."

Dunstan stared at him for a moment, then clicked his heels together and saluted. "I shall certainly look at it, Brother Legate." He spoke as if the words pained him, then he turned and left the hall.

Scalas turned to Kranjick, his frown deepening. "Where did that come from?" he asked.

Kranjick looked as if nothing of particular note had just happened. "Dunstan is ambitious," he said simply. "As are the rest of the 'pragmatists.' It is nothing new."

"*That* was," Scalas argued. "He was looking for a chance to preach his lack of principle in front of an audience. Has something happened to embolden them?"

Kranjick resumed his advance toward the far end of the Great Hall. "No. Dunstan has been a centurion longer than you have. He wishes for a legate's tunic, and thinks that challenging you and the Code will grant him the notoriety that will garner him such a promotion. Or so he believes." The huge man laughed dryly. "Hence why I told him what to study. He has forgotten how advancement in the Brotherhood truly occurs. Popularity in the ranks has little to do with promotion."

"So," Scalas said in disgust, "politics rears its head within the Brotherhood."

Kranjick stopped and turned to face him. "Politics is part of human existence, Centurion. Code or no Code, it was always inescapable. The Brotherhood has endured for the centuries that it has because of the Code—and because we are unmatched on the battlefield by human or alien—but we are still human, and still subject to human frailties, including politics and ambition. Pontakus IX was a Pyrrhic victory that scarred the Brotherhood for all time to come. It made many question whether the Code was worth the risk of death, whether honor was truly more important than life. And many of them were bound to pass those doubts down to those they commanded and trained. It is the way of the galaxy. We can only hold fast to what we know is right, and along the way strive to be better than those who would trample on honor for the sake of advancement or advantage. Is that not what you were taught as a novice?"

Scalas nodded, looking away from his mentor and commander's deep-set, deceptively placid eyes. "I had only hoped that the Brotherhood was somehow immune from such petty squabbling. I have seen little of it so far."

Kranjick chuckled. "That is high praise, as I have striven to keep it out of my legio. But trust me, boy, no one is truly immune. It would have come around sooner or later." He studied Scalas for a moment, a faint smile on his lips. "Perhaps I should have you do some reading tonight, as well. Perhaps refreshing your memory about the aftermath of the Banash War might grant you some perspective. This is not the first such crisis the Brotherhood has faced. It will not be the last."

He straightened, and looked back at the rest of Scalas's squad sergeants. "Get settled back into your quarters," he said. "We will do a detailed after-action report this evening, and the funeral Mass for the fallen immediately thereafter. What time is it, ship time?"

"We synchronized with the Sector Keep three days ago," Scalas said. "We will be fine. I will have the century assembled for the debriefing in three hours."

"Very well," Kranjick said. "Vigilance and Honor, Centurion."

Scalas straightened to attention and saluted. "Vigilance and Honor, Brother Legate," he replied.

$$[\ 4 \ ]$$

THE BATTERED SHIP'S BERGENHOLM FIELDS CUT OUT EARLY. THE drive did not ignite. Fully inert, the near-wreck of the Antares III class starship was slowly falling toward Tokanan's star.

It might pass that star in fifty standard years. If it didn't fall into the photosphere and burn up.

But the ship wasn't *entirely* dead. Somewhere in the blasted ruin of its superstructure, a transmitter started beaming a signal deeper into the system.

———

The legio's chief chaplain, Father Corinus, offered the last blessing over the caskets, committing the fallen Brothers' remains to the ground in hopes of the final Resurrection at the end of time. The surviving Brothers of Century XXXII, alongside the crew of the *Dauntless*, stood at attention, flanking the caskets. Nine men had fallen on Iabreton II. Low casualties, considering how many yeheri they had killed in the action, but it was still a grievous blow to a century.

Scalas stood at the head of the row of closed caskets, dressed in his formal dress tabard, sidearm on one hip, ceremonial sword on the other. It was said that this blade had been presented to the very first centurion of Century XXXII, six hundred years before, by the grateful ruler of Rialexeton VI. Scalas did not know for certain if the story was true—enough time had passed that it could have been only a legend—but none of the other centurions had a dress sword quite like it.

A figure appeared in the door of the chapel, dressed in a tech's uniform, the same as the warrior Brothers' tunics except blue. The man stood at attention and waited, but Scalas was acutely aware of him until Father Corinus finished the prayers and the caskets were lowered into the vaults below the Keep. Ten stories of vaults carved into the mountain held the Brotherhood's Avar Sector dead. Those who had been recovered.

When the last casket had disappeared into the vaults and Father Corinus had pronounced the final blessing and dismissal, the century turned on their heels as one and marched out of the chapel. Not a few eyes turned curiously toward the tech, who held his place, patiently waiting for Scalas and Kranjick. As the two men approached, the gray-haired tech saluted, which was when Scalas saw he had an artificial right hand. Scalas suddenly remembered the man: Brother Henryk Costas, one of Kranjick's senior squad sergeants when Scalas had first deployed as a front-line Brother. Badly wounded, Costas had retired from the line, but had retrained himself as a tech to stay in service with the Brotherhood.

Kranjick returned the salute. "What is it, Henryk?"

"We just received a transmission from a ship at the edge of the system, Brother Legate," Costas replied. "It is from a Valdekan starship identified as the *Mekadik*. She is apparently badly damaged, fully inert, and coasting in toward the sun at minuscule velocity. We have yet to locate her precise position and vector, but the crew aboard the *Boanerges* in orbit believes she's at least three hundred ninety light-minutes out."

"Did the message include what she's doing here?" Kranjick asked.

"Negative, Brother Legate. It appears to be an automated distress beacon, operating on very low power. It was barely decipherable through the background cosmic radiation, never mind Kaletonan's magnetic fields. There might have been more, but if so, it was lost in the noise."

"Very well," Kranjick said. He turned to Scalas. "I could send Dunstan or Soon, unless you would prefer to take it."

Scalas considered. He knew why Kranjick was offering. The men of his century would be brooding over the losses they'd taken on Iabreton II, even more so now that the wounds had been reopened by the funeral. Often such situations were handled by ruthless field exercises or similar training, or even by busy work around the Keep— anything to keep the men's minds and hands occupied lest they slip too deeply into the dark thoughts that can accompany mourning a fallen comrade. A mission might serve the same purpose, help the men get some distance from the deaths, and give them time to process the loss without sinking into despair.

He was tired, and he knew that his century was as well. They'd had days to rest on the transit from Iabreton II, but it had been a hard fight, no matter how quickly it had been over. Yet he would not beg weariness.

"We will go," he said, glancing over at Captain Mor. The starship commander nodded his agreement. "It will give the men something to do."

"We can be ready to lift in six hours," Mor declared, stepping forward even as he signaled his executive officer, Commander Brage.

"Century XXXII will be aboard and ready to lift," Scalas said formally. "Now if you will excuse me, sir, I need to get the men moving and counteract the usual grumbling."

———

Scalas stood next to Mor's acceleration couch on the command deck, fully armored, his mag-boots locked to the deck. "It's a miracle she made it this far," he murmured.

"It's a miracle she survived any of that at all," Mor replied.

The ship displayed in the holo-tank, enhanced by the ship's computer to be visible in the dim starlight over forty astronomical units from the star, was barely recognizable as an Antares III. Her royal-blue, egg-shaped hull was scored and punctured in half a hundred places, and it looked like most of her compartments were open to space. The nose actually appeared to have partially melted. Her drive cones were dark, even in the infrared, and her reactor was apparently cold—the neutrino flux was almost nonexistent. If not for the looping distress call, the *Dauntless* would likely not have been able to track her down at all.

"Can anyone still be alive in there?" Scalas asked.

"It's possible," said Mor. "The Antares III has considerable redundancies, especially when it comes to damage control. There could well still be an air pocket inside somewhere. And there's obviously still some kind of functioning power source aboard, or the transmitter wouldn't be working. So yes, there could be survivors."

Scalas started to turn toward the hatch, though his gaze lingered on the image in the holo-tank. "Well, I'll take First Squad EVA to investigate. Can you get us closer?"

"I could dock with her, if she still had an intact docking collar," Mor retorted. "What kind of scow pilot do you take me for?"

Scalas refused to rise to the bait. He clapped the captain on the shoulder before turning toward the lift in the center of the command deck. "I'll be at Lock Number Ten," he said. "Let me know when we've made rendezvous."

Mor shook his head without looking away from the holo-tank. He had maneuvers to plot.

———

The smashed, ragged hull of the stranded vessel loomed a mere two hundred meters away as Scalas and First Squad exited the exterior lock. They could have gotten the *Dauntless* closer, but there was a respectable amount of debris following the hulk, and no reason to risk colliding with it. The Brothers, with their maneuvering units strapped around their armor's sustainment packs, could avoid the debris much more easily than the starship could.

Scalas led the way, pumping little jets of compressed gas out of his propellant bottles with the control stick that was strapped to his left gauntlet. The *Dauntless* had precisely matched velocities with the hulk, so the transit was easy—a simple, straight-line vector between hulls.

Lettering adorned the stricken starship's flank. The enhanced vision projected on Scalas's visor slit showed him the first few letters, but he didn't recognize them—they were neither Latin nor Trade Cant. Not only was he not sure what language the Valdekans spoke, he wasn't even sure whether the Valdekans were human. He knew only that Valdek was well to Rimward, nearly fifty parsecs.

The main airlock was, as Mor had indicated, blasted to scrap, apparently by a near-miss by a powergun bolt. A direct hit would likely have broken the ship's spine. Whoever the Valdekans were, either their opponents were horrifically incompetent at ship-to-ship combat, or the Valdekan crew was *very* good at countermeasures and point defense.

Scalas retrofired as he came closer, bringing himself to a relative standstill about twenty meters from the mangled hull, directly opposite the blasted remains of the airlock. Scanning for another way in, he spotted a possibility—doors to what was probably a shuttle or lander bay. A fragment or kinetic projectile had punched a long, ragged scar through those doors, leaving an opening that should be just big enough for a man in space armor to get through.

Triggering his jets, he began to drift slowly toward the hole. Even as well-armored as he was, he had to be careful. Strike a structural member or a heavy enough bit of hull plating, and he risked severe injury or decompression. Behind him, the rest of the squad followed in a loose wedge. None of them expected to get into combat aboard the wreck, but enemy boarders inside the hull weren't outside the realm of possibility. Besides, they were Caractacans. If there was one thing they never lacked, it was vigilance.

Scalas came to a relative halt two meters from the breach. It was slightly larger than he'd thought, as the ship was bigger than the *Dauntless* and distances were deceiving in the murky artificial lighting projected on his visor. Still, it could be hazardous to navigate, especially since the space beyond it was dark as the tomb, so he prepared a grapple. The "hook" was a small but powerful electromagnet charged by his suit's power supply, and the gossamer line, impossibly thin, was stronger than two-centimeter-thick steel cable. A quick flick of his wrist sent the magnet flying toward the bay doors. Only long practice and coordination kept the throw from setting him spinning.

The magnet caught and held, and Scalas reeled himself in. As he did, grapples from the rest of his team impacted the hull soundlessly around him.

When he was close enough, he rotated himself so that his boots were pointed at the bay doors, and he triggered their mag-locks. The *clunk* of impact was transmitted through his armor, muted as it was. The mag-locks were tuned to his movement, so he could walk across the warped remains of the bay door relatively smoothly.

He pulled a hand light from his belt kit and shone it through the rent in the door. Unhindered by atmosphere, the light blazed brightly. Just inside he saw a docked transatmospheric shuttle, but whatever had penetrated the bay doors had turned the shuttle's nose into a twisted mass of shredded metal and composite. Farther in, a handful of backup emergency lights emitted a dim glow around the bay's central lift/ladderwell, so Mor was right—there was some sort of functioning power source on board, even if the main reactors and drives were cold.

Bending "down," Scalas took a firm but cautious grip on the edge of the puncture. As tough as the metal weave inside his gloves' palms was, it was never a good idea to take chances in hard vacuum.

He released his mag-locks and torqued himself around the edge and into the bay, keeping one hand locked on the edge of the torn metal, the other on his powergun. Then he let go, pointed his boots at the inner side of the bay doors, and triggered the mag-locks again.

His boots slammed down on the metal, and he could move with relative safety. Kahane came through the hole next, immediately identifiable by his height and girth. The other Brothers were stacked behind him, waiting their turn.

Scalas worked his way around the breach, heading for the nose and the command deck, if it was still intact. This would have been disorienting to someone who hadn't trained in such maneuvers to the extent the Caractacans did. There was a reason the novitiate lasted five years. Like any starship, this ship, when under thrust, was not unlike a tower or a tall building: the drives were "down" and the decks were stacked like floors above them. But in zero gravity, there was no "up" or "down," and Scalas was effectively walking on the inside of a slightly tapering cylinder toward what could, depending on one's perspective, be a ladder up or down or even a bridge or catwalk.

Faint vibrations through his boots told him the other Brothers were following. Again, he knew they would be in a loose wedge. Rescue mission or not, the Caractacans always moved as if ready for a fight.

He reached the catwalk and started to move along it, reorienting himself ninety degrees by first releasing his mag-locks and grabbing the railing before reengaging the locks. Unfortunately, the lift hatch was sealed shut, and it seemed it was going to stay that way as long as the bay remained depressurized.

"We need an emergency lock pod," he said over the short-range comm.

"Coming up, Centurion," a Brother replied. It sounded like Harris. A few moments later, an armored figure appeared through the breach, pulling a compact package behind him. He plodded along the inside of the hull, following roughly the same route that Scalas had.

While they waited, Kahane cast his hand light around the damaged shuttles and the rest of the bay. "Do you notice anything strange, Centurion?"

"Aside from the fact that there are only three shuttles in a hold easily big enough for five times that many?" Scalas asked.

"Yes, aside from that. I don't see any bodies," Kahane said.

"That doesn't necessarily mean anything," Scalas replied. "There wouldn't be many personnel out and about in the launch bay during a space battle. They would have been on one of the command decks, strapped in for acceleration and armored, just like we would."

"I suppose." Kahane didn't sound especially convinced. In fact, he sounded slightly spooked.

Scalas had to admit that the nearly empty, darkened launch bay of a stricken starship in hard vacuum was an eerie place. Every once in a while, the light from one of their lamps would glint weirdly off a bit of wreckage, making it seem like there was movement where there should be none. Even Scalas was feeling the disquiet.

It was indeed Harris who was hauling the emergency lock, and as soon as he arrived, he started setting it up. It was little more than a synthetic tube with a sealer at one end and an overlapping, airtight membrane at the other, hooked up to a compact atmosphere tank that was good for about a dozen cycles before it failed. Which meant they wouldn't be able to get the entire squad inside. Especially if they wanted to get back out without blowing the hatch off.

"Kahane, Harris, Maxon, and Granzow, you're with me," Scalas instructed.

"Fillegron," Kahane said over the comm, "you're acting squad leader here in the bay. Pick five men to hold the breach, and send the rest back to the *Dauntless*."

Fillegron saluted by slapping the buttstock of his powergun, then began to assemble the men in the bay.

Scalas slipped through the barrier and into the emergency lock.

Maxon and Granzow were able to fit in with him, though it was decidedly cramped. It took a few minutes for the small pack to pressurize the lock enough for the safety interlocks on the hatch to release. Scalas, unsure what to expect, kept his powergun ready as he stepped through.

The door opened onto a lift shaft that dwindled into the distance in both directions. The lift itself was nowhere near them, not that it would have helped if it were. Fortunately, using the ladder was no hard task in freefall. Under thrust, it would have been a long, grueling climb, but as it was, Scalas glided up easily, his powergun clamped to his side, only occasionally needing to reach out and briefly grab a rung to straighten his course or continue to propel himself along.

About halfway to the nose, he looked back down at the line of Brothers following him. "Can anyone tell what language these decks are marked in?" he asked. "It looks vaguely familiar, but unless we can decipher some of it, we're going to have to clear the entire ship, deck by deck, looking for survivors."

"I think it's Eastern Satevic," Maxon said. Maxon should know; he had been a professor at the University on Careyn III before the M'tait raid that had killed over eighty percent of the population. "Some of the symbols look familiar."

"Can you read it?" Kahane asked.

"No." Maxon shook his helmeted head. "I might recognize a word or two, but Careyn III was a long way Coreward from any of the worlds where the Satevic languages had taken root."

"We don't need to read the signage," Granzow said. "I served on an Antares III for two years before my novitiate. I know the layout."

For a moment, all four Caractacans looked at Granzow.

"That's quite a coincidence," Kahane said.

Granzow, holding a rung with one hand, shrugged slightly, the motion barely visible in his armor. "There are a lot of Antares IIIs floating around. They were one of the most popular hulls that the

Waiyungari Shipyards turned out in the last thirty years, and at least fifteen major system fleets purchased them in bulk."

"You're a fountain of occasionally useful but otherwise pointless information, Granzow," Harris said.

"Well, this time it turned out to be useful," Granzow said dryly. "And I can't help it if you don't have interests."

"I have plenty of interests," Harris countered. "Starship trivia simply doesn't happen to be one of them."

"Enough," Scalas said. "Granzow, how far are we from the command deck?"

"Another three levels, I think. The primary command center will be wrapped around the lift shaft, with weapons emplacements and auxiliary mech compartments around it."

Scalas looked up the lift shaft. That was fairly standard design for a starship that could be expected to enter combat. Placing the command center deep inside the starship's structure lessened the chance that it could be taken out with a single shot—presuming that a direct hit from a bomb-pumped X-ray laser or kinetic kill munition didn't reduce the entire ship to atomized debris in a fraction of a second anyway.

Scalas pulled himself another three decks up and steadied himself in front of what he hoped was the command center hatch. The Eastern Satevic writing was still indecipherable, but the lights here were green, indicating pressure on both sides of the hatch. He keyed the hatch open, bringing his powergun to the ready as the portal irised wide.

A few dim, blue emergency lights glowed in the alcoves in the overhead, but they didn't illuminate much beyond the general layout of the space that lay beyond. The command center layout was fairly standard for a starship. There was the usual arrangement of acceleration couches and consoles arranged in rings around the compartment, all of which were currently dark. Scalas pulled himself through the hatch and triggered his mag-locks again. His feet solidly on the deck, he moved forward.

That was when the commander's acceleration couch began to turn.

A figure in an armored spacesuit was strapped into the couch. The figure's visor was down, presenting only a dim, featureless, reflective face, and the suit was of an unfamiliar design, blue and green, though definitely of considerably newer manufacture than the old orange suits the Quarisians had been wearing back on Iabreton II.

A distinctly feminine voice crackled from the figure's external speakers in stilted, heavily accented Trade Cant. "You are Caractacans?"

"We are," Scalas replied in the same language. "We received your distress signal."

"Thank the universe!" the woman exclaimed.

Scalas ignored the pantheism. His concerns were with the crew and the ship. "Where are the rest of your crew?"

"I sent all but a skeleton engineering crew to the mid-decks, where we have two decks of hibernation pods," the captain replied, unstrapping from her couch. "We had taken so much damage that I was afraid we wouldn't be able to maintain full life support until help arrived." *If* it arrived went unsaid. "I am Captain Kateryna Horvaset, commanding the RVC *Mekadik* on behalf of the General-Regent of Valdek."

"I am Centurion Erekan Scalas, Century XXXII, Caractacan Brotherhood," Scalas replied. He glanced around at the darkened consoles. "The Brotherhood starship *Dauntless* is just a few hundred meters away, awaiting survivors." He pinned the captain with a stare as best he could through the polarized slit of his visor. "What happened to your ship, Captain?"

"That is why we were making for the Avar Sector Keep, Centurion." She straightened, her own boots' mag-locks fastening securely to the deck. Her helmet came just about to Scalas's chin. "I have a formal message for your commanders, but the short version is that Valdek is under attack by an unknown force, and we are in desperate need of help. We nearly did not escape the system to seek help."

"Then let us evacuate your crew and return to the Keep," Scalas said. If she was telling the truth, that was certainly a grave enough matter that it needed to be discussed with the Brother Legate, not in casual conversation on the wreckage of a starship's command deck. "Do you have enough spacesuits for all of them? It appears that EVA will be the only viable method of transfer."

"We do," she replied. "This is—*was* a Valdekan ship-of-the-line, Centurion. We were all equipped for combat, including explosive decompression, and as you can see, we certainly experienced some of it. I assure you, everyone has their own suit."

"Very well, Captain," Scalas said. "Lead the way. We will evacuate your crew and return to Kaletonan IV. There you may deliver your message to the Brother Legate and the rest of the centurions currently planetside."

There were surprisingly few remaining crew. Horvaset admitted that they had lost several sections' worth to enemy fire when the hull was holed. The starship had also lifted with a short crew—time had been pressing, and she hadn't been due to lift for nearly a week—and the *Mekadik* had been on maintenance cycle when the attack had begun.

Still, it took several hours to get everyone across to the *Dauntless* and situated to Captain Mor's satisfaction. Then, going fully inertialess, the starship lit her drive and left the hulk of the *Mekadik* behind, drifting toward the distant sun.

[5]

For the second time in as many days, the *Dauntless* descended toward the Sector Keep on a thundering pillar of blue-white fire. This time she carried survivors of a desperate space battle with a dire plea for help.

Scalas hadn't seen the message; Horvaset had insisted that it was for the Brother Legate's eyes only. But she had told him and Mor something of what had happened in the distant Valdek system, and both men were grim as they descended. If what she'd said was true, this could have the potential to be another Pontakus IX.

"Look," Mor said, pointing. There was a new spire standing on one of the distant landing pads. "The *Challenger* arrived while we were in the outer system."

The *Challenger* was one of the Brotherhood's newer starships, a sharp-nosed blade nearly fifty meters longer than the spear-shaped *Dauntless*. She was the charge of Centurion Virgil Costigan, who was only still a centurion because of his time in service and his own humility. The man who had almost singlehandedly held off a medium-sized M'tait Huntership's boarding party at Tide's Point Station could easily be seen as a candidate for legate, but Costigan had, if anything, been even more reluctant than the Brotherhood

Conclave for that to happen. They, because of his junior status—having only been a full-fledged Brother for just over six years at that point—he, because he did not consider himself worthy of the post in the first place. He now led one of the Sector's two cavalry centuries.

"If we're going to Valdek," Scalas said, "I expect we'll be very glad to have Brother Costigan and his tanks along."

"*If* this tale is true, you mean," Mor muttered.

Scalas glanced back to ensure Horvaset was not on the command deck. She wasn't, of course; the command deck of a Brotherhood starship was a place for Caractacans only.

"You think it isn't?" he asked.

"Where would any force in the galaxy, aside from maybe the M'tait—who are an entirely different sort of nightmare—get the kind of manpower and ships that she described?" Mor asked by way of reply. "I know, it's a big galaxy, but there's no way any one system can afford to commit that kind of resources just to cross interstellar distances to attempt to conquer another system. It makes no sense. The logistics are ridiculous."

Scalas shrugged. "We shall see."

The *Dauntless* touched down, and Scalas, Mor, and a guard of Century XXXII's Brothers, still in armor and carrying powerguns, descended with Horvaset and her first mate as soon as the pad was cooled enough. This time there were combat sleds waiting—not because the Valdekans were considered a threat, but because the combat sleds were faster. Details had not been sent ahead—that could wait for the formal presentation of Horvaset's message—but the urgency of the visit had nevertheless been communicated, as had the general indication that the stricken *Mekadik* had come looking for Caractacan help.

The tight formation of Caractacans marched the Valdekan officers to the sleds and boarded. There was no formality. The sleds simply rose on their fans, spun about, and roared up the road toward the Keep.

Brother Legate Kranjick was waiting in the Great Hall, along with Centurions Soon, Costigan, and Dunstan, all in armor sans helmets. It was a standard ceremony when receiving supplicants looking for the Caractacans' assistance. If battle was in the offing, a Caractacan had best be in his armor.

Scalas and Cobb flanked Horvaset and her first mate as they crossed the hall to come before Kranjick's imposing bulk. His armor was the same as all the rest, aside from its size. He wore the same magazine pouches, comm units, and sidearm, and his chameleonic coating was currently the same vague gray as the stone of the Great Hall. The only difference was that his armor was more scarred and battered than that of his subordinates. Kranjick had worn the same armor for a very long time.

Century XXXII's honor guard came to a halt precisely twenty meters from the dais with a thunderous crash of thirty armored boots striking the pavement at once. The Caractacans were generally ascetic when it came to ceremony, but when dealing with outsiders, they knew the value of display. The Caractacans were known as the most disciplined and effective of the military brotherhoods in the galaxy, and it was sometimes necessary to remind their visitors of that fact.

In time they would be sure to make that fact known in much more violent ways.

Scalas, Cobb, Horvaset, and the first mate, whose name Scalas could not recall, continued forward. They stopped at the base of the steps, and Horvaset clicked her heels together and bowed to Kranjick. Now out of her armor, she was revealed to be a slender, dark-haired woman with dark, almond-shaped eyes.

The Brother Legate solemnly returned the salute with an open palm over the heart. Strangers rarely saw the weapon salutes that were standard within the Brotherhood.

"On behalf of the Royal Court of the Sovereign System of Valdek," Horvaset intoned solemnly in accented Trade Cant, "I offer greetings to the Caractacan Brotherhood, and bring this plea for aid." She held out a palm-sized holo projector and thumbed it on.

The projector lit, and a regal figure in a square-shouldered tunic appeared.

"To the Caractacan Brotherhood and its leadership, greetings," the man began. Scalas could see little detail, especially as the holo was facing Kranjick. "I am Bozhidar Rehenek, General-Regent of Valdek. I have sent this message out of grave necessity. We are an old world and a proud one, but we are now faced with a menace that is beyond our strength.

"Three weeks ago, as I record this, our system came under attack. A fleet of unprecedented size came from Rimward unannounced and struck at our space facilities before landing ground troops in over-whelming numbers. The outer colonies have fallen, and Valdek itself is besieged. What's left of our fleet is grounded. The rest is now floating debris in space.

"The attacking force, in its demand for our surrender, identified itself as the 'Galactic Unity.' We know nothing about them, aside from their overwhelming numbers and suicidal swarming tactics. That there is no such 'Galactic Unity' should be of no news to the Brotherhood. I fear that we are the victims of a megalomaniac. A megalomaniac with resources we cannot hope to match. To field the forces they have thrown against us, either they must have hundreds, if not thousands, of systems at their command, or else they have completely stripped their own. Our people are reeling, and our defenses are slowly being battered to dust.

"I have sent similar messages to every friend and ally we have within a hundred parsecs, and I have attached to this message the little intelligence we've managed to gather in the chaos of battle. Though it pains me as a sovereign to do this, I place my people at your mercy, Caractacans. Without aid from off-world, we shall surely fall."

The figure bowed stiffly, and the holo winked out, replaced by a montage of recordings, none with any great detail. It seemed that in most cases whoever had recorded them had sacrificed high-definition imagery in favor of enough distance to survive.

The first holo showed a massed cone of ships following a veritable blizzard of missiles and powergun fire toward a deep space station. There were more starships in that one field of view than the Brotherhood had in the entire Spinward Reach. The station disappeared in a glowing sphere of debris, and the recording winked out.

In the second holo, dropships fell toward a dusty planetary surface, as seen from a vantage point just outside a small cluster of domed habitats. The ships landed hard in combat landings that threw up clouds of scorched dust, and swarms of troops spilled out, following angular armored vehicles on crude-looking tracks. In seconds, an entire regiment surrounded the tiny settlement. Some of the troops apparently noticed the person recording, and closed in, weapons leveled. Scalas saw that their armor actually amounted to little more than a chest plate over a plain spacesuit. Then a rifle butt was swung savagely, and the image disappeared.

Horvaset stopped the playback. "There is more," she said, her chin held high, "but I expect that the full reports are not for this time or place."

"Perhaps not," Kranjick said. His face expressionless, he looked to either side of him. "Centurions? Opinions?"

"There has never been an interstellar empire in the entire history of the Great Diaspora that ever amounted to more than a handful of closely spaced systems," Centurion Soon said. He was extremely tall, with the wiry build of a low-gravity worlder who had worked hard to build the muscle to be a Caractacan. "And those soon fell apart, collapsing under the weight of sheer distance and complexity."

"And yet, from those recordings, it appears that someone has at least managed to put together enough resources to *suggest* that they command such an empire," Scalas pointed out. He was wondering if he had been the only one to notice the apparent cheapness of the infantry's equipment. Even Kranjick had not spoken of it. But this was neither the time nor the place for such analysis.

"Does it matter?" Costigan asked quietly. Lantern-jawed and brown-haired, Costigan even looked like the kind of hero that statues were made of. "Someone has demonstrated the power, ability, and willingness to attack one of the most important systems on the Rimward edge of the Avar Sector. That alone should merit our attention."

"Should it?" Dunstan asked. "If I recall correctly, Valdek is arguably at the very edge of the Sector; practically outside our patrol area. Are there not other systems closer by, weaker, that would be stripped of protection against the M'tait and pirates, such as the yeheri that Centurion Scalas so ably defeated a few days ago, if we respond with all the force available to us? And if this General-Regent has indeed appealed to every system within a hundred parsecs, well… that is a considerable relief force. Perhaps we should wait and see, rather than plunge headlong into a war we do not necessarily have a vested interest in."

Horvaset looked suddenly nervous. Scalas suspected she hadn't imagined her request would be met with such skepticism, much less a suggestion that it be ignored outright.

But Kranjick didn't even bother to look at Dunstan; he fixed his gaze on the Valdekan. "You will accompany me aboard the *Boanerges*, Captain."

The woman nearly wilted with relief. Kranjick had just answered her prayers.

"We will lift by nightfall tonight," Kranjick continued. He turned to Scalas. "Centurion Scalas."

"Yes, Brother Legate."

"When we are finished here, seek out Elder Nakamura." His voice was a deep, dry monotone. "You have two days to select nine men from his senior novices to bring your century back up to full strength. Once that is done and the *Dauntless* is fully refitted, you will follow us."

"Yes, sir."

Kranjick then turned his attention to Costigan. "Centurion Costigan. How long until the *Challenger* is ready for lift?"

"We can be ready in six hours, sir."

Kranjick shook his head ponderously. "No. You will not be fully refitted and rearmed in six hours, though your enthusiasm is commendable. I give you two days, until Centurion Scalas has selected his replacements."

"Yes, sir."

Once again Kranjick addressed Scalas. "You are in command in my absence, Centurion, until we rendezvous in the Valdek system. Understood?"

"Yes, Brother Legate." Scalas was proud that he had not even stammered. He could feel Dunstan's eyes on him, but didn't dare look at either Dunstan or Costigan.

Kranjick straightened, towering over his centurions. "We will meet in the war room to go over the rest of Captain Horvaset's intelligence before I leave. *Legio!*" His voice boomed out like a thunderclap. "*Dismissed!*"

———

The rest of the intelligence report was a jumbled collection of raw reports and imagery, clearly assembled in haste, that turned out to be hardly more informative than Horvaset's initial message. There was little in the way of a coherent picture to be gained from it, aside from a very basic idea of the strength of the fleet and army that the Valdekans were facing.

The numbers were truly unprecedented. No conflict had ever involved fleets anywhere close to the size being suggested by the Valdekan reports—at least not since the Qinglong Wars that had led to the destruction of Earth, and it was widely believed that the accounts of the Qinglong Wars had been inflated over time, as history had become legend. It was clear that the Caractacans would not be able to relieve Valdek by themselves—but it was equally clear that their help was needed. And so it would be offered. At the very least, they could buy the Valdekans time.

It was with that conclusion that Kranjick took up his helmet and strode out of the war room, headed for the distant pad where the blunt spearhead of the *Boanerges* pointed at the sky. Kranjick rarely took his war gear out of the starship when at the Keep, allowing for a speedy redeployment when needed. It was a habit that Scalas had tried to emulate.

Soon and Dunstan took their leave as well, Dunstan stiffly refusing to look at Scalas. Horvaset looked uncertain what to do until Costigan quietly suggested that she should probably follow Brother Legate Kranjick if she wished to board the *Boanerges* before she lifted. The captain, looking as lost and flustered as a first-year novice, hurried out, leaving only Scalas and Costigan.

"Congratulations, Erekan," Costigan said after an awkward silence. "I can't think of anyone else Kranjick could have picked among us."

Scalas had still been studying Horvaset's imagery, but now he looked up at Costigan. "Really?" He tried to keep his voice light. "Not even the hero of Tide's Point Station?"

Costigan snorted. "You set in for one suicidal last stand, and by some miracle you survive, and all of a sudden you're a god of war." He shook his head. "I thought you knew me better than that."

"Well, we haven't had much time to catch up since then." Scalas straightened from the display. "People change, Virgil. Warriors grow into roles they might not have foreseen for themselves."

Costigan shook his head. "I'm a fighter, not a leader. Tide's Point Station only happened because I figured I was already dead anyway, so I may as well take as many of the M'tait with me as I could. And it really didn't take much in the way of leadership or tactical acumen, either. It was a holding action in a confined corridor for most of it. 'Bad guys that way—shoot there.' Besides, now I'm a *cavalry* centurion. My tanks, combat sleds, and assault guns will probably have less to do in a defensive action than your infantry shooters."

Scalas chuckled and felt some of his tension draining away. He'd known Costigan since they had both been novices, Costigan a year ahead of Scalas. But their diverging responsibilities as centurions, coupled with Costigan's growing legend as the hero of Tide's Point Station, had made Scalas wonder if the other man had surpassed him to the extent that they could no longer truly be friends. The fact that Costigan certainly didn't think so was heartening, and it relieved some of the leaden weight that Scalas had felt in his chest ever since Kranjick had placed him in command of the legio still in the Avar Sector Keep.

"Don't tell Dunstan that," he said. "He's already insufferable enough as it is." He realized as soon as the words left his lips that he shouldn't speak ill of a fellow centurion, and with shame he resolved to speak to Father Corinus.

Costigan frowned. He hadn't been around Dunstan much since accepting command of Century XXXV and the *Challenger*. "What was that all about back there? Was he honestly suggesting that the Brotherhood refuse a request for aid?"

Scalas sighed. "He's become something of a 'New School pragmatist' over the last couple of years. I think it started back at the Brotherhood Citadel on Caerfaon. It seems that some of the younger generations of Brothers no longer consider the Code to be 'relevant.'"

Costigan's frown deepened. "I'd heard that such ideas were floating around, but I hadn't expected to find them in the Avar Sector Legio."

"Brother Legate Kranjick is well aware of it," Scalas assured him. "We've… spoken about it."

Costigan glanced toward the door where Soon and Dunstan had disappeared. "Can we trust him?"

"Trust this," Scalas said. "Dunstan is a competent soldier, and he's ambitious. I don't think he would willingly endanger his position by stepping too far out of line. He pushes boundaries, but he's not willing to break them entirely. Not yet."

"Well, I'll take your word for it. You are acting legate, after all." Costigan cracked a half-grin at his old friend. "Speaking of which, any instructions before I start to work making sure the logisticians load the right powergun charges back aboard the *Challenger, Acting Legate?*"

Scalas shook his head ruefully. "You know better than that. I have too much work of my own to do to play 'acting commander' power games. Get out of here."

Costigan laughed and clapped Scalas on the shoulder. As ever, it was bruising, but Scalas didn't mind. In fact he punched his friend back, and Costigan winced and rubbed the impact spot.

"You've gotten stronger."

"I'm a centurion," Scalas pointed out. "I *have* to be the strongest in the century."

Before heading out, he scooped up a copy of the intel report. He wanted to study it more closely. Something about what he'd seen was bothering him, he just couldn't say for sure what it was. Maybe, some time in between refitting the *Dauntless* and Century XXXII for launch, and vetting his replacements from among Elder Nakamura's novices, he'd have time to analyze the data in more detail. But he wouldn't hold his breath.

$$[\ 6 \ ]$$

"Centurion, I don't think I've ever seen so many neutrino emitters around one planet," Mor said.

The holo-tank was swarming with tiny fireflies centered on the planet Valdek, each glowing dot representing the neutrino signature of a starship's reactor. Of course, the data they were looking at was ninety minutes old; the *Dauntless*, along with the *Sword of the Brotherhood, Challenger*, and *Vindicator*, was still ninety light-minutes away from Valdek, hovering just above the rings of the most distant gas giant, nearly in the system's Oort cloud, which meant the ships they were currently monitoring would likely have changed orbits and vectors at least twice.

"The intel was certainly dead-on," Cobb muttered. The century's squad sergeants were currently all on the command deck, observing the holo-tank. Scalas had wanted everyone to have a look at what they were facing. "I believe the term *was* 'unprecedented.'"

"Are there any more around any of the outer colonies, Captain?" Scalas asked Mor.

The starship captain shook his head grimly. "It looks like all efforts are being focused on Valdek itself. I suspect there isn't anyone left alive on the outer colonies."

"Too much trouble to secure while they still had a central axis of resistance," Kahane speculated. "One thing is certain: whoever this 'Galactic Unity' is, they are not exactly honorable combatants."

"Did anyone really expect them to be?" Volscius asked acidly. *And since they aren't, attempting to fight with honor would be folly.* He didn't say it in so many words, but his tone implied it strongly.

Scalas felt that Volscius would do better in Dunstan's century, but Kranjick knew about Volscius's attitude—Kranjick knew about nearly everything in the legio—which meant he was deliberately keeping him where he was. Probably to prevent Dunstan from grooming an entirely 'pragmatist' century.

"No," Cobb said coldly. "But there is fighting dirty, and then there's mass murder. This appears to be the latter."

"Any sign of the *Boanerges*?" Scalas asked, forestalling further bickering between his subcommanders.

"Not yet," Mor replied. "We've been looking, but if Brother Legate Kranjick is being cautious, it may take time."

Almost as if it had been timed, the comm console chimed. "We're receiving a tight-beam communication from the *Boanerges*, Captain," the crewman announced.

Mor grimaced slightly, while Kahane and Solanus chuckled. Scalas permitted himself a half smile. "Of course we are," Mor muttered. Raising his voice, he said, "Content?"

"Only a rendezvous vector, sir," the crewman replied. He read off a string of numbers that described a direction, distance, and velocity relative to the ecliptic and the Valdekan sun, Goran 54.

"Navigation?" Mor asked.

The navigator took a moment to calculate the trajectory and where it led. Then he whistled. "Impressive."

"Just relay the information, Nav," Mor said testily.

"Sorry, sir. It appears that the *Boanerges* is presently station-keeping inside the tail of a comet, approximately fifteen light-minutes from Valdek."

Scalas raised an eyebrow. Staying within a comet's tail was not only a difficult maneuver, it was only partially effective as camouflage—not at all like the gas giant they were currently orbiting, which was putting out enough radioactive noise to mask their ships' signatures. A comet was a relatively inert ball of ice and rock, and if someone was really looking, it wouldn't be nearly sufficient to disguise either the ship's neutrino signature or its heat emissions. Even so, if it was the only concealment available that close…

"You mean they were there ninety minutes ago," Cobb pointed out. "Have any of the enemy ships started to move toward them?"

Mor motioned toward the holo-tank. "You can see the display as well as I can, Squad Sergeant. So far, it looks like the *Boanerges* is still undetected."

"Can our four ships fit in the tail with the *Boanerges*?" Scalas asked.

Mor squinted at the holo-tank, bringing up a sensor readout of the comet. It was on its downward fall toward Goran 54, its tail billowing out at an angle to its orbit, pushed out by the solar wind. It still had a very long way to fall before it reached perihelion, so the tail was only about a third as large as it was going to get. Mor's lips moved slightly as he ran numbers in his head.

"I think we can, provided the clods driving the *Sword* and *Vindicator* don't collide with one of us in the murk," he said at last. "I suggest you get to your acceleration couches, gentlemen, and strap in. We'll be maneuvering shortly. Provided that is your chosen course of action, Centurion?" he added, as if just remembering that Scalas was the acting legate.

Scalas only nodded. "We will be below," he said, gesturing to the squad sergeants and starting toward the lift hatch.

———

After a brief exchange of tight-beam burst communications, the four starships went inertialess, lit their drives, and moved out of orbit, pushing to the far side of the gas giant. There, in deep space, with the gas giant and all its radiation between them and the enemy forces surrounding Valdek, the four ships made their vector changes, matching the trajectory and velocity of the comet, before once again activating their Bergenholm fields and pushing deeper into the system at just below the speed of light.

———

When the *Dauntless*'s Bergenholm field cut out completely, she was a very precise two hundred meters from the *Boanerges*, just inside the comet's tail, velocities matched to the point that neither starship appeared to be moving at all.

Mor nodded in satisfaction, especially when he checked the holo-tank and saw the *Vindicator* and the *Sword of the Brotherhood* still maneuvering to close the distance and match velocities more carefully. The *Challenger*, on the other hand, was holding station on the other side of the *Boanerges*, completely relatively motionless, which softened his triumphant smirk.

A small portion of the holo-tank lit with Brother Legate Kranjick's heavy, immobile face. "Welcome to the Valdek system, gentlemen," he said. "Full remote conference, all centurions and ship captains."

In moments, one side of the holo-tank filled with the images of the task group's commanders. Mor thumb-clicked an icon, and his own face appeared, not only in his holo-tank and the holo-tanks on the other ships, but also below, where Centurion Scalas was strapped in.

"We are uploading the last forty-eight hours of the *Boanerges*'s sensor logs to each of you," Kranjick began, "but I will sum up what we have seen. The planet is under near-continual bombardment. We have observed no enemy ships in orbit—it appears that the planetary defenses are still formidable enough to prevent that—but instead appear to be staging in the Lagrange points and making high-velocity runs past the planet to launch dropships, transatmospheric fighters, and kinetic kill munitions. They are being answered with powerguns, heavy particle beams, heavy railguns, and high-energy lasers."

That made sense. Defensive missiles would be too vulnerable during the early stages of launch, as they struggled to build their velocity from low in the gravity well. Though Mor questioned how precisely a railgun heavy enough to be effective from the surface could be aimed at starships moving at or over escape velocity.

"There is a significant amount of debris in high orbit," Kranjick continued, "and some of it is highly radioactive. Captain Horvaset informs me that the density and pattern of the debris is consistent with nearly seventy-five percent of Valdek's fleet having been wiped out in space."

"Rehenek's message said he was sending similar pleas to every ally they had within a hundred parsecs," Soon put in. "Is there any indication that any allied fleets have arrived to lend their assistance?"

It was Captain Trakse, the *Boanerges*'s commander, who answered. "Over the last few hours, we have detected neutrino signatures consistent with small squadrons of starships on the fringes of the system. But they seem reluctant to come deeper in. Either they're waiting for more of a critical mass of ships…"

"Or they're simply too afraid to face that swarm down there," Scalas said coldly.

"No one has seen a fleet this size since the Qinglong Wars, if then," Kranjick pointed out. "There are at least five hundred ships per Lagrange point down there. That would make any starship commander with sense have second thoughts."

"Except for us," Dunstan put in, a bitter note in his voice.

Kranjick's expression didn't change, but his eyes turned several degrees colder. "Indeed," he said. "Suggestions, gentlemen?"

"If we're going to attack, we have very little time to act," Mor said. "The emissions from our passage in-system will reach their sensors in less than ten minutes. At that point, surprise will be impossible."

"Surprise, yes, but misdirection might still be possible," Hwung-

Tsi, the *Challenger*'s captain, pointed out. "A series of short, tachyonic dashes could place multiple false neutrino signatures along multiple vectors around the planet in only a few minutes. They won't know where the real attack is coming from until we're right on top of them."

"Which raises the question," Costigan said, "what is the attack plan? We don't have the firepower to take on five hundred ships at once."

"If I may make a suggestion," said Trakse, "look at the take from the probe on the far side of the comet. A strike force just launched from L2, heading down toward the planet. I suggest that would be an appropriate first target."

"How long until they're on target?" Kranjick asked.

"They do not appear to have engaged their Bergenholms," Trakse said, looking off camera for a moment, apparently gathering data. "At their current rate of acceleration… they will pass perigee with the planet in approximately ten hours."

Mor frowned. Engaging the enemy ships when at their lowest point in the gravity well—and also when they were most likely to be target-fixated on the planet—made sense tactically. But it would also be almost ten hours after the Caractacan ships' presence in the system had been detected.

But Hwung-Tsi was smiling. "I think we can kill two birds with one arrow here, gentlemen."

He explained the broad strokes of his idea, and soon the ship captains were nodding in agreement. Most of the centurions were somewhat more blasé about the plan; any Caractacan commander had to be somewhat versed in all spheres of conflict, be they space, air, or ground, but there were still areas where each had their specialization, and the centurions were ground fighters. The finer points of the plan didn't appeal to their sense of aesthetics the same way they did to the starship captains.

It took only a short time to hammer out the plan's details. There was still a great deal of hard work and calculation ahead, but the general plan of attack had been determined. It would now be up to the starship captains and their crews to execute it.

"We have only a matter of minutes before our emissions reach the enemy, gentlemen," Kranjick said. "Let us be away from this comet before that happens."

The faces vanished from the holo-tank, and Mor got to work.

———

A few minutes later, the *Dauntless, Vindicator,* and *Challenger* went inert barely thirty light-seconds from L3. They immediately lit their drives and began their vector changes. After waiting just long enough for the nearest ship hanging in the Lagrange point to have detected them, all three ships went tachyonic again and flashed away.

———

It was a short hop, only lasting about ten milliseconds. In that time, they found themselves out past the system's Oort cloud. Goran 54 was a speck of light behind them, lost in the vast starfield. Beyond lay the Rim and the myriad points of light that were distant galaxies and globular clusters.

It took a few moments for the navigators to pinpoint their coordinates and relative vector. Then they turned the Bergenholms to negative mass once more and plunged back inward toward Valdek.

Again and again, for hours, they continued their maneuvers. The two elements of starships would go tachyonic, suddenly go inert within a light-minute of one or another of the Lagrange points the so-called "Galactic Unity" was using as staging points, conduct a delta-v burn, then go tachyonic again, outrunning sluggish light and skipping to the edge of the system before doing it all over again at a different place. They could sometimes time their dashes to present the enemy scanners with neutrino signatures close enough together that it appeared that a single, large element had appeared and fled all at once, rather than a smaller element coming and going several times. Such was the advantage of short, superluminal hops.

Every time they cut their Bergenholms, they adjusted their inert vectors to come closer and closer to the attack vector they would need to finally intercept the strike force that was accelerating toward the planet. And after just over nine hours, all five ships had, by way of numerous carefully calculated burns, reached their calculated inert attack vectors.

It was time.

———

The *Dauntless* was once again skimming through deep space, out past the distant gas giant they had first approached when entering the system. That enormous failed star was invisible in the black, too far away to be seen without a telescope, even if one of the Brothers had looked out a viewport.

"Stand by all gunnery stations," Mor snapped. He was still strapped into his acceleration couch, his helmet and armor sealed, as he had been the entire past ten hours. Fortunately, the armor had been designed with such unpleasant possibilities in mind, so he had not had to forgo bodily functions for that long. "Gentlemen," he said, his voice echoing through the ship, "when we go inert again, we will be on final attack vector. Stand by for combat maneuvers." He looked at the holo-tank, tapping controls built into his couch's armrest. "Bergenholm engaging in five... four... three... two... one."

The *Dauntless*'s substantial mass was, for a fraction of a second, measured in negative numbers. She crossed half the system in a tiny fraction of the time it would take a photon to make the journey.

The Bergenholm cut out too quickly for human reflexes. Mor prided himself on his consummate skill as a pilot, but tachyonic trajectories had to be precisely programmed into the flight computer. Any human pilot would never be able to manually control the ship with the precision necessary; in the time it would take to tap a button, the starship could travel light-hours.

The crowded circle of light that was all an unaided observer could see ahead of a tachyonic starship suddenly exploded into the full starfield, and the planet Valdek leapt out at them until it resolved into a variegated sphere no more than a light-second away.

It was an unremarkable planet as inhabited worlds went—at least from what the scans and the Brotherhood's records said. Seas covered only about fifty percent of the planet, and were almost entirely landlocked. Though tectonically inert, the planet was still volcanically active. A string of shield volcanoes stretched across the southern hemisphere. The massive volcano in the northern hemisphere—Gorakovati—dwarfed all of them. It was so tall its peak almost reached beyond the atmosphere.

Little of the surface was visible at the moment. Massive storms had been kicked up by the orbital bombardment, and the near side of the planet was wreathed in flickering clouds, swirling with wildly conflicting eddies as the atmosphere was cooked and hammered relentlessly by high-energy weapons. Mor took the image in at a glance. The planet was not presently his chief concern.

"Deploy the weapons array," he ordered. They were hurtling toward the planet at hundreds of kilometers per second, and closing with the enemy ships at a decent fraction of that. Time was of the essence.

Her drive flaming white-hot before her, the *Dauntless* deployed her weapons constellation. X-ray laser pods drifted outward, held in their relative positions by inertia and careful thruster burns. Missiles shot out of their cells, their seeker heads already looking for targets according to the instructions programmed by the gunnery chief. Decoy bots rushed out to fill the space between ships with thermal, radioactive, and neutrino signatures similar to the starships' reactors. Local space was quickly getting crowded. The Caractacan ships were spaced tens of thousands of kilometers apart, yet that was hardly enough space to keep their weapons constellations from interfering with each other.

The enemy ships were much deeper in the gravity well than the Caractacan starships that were gaining on them, but scanners and remote telescopes showed an enhanced, magnified view in Mor's holo-tank. The enemy ships were sharp-edged, angular, elongated pyramids, painted white with blue markings. There appeared to be about ten of them, though appearances could be deceiving. While it was impossible to hide a ship in open space, there were ways to fill space with so much noise that it could cost a gunner the vital few seconds needed to sort out the junk from the targets. And at these ranges and velocities, with the power of the weapons involved, life and death hung on a margin of milliseconds.

"Powergun batteries and HELs open fire as soon as solutions are reached," Mor commanded. "Missiles as well. X-ray lasers, fire upon minimum safe arming distance." That was not "minimum safe distance" from the target, but from the *Dauntless*.

The powergun batteries and high-energy laser emitters were just reaching the ends of their deployment booms, and soon invisible lines of intense collimated light and lightning-colored bolts of copper plasma were stabbing toward the enemy ships.

The holo-tank flashed red, and an alarm whooped as the ship shuddered and rang like a bell. "Grazing hit, HEL, Quadrant Four," the damage control officer reported. "Hull breach." He paused, listening and scanning his screen. "Contained. No major damage."

The impact had more than likely been from a snap shot that had just barely managed to burn through the hull. The Caractacan ships had one major advantage over the enemy starcraft: though the enemy had to have known they were coming, after the last ten hours of ghost echoes, they would not have known exactly when or where. The attacking Caractacan starships had outrun the lightspeed signals that would have warned their targets they were coming, right up until they had cut the Bergenholms. That gave them a few seconds' head start, and that might be all it would take.

In the holo-tank, the bright, flashing lines of laser pulses and powergun bolts rained down on the enemy craft. One took a powergun bolt to the drive bay and detonated silently, hypervelocity packets of copper ions destroying the drives' magnetic plasma containment fields. Another ship caught half a dozen laser pulses that punched through hull metal and anything on the other side. A gout of vapor puffed from the ship's flank, but other than that it was apparently unhurt. But many of the shots were misses, either because of poorly predicted target vectors, or because they had been aimed at decoys. There was no time to worry about distinguishing the real ships from the fake; when fractions of a second count, *every* target that can be engaged, must be.

Two more starships flared white and vanished, turning into miniature suns under the impact of X-ray lasers, which transferred as much energy to their target as a direct hit from a thermonuclear weapon.

Meanwhile, the distance between the two forces was shrinking rapidly. The Caractacan ships were braking at less than a half gee—in part to present their drive plumes as additional defensive measures—but they were still moving several times faster than the ships they were pursuing, the ones that had moments ago been focused on attacking the planet.

As the enemy ships neared the planet, locked into their approach vectors, a storm of fire erupted from the surface below. The lead enemy ship was suddenly connected to the cloud tops by a bright, gossamer line of greenish light… and was abruptly cut in half lengthwise. A moment later its reactor, breached by the particle beam, detonated in a brilliant, silent flash.

Caught between groundside defensive fire and an unexpected attack from above, the remaining ships suddenly went inertialess and flashed away, rapidly accelerating to near lightspeed, making for the L4 point, between Valdek and its second moon. The only ship that continued on its previous vector was the one that had been holed by multiple HEL pulses. It was apparently dead.

Mor was about to issue the order to follow suit. Staying inert above the planet would only invite a counterattack from one of the Lagrange points, and the Caractacans would then find themselves in a similar position to their latest adversaries. And he had no concern about retrieving the X-ray laser pods, as they'd deployed few enough to be expendable.

But before Mor could say a word, Kranjick's face appeared in the holo-tank again. "All Caractacan ships, stand by for high-gee braking maneuvers. We have been contacted by the General-Regent, and he has requested that we descend to the surface."

"Brother Legate," Hwung-Tsi protested, "that will put us at a disadvantage. We would be at the bottom of the gravity well."

"He has assured me that the situation is far more dire on the surface than in orbit. We may require the starships for close support." Kranjick paused. "It is true that we will not have the velocity or mobility advantage that we might have in space… but if the planet is lost under us, we will have accomplished nothing. Prepare to descend."

Mor clenched his jaw, as much in anticipation of the upcoming maneuver as in dissatisfaction with the prospect of descending to a planetary surface while there was still a space battle going on. But he was a Caractacan Brother, and he followed orders.

He keyed the "All Decks" comm. "Stand by for high-gee maneuvers," he said. "Six gees to commence in… three minutes."

[7]

THE DESCENT WAS ROUGH, BUT THE FEROCIOUS BUFFETING OF A STEEP dive into the roiled, storm-wracked upper atmosphere of Valdek seemed almost gentle compared to the extended six-gravity braking maneuver that had been necessary to slow the ships to below escape velocity so they could be captured by the planet's gravity. They whipped around the far side of the planet—only to encounter a formation of twenty more long, pyramidal ships plunging toward them from the L2 point.

As their descent turned into a powered dive, HELs and powergun bolts stabbed at them from above, their brilliant light scoring lines through the attenuated air that would have been impressed on retinas for some time after, had anyone looked directly at them. The thunderous concussion of an energy weapon's passage, explosively super-heating even the thin atmosphere at that altitude, rocked the *Dauntless* with a near-miss. Only the persistence of the decoys above, the high relative velocities, and the increasingly heavy counter-fire from the surface kept the enemy ships from scoring a direct hit.

Even so, Mor saw the blast of a powergun bolt pass close enough to the *Vindicator* that it tossed the starship hard to one side, almost knocking her out of control. He couldn't spare the attention to watch more closely, but he expected that the *Vindicator* had sustained some serious damage on one flank from the blast and thermal effects alone.

Particle beams lanced up from below, hammering their own tunnels through the atmosphere, and Mor had to thrust hard to steer around the narrow columns of high-energy ions and their accompanying hurricane turbulence. He was tempted to curse the gunners down below —until he saw one of the attacking cruisers above pinned by three beams, a fraction of a second before it exploded.

And then *Dauntless* was plunging into a billowing thunderstorm, and he had other problems to worry about.

Lightning nearly as intense as the powergun and particle beam fire flashed through the clouds, and thunder rocked the starship. Intense crosswinds, moving at well over three hundred kilometers per hour, tried to spin the vessel out of control. If not for the starship's powerful sensors she would have been blind in the dark gray clouds that swirled violently around her hull, lashing her with hail, rain, and particulate matter thrown into the atmosphere by the bombardment.

Though physically he was doing little more than tapping controls with his fingertips, Mor was drenched in sweat as he tried to compensate for every gust, especially as the ship's velocity continued to fall as she got deeper into the atmosphere. The red glow of her meteoric descent into the stratosphere had faded, and soon she would be standing on her tail, descending on her drive plume. At that point she would be fully vertical, and flight would become even more treacherous as the tearing winds tried to snatch the ship off balance.

The *Dauntless* dropped out of the clouds, descending into driving rain that was instantly turned into steam and plasma by the white-hot flame of her drive. The gray of the storm was lit by another brilliant line of blazing green as another of the groundside particle beam weapons fired on the enemy ships overhead, invisible to the naked eye through the swirling overcast.

Mor spared a brief moment to switch the holo-tank to an

enhanced view of the scene below. He needed to know where they were going, and what they were dropping into.

The *Dauntless* was currently three thousand meters above the ground. Below stretched a broad plateau on the shoulder of Gorakovati, the gigantic northern shield volcano.

The entire plateau was a war zone.

At one end of the plateau, just where the steeper slopes of the volcano began to flatten out, hulked a sprawling fortress, an edifice that dwarfed the Avar Sector Keep. A gigantic central dome was surrounded by multiple concentric rings of defensive emplacements, including massive spherical emitters for particle beam weapons and HELs. The long, crane-like structures mounted on the slopes above had to be the railguns.

Only three of those defensive rings now stood, though the remains of at least three more could be seen, broken and in some cases still burning fiercely despite the rain and wind. The ground beyond the third ring had been churned and cratered by armored vehicles, artillery, and explosives. If there had been any vegetation growing there before, it had been crushed, blasted, or burned to ash. Surely nothing lived for kilometers around the planetary fortress except what was contained in armor.

The enemy dropships stood on the opposite edge of the plateau. These were smaller, squatter versions of the starships above—blunt, angular pyramids squatting on heavy landing jacks—and were surrounded by dug-in artillery, supply dumps, and vast staging areas for troops and armored vehicles.

"Gunnery," Mor called out. "I want powergun batteries deployed for atmospheric employment. If we're going to fly over those positions, I expect we're going to take some fire." Especially since they weren't flying as fast as he would have liked. They were still moving laterally at considerable velocity, but not so fast that they couldn't be targeted and hit, especially with the blinding light of their drive to shoot at.

Kranjick's face appeared in the holo-tank again. "Valdekan

Command is transmitting a flight path, gentlemen," he said, his voice as slow and bored-sounding as ever, even after what they had just been through. Mor knew about some of what the Brother Legate had seen during his long years of service. The man's air of boredom was come by honestly, though he had always suspected that it was also simply a part of Kranjick's leadership style. Kranjick knew the men couldn't get overly excited as long as their commander sounded bored. "They strongly suggest that we stick to it, as ground-based batteries will be engaging the enemy on the ground to help cover our approach."

Almost before he had finished speaking, elevated gun positions on the flanks of the mountain opened fire, the railgun rounds dimly visible as streaks of dull red as they went hypersonic before leaving the barrels. They struck the fortifications set up around the dropships and several of the breaches in the fallen defensive rings with catastrophic force, hitting with brilliant flashes that looked almost like small thermonuclear charges.

Mor wasn't going to leave it at that, however. The *Dauntless* had a better vantage point anyway. "Gunnery, identify probable powergun and railgun positions and engage at will. Prioritize what can do the most damage to the ship."

"Yes, sir," replied Gunnery Chief Carne. A moment later, the thunder of the powergun discharges rumbled faintly through the hull, and in the holo-tank, brilliant blue-white bolts flickered down from the sky, striking so fast that they looked more like lightning flashes than discrete projectiles. Armored vehicles and gun emplacements erupted into brilliant fireballs wherever the bolts touched.

Even so, the Caractacans couldn't hope to suppress *all* the enemy ground fire. The starships had more powerful batteries, elevated position, and more capable scanners, but the enemy had more weapons by far. Answering plasma packets immediately stabbed skyward at the approaching hulls.

The Caractacan starships' countermeasures kicked in just as quickly, making hash of any active targeting systems. The inclement conditions helped. But when the target is a ship the size of a skyscraper, balanced on a pillar of actinic fire, there is only so much that countermeasures can accomplish. The *Challenger* was hit the hardest, hammered by nearly a dozen powergun bolts as she roared overhead. The bolts weren't ship-killers, but she shuddered under the impacts, her drive flickered, and began to drop faster. Mor hoped that meant that she was trying to get lower to evade, not that she was losing power.

All five ships replied with a withering storm of powergun fire, every shipboard battery opening fire until the assault looked almost like sheet lightning. The emplacement that had scored its hits on the *Challenger* vanished in a superheated cloud of atomized metal and rock.

And then the ships had passed over the enemy lines and were descending on the fortress itself. They had all been tilted slightly toward the mountain, utilizing their main drives for both lift and forward thrust, but as they neared the massive, clamshell doors of the armored spaceport's landing pads, they started to come fully vertical. Their lateral velocity slowed to a near standstill, and they began to slowly drop toward the enclosed pads. Only then did their batteries cease fire, though the roaring flames of rocket artillery exhausts and the dully glowing streaks of ground-based railgun rounds were still sailing off into the gray of the storm, toward enemy emplacements now invisible to the naked eye. They were now receiving only sporadic laser, powergun, and missile fire from the enemy lines, and the missiles were being easily swatted out of the air by the point defense lasers of both the Valdekan fortress and the Caractacan starships.

Mor turned his attention to landing the ship. The pad below him was completely obscured by clouds of vapor from the silo's cooling systems—he was, after all, about to land on the sun-hot drive plume —but the holo-tank showed him that the pad was sunken a good three hundred meters below the surface, and the silo above it was not exactly spacious.

He was thankful that at least he was not trying to land the damaged *Challenger* or even the *Vindicator* in such a small bay.

A tap of a finger fired thrusters for a split second, nudging the big ship to one side and bringing the dotted line of thrust in the holo-tank more in line with the centerline of the silo. This was now entirely an instrument approach. The billowing clouds of condensation made an approach by eye impossible.

Slowly, her drive thrumming through every beam and plate, the *Dauntless* descended into the dimness of the landing silo. The roar of her drive reverberated in the enclosed space, shaking the ship's hull even more and creating an all-consuming blast of noise that was almost intolerable. But at last Mor felt the faint jar of contact, the indicator in the holo-tank demonstrated that the starship had come to rest on her landing jacks, and the thunder quieted.

He was suddenly aware that a voice was coming over the comms. "All Caractacan starships," the voice said in accented Trade Cant, "be advised that we will be closing the overhead bay doors. This is for your protection. We are being bombarded at semi-regular intervals by enemy ships in space and are receiving some effective rocket artillery fire from their positions beyond the defenses. *Do not* attempt to launch without coordinating with Planetary Defense Central."

Whatever came next, they were committed.

Scalas did not enjoy space combat. He couldn't say he especially enjoyed spaceflight at all. When he was on the ground, leading his century, he was in control of his own fate—as much as a man ever could be. But strapped into an acceleration couch aboard the *Dauntless*, feeling every thruster burn and maneuver, he was helpless, unable to lift a finger to aid or hinder anyone. And that was not to his liking.

He knew he was far from alone. Most of the Caractacan ground fighters felt the same. Every one of them had received cross-training in space and atmospheric flight during their novitiate, but for some, that only made the lack of control worse. Like Scalas, they couldn't wait to get out of the couches and on the ground, their feet under them and their powerguns in their hands.

As soon as the light above Scalas's couch turned green, he slapped the release on his safety harness and got up, his joints creaking slightly, his muscles protesting. The life of a Caractacan Brother was not an easy one, and the deorbiting maneuver, followed by atmospheric entry, had not been gentle. But with a roll of his shoulders, he drew his powergun from its rack next to his couch, drew himself up straight, and strode toward the exit hatch. Most of his First Squad joined him, while the others began to ascend from the lower troop decks. They faced the hatch with a grim silence that mirrored his own.

He'd had a replica of Mor's holo-tank display piped to him throughout the space battle and the descent, so he knew what they were facing out there on the defensive lines. Even five hundred Caractacans would be hard-pressed to put a dent in *that*.

"Squad sergeants!" he barked as he walked, his voice amplified by his exterior speakers. "Squads Two through Five, muster on the troop decks and stand by. Squad One will debark with me and make liaison with our hosts."

He got his acknowledgments as he came to the debarkation hatch and touched the opening control with one gauntleted hand. Like the rest of the Caractacans, he was in full combat armor already; true to their training, the Brothers had landed ready to fight.

The hatch irised open, revealing a gangway reaching through still-swirling clouds of coolant mist. There was no one on the gangway, and it vanished into the murk beyond. Scalas squinted behind his vision slit. He didn't expect the Valdekans to betray them and set an ambush, but Caractacan training taught the Brothers never to allow themselves to become complacent, even among friends.

There *were* no friends, really. There were Brothers, enemies, and those the Brothers were sworn to protect. That was all.

And enemies often were not above using those under Caractacan protection to try to get at them.

He allowed none of these thoughts to show in his body language as he strode out onto the gangway, and even though his face was hidden behind the jutting prow of his helmet's visor, he kept his expression neutral. He held his powergun easily in his hands, the barrel slanted down and to one side, but ready to be snapped to the butt-stop on his pauldron in a split second. His eyes searched the fog, his every muscle tensed just enough to throw him into a sprint as soon as a shot came out of that mist.

As he moved along the gangway, he was dimly aware of the distant thunder of friendly and enemy artillery batteries continuing to exchange fire. When a heavier series of impacts shook the decking beneath his feet, he assumed that the ships that had come after them from the L2 point were taking the opportunity to fire the salvo that their predecessors had been unable to. The noise was increasingly muted, however, as the great clamshell doors over the landing pit slowly closed.

The portal at the far end of the gangway loomed out of the haze, lit by yellowish glow rods. A trio of figures were standing on the other side, stiffly at attention and well back from the coolant gases; his helmet display indicated those gases were still hotter than any human being outside a suit could survive.

The central figure wore a sidearm at his hip, while the two on either side held coil guns at port arms, the power cables arching over their shoulders to their power packs with parade-ground precision.

Scalas was well aware of the figure he cut as he came out of the billowing coolant fog. His armor had taken on a shifting shade of dark gray to black, his centurion's bars a faded, slightly lighter shade of the same gray on his pauldrons. His vision slit was nothing but a dark line of faceless watchfulness. Ammunition packs bulked around his belt-line, and in his hands he carried his powergun, shorter and stubbier than the long-barreled coil guns the honor guard carried, but capable of much more than the gauss weapons.

The double file of similarly armored figures looming behind him would be no less intimidating. Especially since the honor guard was only partially armored, dressed in mottled camouflage utilities, with open-faced helmets and chest armor. Lightweight exoskeletons were strapped to their hips and legs, unpowered, intended only to support the not-inconsiderable weight of the coilgun power packs. The downside of the exoskeletons was that they were stiff and limiting, lacking the full articulation of Brotherhood combat armor.

The man with the sidearm saluted stiffly, bringing a hand to his temple, palm out. "I am Major Athanasi Stojanek," he announced in halting Trade Cant. "Valdekan Ground Forces."

"Centurion Erekan Scalas, Century XXXII of the Caractacan Brotherhood," Scalas rumbled in reply, raising the muzzle of his powergun to return the salute.

The major cut his salute. "We are glad to have you here, Centurion. Come with me, please." He turned on his heel and started down the vaulted corridor behind him. "The starport commander is meeting your legate in the central staging area. I am instructed to bring you there."

Scalas turned to Kahane. "Pick five men to come with me. The rest stay here and secure the gangway until we know where the rest of the century will be going."

Kahane nodded and turned to call out the centurion's escort. The five Brothers he'd chosen, one of them toting an MT-41 1.5cm support powergun, stepped forward and joined Scalas as he turned and followed the Valdekan honor guards. Kahane wasn't getting complacent, either; sending one of the two squad support gunners along with the centurion was a message. And from the look on one of the honor guards' faces, the message had been received. That heavy powergun could do some appalling damage.

The officer led them down the corridor to what was unmistakably a tram station. A car was already waiting, and in moments the honor guard and the Caractacans were aboard and being whisked down the long length of the starport. More stations flashed by, one for every cluster of three or four landing pits.

The car hissed smoothly to a halt after only a few moments, and the officer stepped out and waited at attention for the Caractacans. Scalas followed him out, looking around at the gigantic underground staging area before him.

The chamber might have been a grand lobby for a civilian starport if it hadn't been on the flanks of a planetary defense fortress. Carved pillars held up the domed roof, studded with glowing sconces elaborately sculpted and programmed to flicker as if they were ancient lanterns. Vaulted, armored windows let in a dim, gray light from above, momentarily brightened by the flash of an explosion or the ripping, glowing passage of a railgun round. Train stations stood at each corner of the compass, and Scalas quickly figured out where each one led. The north and south stations led to either end of the spaceport. Westward led back to the central dome of the fortress while the eastern station led outward, toward the outer defensive rings.

At the moment, the entire vast space was a mass of seething humanity in various levels of camouflage and combat armor. One quarter of the chamber appeared to have been turned into a field hospital, packed with wounded who were being hauled in from the defensive station. Screams of agony contended with the murmur of nervous soldiers wondering what was going to happen next and the unintelligible shouts of officers and NCOs directing their men. The marbled tile floor, a contrast to the utilitarian gray metal of the landing pit, was spattered with dark stains and scored with deep scratches. The Valdekans had not been overly careful moving equipment while under siege, and these were definitely not the first wounded to have passed through.

The liaison officer led the way through the crowd, shouting in the local dialect to clear the way. Not that his shouts were particularly necessary; the looming, armored forms of the Caractacans were as threatening as they were reassuring, and the Valdekan soldiers stepped aside quickly.

Thanks to his size, Brother Legate Kranjick stood out clearly even amid the sea of humanity. Often legates had standards that could be lifted on telescoping mounts to serve the same purpose, but Kranjick had always foregone that particular bit of heraldry. He was not a man for display—even a situation like this, where some might have bolstered the locals' morale—and yet he was something of a morale-boosting display unto himself.

The legate's emotionless vision slit turned like a gun turret to lock onto Scalas as the six men from Century XXXII approached. His laconic voice crackled over the battle net. "Centurions, with me. The General-Regent wishes to speak with us before we deploy. The rest can wait here. I will leave it to individual initiative if they wish to render aid to the wounded."

Scalas saw that Soon was already standing next to Kranjick, along with a tall, pale Valdekan officer. Horvaset and her bridge officers had joined them as well, dressed in their shipboard spacesuits. Costigan and Dunstan were making their way through the crowd. Costigan had the same five-man honor guard as Scalas, Soon, and Kranjick. Dunstan, however, had half a squad with him.

The pale Valdekan officer was standing stiffly at attention, his head only barely coming to Kranjick's pauldron. He clicked his heels together as the centurions gathered around. "The Duchess and the General-Regent are in the command center, gentlemen, madam. If you will follow me?"

He turned and led the way toward the tram station that Scalas had pegged as the one leading back toward the central dome of the fortress. The Valdekan kept his back ramrod-straight and didn't spare a glance for the hordes of wounded men—men with limbs blown off, their flesh charred, or nearly flayed alive by shrapnel. Scalas was not a squeamish man, but he was glad that his suit filtered out the odor of burnt flesh and blood. Putting the field hospital here was not a good idea. How many of the men embarking for the defensive perimeter had to go past that screaming charnel house on their way to fight and die? Morale would be at an all-time low before they even got on the train.

Perhaps the Valdekan commanders were simply not all that competent. Or perhaps they were even more hard-pressed than the Caractacans knew. Scalas wondered at that as they headed deeper into the fortress. And he wondered if any of them would leave this world alive.

[8]

THE FORTRESS'S COMMAND CENTER WAS NOT LARGE. IT WAS ROUGHLY the size of the *Dauntless'* command deck and looked much the same: a central holo-tank ringed by two dozen smaller consoles, all facing it. The air crackled with comm chatter in Eastern Satevic, a babble of what must have been status reports, requests for support, targeting instructions for the artillery and the planetary defense batteries, and coordinating instructions.

Scalas took a half step closer to the holo-tank, peering at the picture of the battle within. It glittered with a mass of unfamiliar glowing symbols, but none were so different from those used by the Caractacans that he couldn't decipher them. And if he was reading the symbols right, the situation was worse than he'd thought.

The picture that he had gotten on the way down had been incomplete. He'd had only the *Dauntless*'s targeting information and flight data to work with, and that had been limited by the weather and the electronic warfare seething invisibly throughout the atmosphere and the orbitals. Now there was more information available. The tank was being fed not only by direct observation, but also from reporting that was coming in from the surrounding defensive positions.

And according to that reporting, vast legions of enemy troops and armor surrounded the plateau. The army besieging this particular Valdekan planetary defense fortress alone numbered in the hundreds of thousands, and that wasn't even taking into account the size of the fleets in the Lagrange points, or ground forces on other parts of the planet.

Who can afford to carry these numbers across interstellar space to make war?

Even with an entire system's resources available, the logistics alone were mind-boggling. It took massive numbers to try to control only one planet; to attempt to exert control over multiple worlds... This was why most attempts at interstellar empire in galactic history had collapsed relatively quickly, and none of those had tried to conquer by brute force.

Scalas took all this in at a glance as he continued to follow Kranjick, Horvaset and her officers, and the rest of the legio's centurions toward the far side of the command center, where two figures awaited them.

The first was a squat, heavyset man with white hair, a stubby nose that looked like it had been broken many times without reparative surgery afterward, and a thick mustache. In his prime, he must have been a formidable man, but now he was pale and wan, held upright by a medical exoskeleton that was pumping several tubes worth of fluids into him. The white coverall he wore beneath the exoskeleton bulged in several places, where Scalas assumed bandages and healing packs had been placed. It was clear this man had been badly wounded. And yet here he was, on his feet, his eyes still alert despite the pain that was written on his craggy features.

The second figure was a woman, taller than the man, her graying hair pulled back behind her head in a tight bun, wearing a high-collared, vaguely military tunic over her own white coverall. As the Caractacans approached, she glanced at the wounded man and moved to stand close behind his shoulder. There was concern in that look, but it was quickly disguised as she adopted a cold, businesslike mien, facing the advancing armored warriors.

"You must be the legate," the old man said. His voice was scratchy and hoarse, but Scalas recognized it from the recording of Horvaset's message. This was Rehenek, the General-Regent of Valdek. "I would welcome you, but it would seem hollow given what's happening here. Not that we are ungrateful that you have come, but I fear that there is little you can do for us now."

"What exactly *is* happening here, General-Regent?" Kranjick asked. He had removed his helmet, and Scalas reached up to do the same. One by one, the other centurions followed suit. "Who is this 'Galactic Unity'? Where are they getting the resources for a campaign of this magnitude?"

Rehenek sighed and motioned for them to follow him. "That is a tale better told away from all of this," he said, waving to indicate the cacophony of activity in the command center.

He led the way through a narrow door, directly opposite the lift they had entered by, and into a small, private briefing theater. Rehenek walked—or steered his exoskeleton—stiffly toward a small console mounted to the wall to one side of the door. "It will be easier to show you than tell you, I think," he said.

They stood together, the centurions encased in their armor, the General-Regent in his exoskeleton, a nightmare assembly of mechanical men, some fever-dream of the Qinglong cultists, as the lights dimmed. Then a holo sprang up from the floor, surrounding them. The entire room was a holo-tank, one that a viewer could stand inside.

The holo flickered to life, and the room seemed to vanish.

———

They appeared to be standing in space, above a deep-space station. If the size of the star was any indication, they were another five light-minutes out from Goran 54. The station was a bog-standard ring construct, with just enough radius to give about a half-gee spin gravity without too much Coriolis effect destroying the crew's equilibrium, and there was nothing particularly interesting about it. It could have been a research station, or a listening post, or even a comms repeater. Some star systems still used manned repeater stations, reasoning that failures could be fixed more quickly by a living crew.

But in an instant, everything changed. As the station rotated placidly in the dark of space, lit on one side by the distant sun, the space around them was suddenly full of ships.

There had to be at least five hundred of them—the same blunt, brutal, elongated pyramids that the Caractacan ships had fought above the planet. All of them painted white with a blue emblem of a barred spiral, surrounded by what might have been either wings or laurels, backed by crossed swords. The ships had cut their Bergenholms within less than a light-second of the station.

Without pause, the leading starships opened fire with powerguns, not even bothering to deploy a weapons constellation. The blue-white plasma packets flickered between starships and station, and in moments the station itself was dead, blackened and holed in a hundred places, spewing atmosphere. Still the ships did not cease fire. They continued to bombard the ring station until it was blasted into fragments no larger than a personal air skiff.

The recording froze. "That was Research Station Five," Rehenek said, "a private concern owned by one of the universities here on Valdek. The holo you just watched was recorded by its remote sensor satellites, which were transmitting constantly to the university here on the planet."

"If it was a research station," Soon asked, "why destroy it?"

"As a message," Rehenek said grimly. "Watch."

The holo abruptly changed. None of the Caractacans so much as flinched as a gigantic face suddenly filled half the briefing room. The face was male, human, roughly middle-aged. There was a tired sort of wisdom in the expression, though when Scalas looked at the man's eyes, he was struck by their nearly inhuman coldness.

"By now, you will have detected the destruction of thirty of your outer-system space stations," the man said. He was using a strange variation on Trade Cant; it was understandable, but only just. "While the loss of life is regrettable, it was necessary that you understand the gravity of your situation. The Galactic Unity is here to take possession of the Valdek system. While this is, ultimately, for the greater good, the object lesson in the short-term consequences of resistance should adequately communicate that you *must* cooperate. While I am certain that, given time, you will come to see the salutary effects of joining with the Unity, understand that any resistance *must* be crushed. And it will be, without mercy. The establishment of the Unity is far too important for sentiment to get in the way. And the Unity is already powerful enough that one system alone cannot stop it.

"*Nothing* can stop it."

The recording ended. For a long moment, the briefing room was silent and still.

Then Rehenek spoke, his voice heavy. "You have seen only a small fraction of their forces. There were over three thousand ships in the first attack. Some have left. Some have come into the system since. They are not the most advanced designs, or the best-built ships, but their numbers are overwhelming. Our defense fleet was destroyed in a matter of hours. The Ithogen task force that came to our aid five days before you arrived was wiped out in less time than that.

"They have little tactical subtlety, either in space or on the ground. Massed movements and massed firepower are the keys to their success. And they have more bodies and more firepower than we can withstand. Than *you* can withstand."

"Why did that man look familiar?" Costigan asked thoughtfully.

"Probably because he was once a hero," Rehenek said. Scalas glanced at him keenly, hearing bitterness in the man's voice. "Geretesk Vakolo and I fought the M'tait from one end of the Tyrus Cluster to the other. I counted him a friend. Once."

Costigan nodded. "Yes, Vakolo," he mused. "I remember now. I hadn't realized he was still alive."

"He was badly wounded on Nekophor, but not killed," Rehenek said. "I was there when we retrieved him and got him off the planet. I hadn't seen or heard from him since—until now."

"Where is he from?" Kranjick asked.

"The Sparat system, about five parsecs away."

Kranjick frowned. "I thought Sparat was sparsely populated. How could they muster this kind of force, not to mention the support infrastructure to send it across light-years?"

Rehenek's expression grew even more haunted, if that was possible. "This is how," he said quietly, and pressed another control.

The holographic image of a dead body appeared on the floor. It was dressed in the same cheap space suit and armored vest that Scalas had seen in Horvaset's recording. A weapon lay next to it—a cheap, crude-looking cone-bore rifle. The helmet had been removed, revealing an olive-skinned, heavily browed face with a shaved head.

The holo disappeared and was replaced by another—another corpse. This one was in a different place, and the lower half of this man's body had been completely blown off. But once again the helmet had been removed, and the face...

The face was identical to the one before it.

The Caractacan reactions were all carefully controlled through discipline and practiced military bearing, but Scalas frowned slightly.

Rehenek flicked through more images, more dead bodies. The faces changed occasionally, but all told, Scalas counted only four distinct sets of features among nearly two dozen bodies.

"We have retrieved only a tiny fraction of the remains on the battlefield," Rehenek said, "but the trend is clear. These are not recruits. They are clones."

"I still don't see how it's supportable," Costigan said. "The resources to raise this many clones... Even just the time involved. This had to have been started a generation ago. Maybe more."

Rehenek shook his head. "I was on Sparat several times during the Tyrus Cluster campaign, and I saw no installations that could be raising and training this many clones. There weren't even enough people on Sparat to produce this many, at least if they used the methods we understand, even were they all convinced to ignore the moral and ethical issues." He shook his head again. "No, something has changed. Vakolo has discovered some new method, some new technology that allows for rapid gestation. There is no other explanation."

"How?" Soon asked. "Genetic copies or not, they're still humans. They're not simply bots that one puts together on an assembly line."

Rehenek looked like he might have shrugged had he not been immobilized by his medical exoskeleton. "We don't know. All we know is what is before us: hordes of the same few men, over and over and over again, in such numbers that Vakolo's threat is far from idle. We cannot resist them, not for much longer."

His words hung in the air as the Caractacans considered the ramifications. They stood on the surface of a doomed world.

"Five centuries, even of Caractacans, cannot turn back an army of that magnitude, General-Regent," Kranjick rumbled.

"I know, and I am sorry," Rehenek replied. He switched off the holo and stiffly moved toward the door. "At first I hoped you could help defend us. But that was before the Ithogen ships were smashed to floating debris and every other force since has either fled before entering the system or engaged briefly and *then* fled when they saw the numbers they were up against. Before we lost hope."

He turned, slowly, to face Kranjick once more. "I did not ask you down to the surface to help fight our last stand, Legate. I asked you down here so that you could help me with one final task."

———

The Duchess was waiting, Horvaset standing at parade rest at her side, when they came back out into the command center. The holo-tank was flashing with alerts; another wave of ships was passing overhead from the L3 point, and an alarm was going out throughout the fortress to brace for another bombardment. More symbols flashed as the ground-side defensive batteries began to fire. Yet the stately, gray-haired woman was serene among the chaos and destruction that was shuddering through the fortress, causing faint vibrations in the floor and walls.

"Particle Cannon 52B just suffered a meltdown," she announced calmly. She was speaking to Rehenek, but in Trade Cant so that the Brothers could understand.

Rehenek grimaced. "That makes three in the last week. Casualties?"

"Fifty percent," was the calm reply.

"It could be worse," Rehenek said, as much to the Caractacans as to himself.

"Did you ask them?" the Duchess asked quietly.

"Not yet," Rehenek replied. He turned back to the Caractacans, putting his arm stiffly around the Duchess. It looked like it pained him, and the concern that crossed her face as she gently leaned into him, obviously trying to take some of the tension off his arm, spoke volumes.

"We have been fighting these last few days only to buy time," Rehenek said. "As you have seen, Valdek is lost. When we sent the *Mekadik*, we hoped that the Caractacan Brotherhood might lead a coalition of allied forces to drive the enemy off. That is no longer possible, I think you can agree. So, now we ask not that you fight for us, but that you help some of us escape."

"You wish us to take you off-world?" Kranjick asked. As always, his voice was flat and grim. If he harbored thoughts of reproach for the planet's leadership fleeing and leaving their people behind, he did not allow them to show.

"No," Rehenek said. "I will not leave my world. I will stay to the end. I am General-Regent of Valdek. My place is with my people."

"And I will not leave him," the Duchess said, as Kranjick turned his eyes on her.

"We wish you to take our son," Rehenek said. "He will be our government in exile, along with as many of his troops and their families as you can take. Please, take him away from here, out of the clutches of this so-called 'Galactic Unity.'"

"His escape is our world's only hope." The Duchess's voice was low and full of pain.

Kranjick nodded, acknowledging both the General-Regent's request and his courage in staying behind. "Is he prepared to depart?"

Rehenek smiled grimly, and Scalas could see a combination of pain, weariness, and deep pride in his face. "Hardly." He pointed to the holo-tank, indicating the outer defensive rings. "He is out there. With his men."

Even as he spoke, blinking, blood-red indicators showed another wave of Unity ground forces moving forward from the wrecked outer defensive lines, seeking to take advantage of the disruption caused by the latest orbital bombardment.

Kranjick looked to his centurions. "Then I think we had best get moving, gentlemen."

[9]

THE SPACES BETWEEN THE DEFENSIVE RINGS OF THE VALDEKAN planetary defense fortress had largely been designed to act as staging areas for react forces moving out to the outermost ring. With the notable exception of a M'tait raid nearly a century before, no force in history had been able to get past that first line of defense. The surface-to-space batteries were thick enough that any direct assault from orbit or air would be wiped out, and the fortifications and fire-power available on the outer defenses were more than enough to stop any pirate forces cold.

Even so, the designers had been prudent, not relying only on that first line of defense but creating a more robust system in case the unthinkable ever happened. And the troops currently dug in along Defensive Line Three, which was now the front line, were extremely glad of it. They would have all been slaughtered long ago otherwise. Many of the men they had known, trained, and fought beside already had been.

They were hunkered down in the deepest parts of the defenses as the ships above and the batteries below hammered at each other. The entire universe seemed like it was being torn apart. Plasma bolts and kinetic projectiles tore howling holes through the atmosphere, with thunderous reports that were loud enough to deafen even beneath ten meters of reinforced steelcrete.

And then one of the defensive positions, essentially a sub-fort on Section Eighteen, took a direct hit. Whether it was from a kinetic kill munition, a missile, or even a shipboard powergun made little difference. All that mattered was the position was now a smoking mass of mildly radioactive wreckage above a glowing crater. And that position had been one of the linchpins of the entire section. With that fort knocked out, there was a gap in the defenses. A small one, but a critical gap, nevertheless.

To make matters worse, Section Eighteen's commanding officer had been killed the day before. There hadn't even been enough left of him to bury. The next senior officer had wisely deferred to the senior warrant officer; he might have been enlisted, but he had more combat experience, both on- and off-planet than most of the rest of the officers combined. He had even been in the Tyrus Cluster. And now, as soon as the raving, world-ending destruction of the bombardment ceased, the warrant officer was moving up and down the line, grabbing soldiers and shoving them toward the still-hot remains of the sub-fort, even though the dust and debris was still coming down from the sky after the impact. He knew that the end of the bombardment didn't mean they had breathing room. In fact, it meant just the opposite.

It meant the next wave was coming soon.

———

Everyone on the wall had been too deafened by the world-shaking exchanges of firepower, not to mention the hurricane winds scouring defenses and blasted landscape alike, to hear the rumble of vehicles advancing across the pulverized dead zone between Defensive Line Three and what had been Defensive Line Two. Nor could they see the approaching convoy; the wind-blown ash, dust, and smoke reduced visibility to less than half a kilometer. Sensors could penetrate the miasma, but the naked eye saw only swirling curtains of black, gray, and brown.

But the sensors didn't lie. Out there in the wind-whipped murk, a line of two hundred tanks, three hundred assault vehicles, and three hundred scout tracks rumbled forward. All were based on the same basic design: bulky, squared-off wedges of armor on shrouded tracks, with pyramidal turrets sporting railguns of calibers ranging from 30mm on the scout tracks to 70mm on the tanks. The bore sizes weren't impressive until one took into account the incredible muzzle velocities those gauss weapons could produce. The Unity's vehicles were ugly, brutal, mass-produced things, but their weapons had power to burn.

And there were a *lot* of them. Quantity has a quality all its own.

The first railgun rounds began to impact the wall near the firing ports, blasting huge chunks out of the steelcrete and leaving pits that glowed with the heat of their sheer kinetic energy. In reply, missiles streaked out of box launchers on top of the wall and disappeared into the murk. Most hit. Some scored kills, the fiery deaths of armored vehicles visible as dim flashes and lurid glows out in the smoke and dust. But too few of the incoming armored vehicles were stopped, and the rest continued to advance. A second wave of hypervelocity projectiles then obliterated the box launchers, blasting them to fragments that still retained enough velocity to kill a man dead a kilometer behind the line.

The warrant officer was fighting back despair. His men had to see him leading, to see his faith that they would hold. They had to see his unerring confidence that the Unity would not get through this time.

But his hopes waned each time another of his heavy weapons went silent. The scanners, displaying their take on a green-tinted screen set into the wall of his tiny command post, showed the tanks bearing down on the wreckage of his sub-fort. He could engage with the firing positions and heavy weapons he had left, but he would likely lose those positions almost immediately, and with them his remaining heavy weapons, in a blizzard of hypersonic steel and tungsten slugs.

And then it would all be over.

The tanks had already demonstrated that, as ungainly as they looked, they were extremely agile. They could easily climb over debris and obstacles. They would roll over the wreckage of the sub-fort and be in the rear in a matter of minutes. Maybe an hour.

Defensive Line Four would become the front line. Some of the forces manning Defensive Line Three *might* make it back to join the remaining defenders there. Might. But most wouldn't. Not once the enemy was running rampant inside the line. And these men facing the assault at the breach point… they certainly wouldn't.

The warrant officer kept all these thoughts hidden behind a dull, flat face as he directed fire as best he could. And as the tanks got nearer, he left the command post and ran to one of the forward positions.

If he was going to die, he was going to die fighting.

By then, the noise of the Unity vehicles' treads was audible even inside the wall. He could feel their dull rumble through the soles of his feet, while the crackle and boom of missile, powergun, railgun, and coilgun fire thundered outside.

It was why he almost missed the other sound.

———

The dull, earthquake rumble turned heads on the inner walls, nearly a kilometer away from the increasingly desperate fighting on Defensive Line Three. Not everyone could tell what it was at first. Only some of the older men knew the sound, and they reminded their subordinates and juniors about what had arrived less than a day before.

Riding on columns of actinic fire, five Caractacan Brotherhood starships rose majestically out of their landing pits. No sooner had their nose cones risen above the landing pads' clamshell doors than their targeting systems were already at work.

The *Dauntless* was slightly ahead of the other four ships. Her powerguns were the first unmasked, and her targeting scanners cut through the storm kicked up by the bombardment to start picking out targets as she accelerated toward the sky. Brilliant lines of blinding, blue-white discharge flickered from her emplacements, reaching out toward the savaged outer defenses, slapping the landscape below with vicious cracks of thunder as they passed, just below the speed of light.

The targets weren't the tanks and fighting vehicles moving toward that breach in Defensive Line Three. Not yet. The *Dauntless* wasn't high enough to have a shot at them yet. But some of the artillery wasn't deep enough in defilade to protect it from the raving bolts of sun-hot plasma the starship was spitting. Rocket artillery vehicles suddenly turned into pearlescent balls of fire as they were struck. A lander burst, showering fire and fragmentation across an area roughly half a kilometer across, as strobing lightning played across the line of Unity positions near the edge of the plateau.

The starships accelerated skyward, continuing to hammer every potential enemy heavy weapons position with devastating fusillades of powergun fire. Those Unity troops who survived only did so by hugging the earth and diving into trenches and fortifications. Only the vehicles that were well dug-in, or still in their excavated, fortified staging areas, survived that storm of sun-bright destruction.

Five hundred meters up, the ships slowed their climb, but their rate of fire didn't decrease. They still rained destruction down on any Unity troops and vehicles they could see.

Return fire was beginning to reach for the towering ships on their tails of blue-white flame. The *Boanerges* took several powergun shots and a railgun hit, and she staggered under the impacts. All five ships responded in kind, even as a dozen HV missiles were swatted out of the air by point-defense lasers. The bay doors on the starships' flanks irised open, and blunt cones shot out like bullets before flipping nearly end over end and igniting their own main drives as they plummeted toward the breach in Defensive Line Three.

Only then did the starships begin their descent back down toward the spaceport to get out of the line of fire. Meanwhile, the Brotherhood dropships roared toward the breach where the defenders of Section Eighteen were making their final stand.

———

Scalas really, really disliked these short-range drops. Kahane flat-out refused to even call them "drops;" he referred to these short-range, in-atmo drops as "shots." And it was as good a description as any. They happened so fast they were over almost before they started. By the time his inner ear had recovered from the abuse of the hard skew-flip and the equally brutal kick of the main engine firing, they were almost on the ground. He had only about two seconds to regain his equilibrium before the dropship landed hard, compressing its landing jacks almost all the way to the pneumatics' limit with the impact, and then the doors were falling open and he was slapping his harness release, ripping his powergun out of its rack, and pounding down the ramp.

Landing in the middle of the Unity assault force would have been suicidal, especially against those kinds of numbers. Even facing the yeheri on Iabreton II, they hadn't landed in the midst of the opposing force—and the yeheri hadn't had tanks. Instead the dropship pilots had landed them with precision right on the inside of Defensive Line Three, lined up on either side of the breach where the sub-fort had once loomed above the wall.

Scalas had been getting the real-time feed of the battlefield piped to him as he'd been strapped into his acceleration couch, so he knew precisely what they were getting into. That was why he slung his powergun and grabbed an extra HV missile launcher as he moved down the ramp. They had a lot of tank-busting to do. The bulky, slightly boxy launcher was a four-shot job, with each missile individually encapsulated. He didn't have the reloads, but Torgan had grabbed those while he'd followed his centurion down the ramp.

The ground was a mess, a mix of mud, ash, and shattered rock. The blowing dust in the brutal winds kicked up by energy weapons and hypersonic projectiles was sticking to the mud left over from the driving rain of the storm that had passed after they'd landed, but the ground was soft underfoot, making it hard to run. Yet run he did, making for the edge of the crater, where the air still rippled with heat.

His armor would protect him from the heat and the rads. It wouldn't protect him from the direct fire of a tank that made it through that breach.

A fusillade of heavy-caliber fire hit the wall in front of him, where the defenders were still putting up a hell of a fight. Debris shot skyward with the impacts. The shockwaves rolled over the top of the broken wall and the wind snatched at him as he ran into its teeth, but he didn't miss a step, just kept clambering up the pile of detritus toward a firing point.

Behind him, the thunder of the *Challenger*'s bigger, hemispherical dropships was dying away. Costigan's century had landed farther back than the infantry units, and for good reason.

Scalas dug in as the slope got steeper and the footing more treacherous. The battle on the other side of the wall was getting more intense, and he could *feel* the rumble as one of the Unity armored vehicles approached the breach. The defenders were crumbling. The enemy was getting through.

He reached the top and dropped to a knee just behind the cover of a broken section of wall where the curving portion of one flank of the sub-fort still stubbornly stood. Hefting the weighty HV missile launcher to his shoulder, he took a deep breath to steady himself, then took a step forward with his off foot and leaned out, searching for a target.

Immediately, the blunt prow of a battered, gray-and-brown-painted tank appeared, not even fifty meters away. It was a short shot, barely far enough for the HV missile to arm itself before impact.

And the sheer kinetic energy of the missile's impact should do *some* damage, at least.

The missile launcher had a shoulder pad specifically designed to fit against Caractacan pauldrons. It nestled against the powergun shoulder stop perfectly, and the flip-out sight was easy to acquire, even as he hastily put the crosshair on the advancing prow of the armored vehicle. Someone up on the wall was peppering the tank with powergun fire, blowing pits in the armor, but an infantry powergun just didn't have the juice to get through a tank's hide.

Scalas held his fire for a fraction of a second, waiting for a better shot. The front glacis plate of a tank was a bad target, even for an HV missile. Too much chance that it would glance off. But if he waited too long, that thing was going to get through the breach.

"Backblast!" he roared, his helmet's exterior speakers amplifying the words, and then he fired, just as the base of the turret came into view.

The fat, pyramidal turret had already been turned toward him, and it looked almost as if he was staring right down the barrel of its long railgun. He half expected to die right then and there. As good as Caractacan armor was, a direct hit from a 70mm railgun would turn him to mist. But the Unity gunner either didn't see him—the armor's chameleonic coating him amid the rubble—or was simply too slow.

The HV missile struck the turret ring so close to its firing that it almost seemed instantaneous. In the same heartbeat that Scalas squeezed the trigger, the tank's turret blew apart, the sheer force of the HV projectile blasting the debris away from the breach, tumbling and whistling through the air.

The tank's power systems surged in the backlash of liberated energy from the destroyed turret—the railgun must have been charged up for a shot—and capacitors in the back deck exploded with a rippling series of bright flashes, even as Scalas switched to his secondary tube and inched forward, looking for another target.

He was just behind two of his men who had formed a similar hunter-killer team, crawling up the slope of the crater inside the breach itself. The gunner lifted just his head and his launcher above the lip of the crater, sighted in, and fired. A booming detonation sounded on the other side of the wall as another tank exploded under an HV missile impact.

Caractacan Brothers always hit what they aim at.

Scalas shifted his aim, spotting what looked like an infantry assault carrier trying to move around the far side of the tank he'd killed, and fired. This HV missile had a bit longer to arm, and it blew a glowing hole through the carrier's flanks. The men inside were sucked out through the exit hole. What was left of them, at any rate.

Then a powergun bolt slammed past his head from behind with a blinding flash and a tooth-rattling thunderclap, accompanied by a howling roar that was definitely not the rattle of Unity treads.

The lead tank of Century XXXV would always be Costigan's. Its rounded prow looked sleek and deadly compared to the blocky wedges of the Unity tanks, and its domed turret seemed to almost blend into the hull. It glided forward on a thin cushion of air, its fans roaring, dust and ash billowing out from beneath. The stubby powergun muzzle protruding from the turret flashed again, and the shockwave slapped more dust away from its path, scouring the Caractacan infantry's armor with grit.

The lead tanks formed a wedge as they pushed up the slope toward the crater, and the two infantry Brothers on the crater lip had to scramble to get out of the way. The Destrier was well-designed, but as with any tank, it had limited lines of sight. A friendly could get turned to mangled paste beneath the steel skirts of one of those one-hundred-fifty-ton behemoths just as easily as an enemy.

Three heavy powerguns quickly turned the breach into a hell-storm of sheet lightning. The gunners traversed their muzzles back and forth, tripping the weapons as soon as their sights crossed an enemy vehicle, and the autoloaders dropped in new cartridges as soon as the remains of the first were ejected. The R-17 Destrier's main gun was semi-auto, designed to facilitate rapid engagement, and built to the highest tolerances.

As Costigan's tanks drove through the breach, continuing to lay down a curtain of powergun bolts, the rest of the century's tanks followed. They were badly outnumbered, but Costigan was holding to the Caractacan battlefield doctrine of speed, surprise, and aggressiveness.

Scalas didn't wait around to watch. "Squads One and Two, with me!" he roared. The other three would take cover inside the wall and stand by until he knew where to deploy them. He turned and dashed along the wall, heading for the nearest set of stairs. The fight wasn't going to wait for him and his men to gawk at the power of the Caractacan tank charge.

He took the steps two at a time, bounding up toward the rectangular armored hatch, his powergun knocking against his torso armor while the HV missile launcher swung on its sling and beat at his sustainment pack. His breath was rasping in his throat, and his armor was turning up the oxygen mix to compensate.

At the top, he hammered on the hatch. The only response he got was the rolling thunder of powergun discharges and the flat *cracks* of railgun fire. It would have been deafening if not for his helmet. Irritated, he hammered harder on the metal, and seriously considered calling Vargas up with a breacher charge. The fight was going on in earnest, and he was stuck banging on a hatch.

But before he could decide to blast the hatch open, it unlatched and swung inward. Instinctively he stepped aside, out of the direct line of the hatchway itself.

Which was probably wise. Four Valdekan soldiers were crouched inside, barricaded on the short passageway to the hatch, rifles trained on the opening.

"Friendlies!" Scalas bellowed, his helmet amplifying the word into a battle roar that could be heard even over the cacophony of the ongoing tank battle on the other side of the wall. "Caractacan Brotherhood!"

The men inside spoke rapidly in Eastern Satevic. With a sinking feeling, Scalas realized that it might be the only language most of these men spoke.

"Caractacans!" he shouted again, hoping the name at least was recognizable.

"Caractacans!" a voice inside called back. The words that followed were gibberish to Scalas's ears, but the tone wasn't threatening, and what might have been a noncom waved them forward as the other Valdekan soldiers lowered their weapons.

Scalas stepped through the hatch, followed by the rest of his squad. "Where is your commander?" he asked. He hoped that the other squad sergeants were keeping their heads and making sure that what little communication was possible was established with the Valdekans in the defense.

The Valdekans just looked at each other blankly, then back at him.

Behind his visor, Scalas grimaced. Yes, they only spoke Eastern Satevic.

He tapped a key on the inside of his vambrace. When he spoke again, his voice reverberated down the passageways, making the nearby soldiers flinch and cover their ears. "Does anyone here speak Trade Cant?"

After a moment's deliberation, the noncom keyed his comm and spoke rapidly, holding up a hand to Scalas. Scalas gritted his teeth and waited. There was a battle going on, and his friend and his men were in combat, while he stood here and waited for a translator. He briefly considered simply driving on to the nearest firing ports, but he held his place. If he couldn't establish communication and rapport with the Valdekans, he and his men might do more harm than good.

An older man jogged up the passageway, then halted and reported in front of the noncom. His hair was mostly silver, he had deep lines around his eyes, and he wore the insignia of a corporal on his flak vest. The noncom pointed to the looming, armored figures in the passageway and barked something in their own language.

The corporal turned to face Scalas. "I speak Trade Cant, a little," he said. "I am Corporal Slovo Viloshen."

"We need to see your commander, Corporal," Scalas said. "Or at the very least, we need to know where to deploy to do the most good."

"Come with me." Viloshen turned and jogged back down the passageway.

The hall was narrow, the ceiling low, and Valdekan soldiers were hustling back and forth, moving to reinforce or resupply positions along the wall, making it difficult for the armored Caractacans to move quickly. But they soon reached a pillbox set into the side of the wall, about twenty meters up from the killing ground below, where Valdekan soldiers were manning heavy powerguns and what looked like a couple of remote control units for HV missile launchers. There was no using an HV missile launcher from directly within this enclosed space; the backblast would kill every unarmored man in the chamber.

Viloshen called out, and a blond-haired man with a rifle in his shoulder, standing between two heavy powergun mounts, turned.

"This is Warrant Officer Coram Raskonesh," Viloshen said to Scalas. "He is commander."

As Raskonesh stepped back from the firing port, Scalas moved up next to him and peered out the firing slit. Two of the Caractacan tanks were dead and burning. Costigan's standard still fluttered from the turret of his own tank, so he was still alive, though his vehicle's chameleonic coating was already showing new scars. As Scalas looked on, he saw a railgun round glance off Costigan's turret, immediately answered by a thunderous flash of a powergun bolt. The tanks were very much still in the fight, firing so fast that their barrels were glowing, and the combat sleds were moving through the gap behind them, the HV missile pods on their back decks adding their own fire.

It was a contest of firepower and reaction time.

The killing ground between Defensive Line Three and what had been Defensive Line Two was flat, without defilade or cover. Up against the Unity's numbers, the Caractacan armor should have been mowed down quickly.

But the Destriers were faster and more agile than the lumbering Unity tanks, and they could stand up to multiple railgun hits, while their powergun bolts killed wherever they struck. Their turrets, too, were made to move as fast as a gunner could react, making the Unity tanks' crude railgun turrets seem to move in slow motion by comparison.

At first the Unity armor continued to try to advance even in the teeth of that the Brotherhood's deadly storm of energy. Only when their strength had been cut by nearly a third did they fall back, moving as a unit, firing back over their back decks and dumping smokescreens that were all but useless against the scanners aboard the mammoth Destriers.

Costigan did not pursue. He had lost three of his tanks, which for a cavalry century was no small loss. Besides, he knew as well as any of them that they were not here to win this war.

Scalas straightened and turned away from the slit to face Raskonesh. "Where is Commander Rehenek?" he asked. "We need to find him."

Viloshen translated, then said to Scalas, with a bit of a chuckle, "He was here, but probably no longer. He always looks for the hardest fight. It is like he can smell it. He will be moving to where the next big attack will come."

"Where would that be?" Scalas asked. If Viloshen was telling the truth, they might still be able to intercept the man.

Both Viloshen and Raskonesh shrugged. "Only he knows," Viloshen said. "He does not tell."

Kahane snorted. "This is great. A simple retrieval turns into a manhunt."

"It was never going to be 'simple,'" Scalas replied. "We just have to find him. If that means rushing to every hotspot on the line…"

A titanic impact made the ground itself shudder. A moment later came another. Through the blowing dust and smoke, Scalas saw flashes in the distance, in the direction of the Unity survivors' retreat.

"They regrouped quickly," he said dryly.

Viloshen shook his head. "No, now they change tactics. They bombard wall, infantry come up behind bombardment. Try to get into breach and through to take defense positions."

"Centurion," Dravot said, "these men would have been overrun if we hadn't arrived when we did. With that gaping hole in the wall, they're not going to be able to hold on their own."

Scalas knew Dravot was right. The Valdekans looked exhausted and shell-shocked to a man. Smoke drifted through the passageways, and as he looked down the line, he could see dim light that was not the interior lamps. Some of the incoming railgun rounds had penetrated the wall, and in more than one place. And even if it were possible that the Valdekan defenders might manage to hold on their own, a part of him rebelled at just leaving them to their fate, no matter what the mission given by the General-Regent might be.

He keyed his comm. "Brother Legate, this is Centurion Scalas."

"Kranjick," came the reply.

"The Valdekans are reporting that Rehenek has likely moved on from the breach, sir. He has been running from trouble spot to trouble spot, so he's probably detected another potential breach elsewhere in the fortress's defenses. However, there appears to be a renewed attack on the way to our current location. I am requesting permission to aid the Valdekans in repelling it before we go looking further for Rehenek. These men won't hold long without us."

There was a long pause. "Our primary objective is to secure Commander Rehenek and get him off-world," Kranjick said. "But… it is in accord with the Code to aid those we can, when we can. We will help the Valdekans secure the breach as best we can before moving on."

"With all due respect, Brother Legate," Dunstan put in, his tone putting the lie to his words, "you said yourself that we cannot hold this world's defenses. Even their own General-Regent said as much.

We should lift, find Rehenek, and get off-world. To do anything else would be to throw Brothers' lives away after men who are already dead."

Kranjick's voice was mild as ever. "And how do you suggest we convince a commander, one who has put himself at great personal risk, deliberately throwing himself into the thickest of the fighting, to cooperate with us when we left his men to die in the teeth of a renewed assault? Your recommendation smacks more of self-preservation than 'pragmatism,' Centurion Dunstan. No. Not only does honor demand that we help the Valdekans here, where we have already landed, with the foe already at our doorstep, but prudence suggests that it might make our ultimate mission easier."

Scalas glanced at the indicator in his helmet. Kranjick had shifted the conversation to the command-only net. The rest of the Brothers could not hear this argument; it was solely between the Brother Legate and the centurions.

"I repeat: we will assist the Valdekans against this assault, then proceed to search for Commander Rehenek once the breach is secured," Kranjick finished. "Dropships are to lift and return to the spaceport immediately, lest we lose them to the bombardment."

Dunstan did not reply, but Scalas could imagine him fuming.

"Acknowledged," Scalas said into the momentary silence. "Thank you, sir." He turned to Raskonesh. "Where are your defenses the weakest?"

[10]

THE WALL SHOOK, REVERBERATING WITH THE HEAVY *THUD* OF another nearby impact. Dust sifted down in a steady, if quavering, stream. The bombardment had been going strong for at least an hour. That none of the dropships had been hit on the way out was a minor miracle, especially given how late some of them had lifted.

It had taken only a scant few minutes to get his century's squads set in, reinforcing the most likely spots where the Unity infantry would come. Since then, it had been a matter of waiting, peering out through firing slits and cracks in the wall at the smoking, dust-scoured no-man's land between the wall and the enemy.

"How long do they usually keep this up?" Scalas asked Viloshen.

Viloshen was looking out into the haze, sitting on an ammo crate, his sleek K-74 powergun across his knees. His fatigues were ragged and covered in dust, but his weapon was nearly spotless. Scalas had seen him take out a rag to wipe the dust and soot off it twice already.

The older man shrugged. "They do not set patterns," he said. "Smart, that. They pound wall with fire until they are ready."

Scalas nodded in reply. He had not removed his helmet, making him appear to be a hulking, armored statue, faceless and grim. But the stark prow of his visor and faceless eyeslit did not seem to bother the Valdekan corporal.

After a moment, he spoke again. "Aren't you a little old to be a corporal?" he asked. "I'd think a man of your age might be a warrant officer—or a colonel."

Viloshen chuckled. The sound of amusement was jarring in the tension within the revetment, as the thunder of the bombardment continued outside. He shook his head. "I was corporal when I mustered out from my term of service, many years ago," he said. "I took berth as spacer, on deep-space trade vessel." His chuckle died, and his pale eyes looked somewhere far away. "I was lucky to be on home leave for *Iveniya*'s latest voyage. Sure that he was destroyed in orbit." He shrugged again. "I join up again. They give me last rank I had."

Scalas nodded solemnly. It was not a new story. He had been in countless wars on countless planets in the ten years since his noviuntiate had ended. In the really grim ones, the truly desperate fights, you could always find men like Viloshen. Men who had served their time in their youth, gone on to other things, and been called back when the war got bad. Some came willingly, like Viloshen. Others were dragged back into the ranks, kicking and screaming. Some recalled their training and were better soldiers than they ever had been when younger. Some resented their recall so much that they became a danger to themselves and everyone around them.

Scalas pegged Viloshen as one of the former. Especially given the almost obsessive way the man kept his weapon clean.

Raskonesh ducked through the hatchway to join them. The hatches between pillboxes had been designed to be defensive chokepoints; they could be sealed, with firing ports that could only be opened from the inside. Presently the hatches were all open, to allow for easier communication and movement within the defenses from hotspot to hotspot. But if the Unity forces penetrated the line, they would all be locked down.

Raskonesh, younger than Viloshen by most of a decade, dropped onto another ammunition crate with a gusty sigh, knocking some of the dust off his trousers. His weapon, another K-74, was noticeably dirtier than Viloshen's, but he soon pulled out a rag of his own and started to wipe it down.

Dirt rarely affected a powergun much, but when it did, it could be catastrophic. There were nightmarish stories, told far more often than they ever actually happened, about obstructions in the workings managing to divert the energy of the bolt just enough that some of it leaked out somewhere besides through the barrel.

Needless to say, the shooter in such stories did not survive.

Raskonesh looked up at Scalas. His dark eyes, set in sunken sockets, were almost black, in stark contrast to his fair hair. His cheeks were hollow, as if he had not eaten well for days. It was entirely possible that he had not. Blond stubble showed on his jaw, though only when the light was right.

He said something in Eastern Satevic, speaking directly to Scalas's faceless helmet.

Viloshen translated. "What is it like, joining one of the brotherhoods?"

"That depends on the brotherhood," Scalas replied. "Some still hold to their Code and the principles they were founded on—to protect the weak and defenseless, to punish aggressors, to provide some kind of deterrent to the pirates, megalomaniacs, and M'tait of the galaxy. Others have become mercenaries, hiring out to the highest bidder. Others are little better than pirates themselves."

"They say the Caractacans hold to their Code," Viloshen ventured.

Scalas nodded, even as he thought of Dunstan, and even Volscius. *How much longer will that be the case?*

"The Caractacan Brotherhood takes care in our training to pass on our philosophy and principles. We train in that as much as in the arts of war. Caractacus Regnus, our founder, wanted to call it the 'Artorian Brotherhood.'"

This was met with blank stares from both Valdekans. Of course; they had no idea who Artorius was.

"Artorius was a legendary figure from Old Earth," Scalas explained. "A warrior king. He gathered all the finest warriors of his country around him and gave them a code and a purpose. He said that Might must always serve Right. Caractacus believed in that too, down to his very bones, and he gathered legates and elders around him who believed the same. They handed down the Code to the novices and the Brothers who followed."

He turned his gaze far away as he recited the words every novitiate learned by heart. "To fear God and obey His commandments. To protect the weak and defenseless. To help the poor whenever possible. To refrain from the wanton giving of offense. To live by honor and for glory. To despise pecuniary reward. To fight for the welfare of all. To obey the superiors of the Brotherhood. To guard the honor of our Brothers. To eschew unfairness, meanness, and deceit. To keep faith with our given word. To always speak the truth. To persevere until the end in any enterprise begun. To never flee before the enemy."

The Valdekans in the pillbox listened quietly to Viloshen's translation. Dravot and Powell, stationed at the firing slit with their BR-18s, and Geroges with his MT-41, listened in silence. Scalas spared the younger Brothers a glance. He remembered that Kranjick had always led his century in the recitation of the Code before insertion, and he felt a momentary pang of failure as he realized that he had let his mentor's tradition slip. He really should start doing that again.

One of the younger Valdekan soldiers, a skinny kid whose fatigues seemed to almost hang off his bones, asked a question. Viloshen translated. "He wants to know if the training is hard."

All the Caractacans in the pillbox chuckled at that. "It was the hardest thing I had ever done," Scalas said, "and I had been a Vitorian Commando."

That drew a whistle from Raskonesh when it was translated. The Vitorian Commandos were not nearly as well-known as the Caractacans, but their actions against the cultist insurgents that had nearly taken over the Vitor system were known for parsecs around. They were hardened, ruthless men of war, driven nearly to collapse in the selection process. To hear a former Commando admit that the Caractacan novitiate was harder had to be an eye-opener.

"To be a Brother, you have to learn *all* the arts of war," Scalas continued, with Viloshen translating. "In space, in the air, on the ground, even on the water. That's why the novitiate is so long. Five years of training and fighting, right alongside full-fledged Brothers, in every environment and every situation your Elder can find to throw you into. You learn what it's like to march for a week on two days' rations. You discover just how long you can last in vacuum without a suit. And when you're done, and you take your oath as a Brother, you learn that there's still more to endure, more training to go through."

A few of the Valdekan soldiers on watch had turned to look at Scalas as he spoke, only to be snapped at by Raskonesh. Heads snapped back toward the front.

Raskonesh asked another question. "What about family? When is your term of service over? Or does your family stay at your headquarters?"

Scalas shook his head. "There is no term of service. Once you finish your novitiate and take that oath, you are a Brother for life. Or until you disgrace yourself and your century badly enough to be cast out. As for families… they are not forbidden, or even frowned upon, necessarily. But few have attempted to start them. Our patrols are too long, too far out. Those who have married and tried to raise children have had a hard time of it."

One of the soldiers, a squat, slovenly young man, asked a question. Raskonesh upbraided him acidly, but Viloshen translated anyway. "What must a man do to be cast out?" he asked.

"Show open cowardice in the face of the enemy," Scalas said flatly. "Lie. Cheat. Steal. Break your word."

"Murder?" Viloshen asked. "Rape?"

"Those are not punished by exile," Scalas said grimly. "Each Sector Keep has its own gibbet."

There was a hush in the pillbox at that, broken only by the continuing rumble and thunder of the bombardment.

"What about the other brotherhoods?" Viloshen asked, perhaps only to change the subject. "You said that not all were the same."

"There are many," Scalas said. "More than any man can really say. The galaxy is a big place."

Viloshen translated another young soldier's question. "Have they ever fought each other?"

"It has happened," Scalas admitted. "It is a great shame and is not spoken of. No matter how far the opposing brotherhood has fallen."

Scalas cocked his head, listening. The others all followed suit. The noise of the bombardment had changed, subtly. It was dying away, the steady drumbeat of impacts no longer making the entire wall shudder.

"They are coming," Viloshen announced.

"*Vrykolok*," Raskonesh spat, heaving himself to his feet and moving to the firing slit with his powergun held at the ready, though he kept back from the slit itself.

"What does that mean?" Dravot asked Viloshen.

Their interpreter was moving to the slit himself, squinting out into the hellscape of no-man's land. "The *vrykolok* is dead man that has gotten up and walks around," he said. "No mind, only puppet strings. Old fairy tales, from before times. From Old Earth. But name fits these soldiers. You will see."

Scalas moved to the firing port, putting his helmet's image enhancers to the test. The view was slightly less murky than it had been before, but it was still covered in thick smoke and dust.

For the most part, there was nothing to see anyway. No-man's land was still just a blasted field of wrecked vehicles, craters, and less-identifiable detritus. Costigan's tanks and combat sleds had withdrawn back through the breach; they would be needed as a react force if things got too hot. Kranjick had no intention of letting his heavy support get pinned down by digging them in on the enemy's side of the wall.

But then Scalas thought he saw fleeting movement in the murk. He zeroed in on the area and searched. At first his efforts were in vain, but then he made out a human shape scuttling behind the smoldering hulk of a Unity armored assault carrier. If that was one of the Unity soldiers, he wasn't wearing the spacesuit and flak vest that Scalas had seen before. This man was camouflaged—and camouflaged well.

Scalas continued to scan the battlefield. Now that he had an idea of what to look for, he spotted more of them. Draped in grayish camouflage ponchos, the Unity soldiers were slipping between the craters and the wrecks, keeping behind cover and concealment as much as they could, even while the waning bombardment was supposed to keep their enemies' heads down.

He spotted one out in the open, running from cover to cover. Lifting his powergun to his shoulder—the holographic sight was slightly offset to make it easier to fire with an enclosed helmet—he fired.

The ear-splitting *crack* of the powergun's discharge was muted inside his helmet, but the flash lit up the gloom cast by the flying dust and smoke. The running Unity soldier was knocked off his feet, a blackened hole through his torso, his camouflaged poncho catching fire.

As if that powergun shot was a signal, the ground before the wall suddenly erupted with enemy muzzle flashes. The Unity soldiers opened fire en masse at any opening in the wall they could see, their cone-bore rifles flinging a storm of hissing, high-velocity projectiles against the steelcrete face of the fortifications with a noise like a heavy rain.

One of the Valdekan soldiers had been standing too close to the slit. He toppled backward, his head snapping back with a spray of blood and fragments as a needle-tipped projectile punched through helmet and skull. His corpse fell heavily to the floor, even as a second man died the same way. The cone-bore shots moved almost as fast as a coilgun round.

Just before Scalas reflexively ducked below the lip of the firing port, he saw what looked like the entire stretch of no-man's land get up and charge forward. There were hundreds of the enemy soldiers, all of them clad in grayish camouflage ponchos, open-faced helmets, and camouflaged balaclavas, and as one they were running toward the wall, firing from the hip on full automatic. The sheer volume of fire was enough to guarantee that they would hit *something*.

Bracing himself, reminding himself of the Code's admonishment to never flee before the enemy, and knowing that his helmet was better-made than the Valdekan infantry helmets, Scalas straightened, shouldered his powergun, and opened fire.

His first bolt took the closest man in the face, the energy dump blowing off his helmet and a good portion of his skull. The corpse dropped to the ground, only to be trampled on by the horde behind him. Scalas's second shot took the next man high in the chest. Whatever body armor the Unity troops might have been wearing, it was no proof against a 1cm powergun.

A cone-bore round glanced off Scalas's helmet with a brutal impact. The pain was sharp and sudden, but far preferable to the damage that would have been done had that shot penetrated. He answered with a rapid string of powergun bolts, line-straight lightning hammering running, camouflaged figures off their feet with ravening, explosive bursts of sun-hot energy.

Geroges opened fire beside him, the thunderous crackle of his heavy MT-41 making it sound like the very air was being torn apart. In a way it was. Powergun charges soon sheeted across no-man's land, blasting apart whatever they touched and burning everything around the impact points.

Another Valdekan fell. Powell crashed onto his back, a splintered hole through his vision slit. Caractacan armor was good, but it didn't make a man invulnerable.

There was nothing in this life that could.

Then Raskonesh shouldered his way between the Caractacans and heaved a blocky, multi-barreled grenade launcher against the firing slit. Ignoring the roar of cone-bore rounds hitting the wall and snapping through the firing port, he opened fire.

Compared to the world-ending noise of powergun bolts, the grenade launcher sounded muted, almost silent. But it fired rapidly, each barrel pumping out a fat lozenge of molecular explosive wrapped in notched, monomolecular wire. And the Valdekan warrant officer was a good shot. He gauged his distance and his spread with a precision that spoke of long practice. Not all of the grenades made it to their targets—there was too much powergun fire roaring through the air, and it was inevitable that a few of the tiny bombs would fall into the line of a bolt—but even the aerial detonations were impressive, though they did little to slow the oncoming horde.

Those grenades that did find their mark landed in a sweeping pattern across the Unity front, which was now less than a hundred meters from the breach. Their thunderous explosions rocked the defensive positions with brutal shockwaves, and the overpressure and hypersonic fragmentation tore the Unity clones to bloody shreds, armor or no.

Still the Unity troops did not disengage. Their fire slackened, if only because fewer and fewer bodies were able to continue the charge and keep shooting, but they kept coming. It was just like Viloshen had said. These men acted like they had no sense of self-preservation at all.

Then the first of them were at the breach.

"Dravot, Geroges, Viloshen, with me," Scalas snapped. He pulled away from the firing slit. The cooling fins around his powergun's muzzle shroud were glowing a dull red, and heat waves were rippling off the weapon. He keyed his comm. "All squad sergeants, I need reinforcements at the breach. Now."

He had chosen his position, the last intact pillbox on the east side of the breach, deliberately. He had to suspect that Raskonesh had, as well. The warrant officer was already moving, cradling the heavy grenade launcher in his hands, reloads hanging in several satchels from his narrow shoulders, hefting the launcher so that he could reach the last hatch before the breach. Scalas reached around him and grabbed the latch, prying the armored door open.

Beyond, the passageway ran a short, angled twenty meters before opening up onto nothing.

Well, not exactly nothing. Twisted reinforcement bars and shattered steelcrete, still warm hours after the hit that had taken out the sub-fort, framed a long drop toward the crumbling slope that led down to the bottom of the debris-choked crater that formed the breach. Both Caractacan and Unity tanks had crushed paths through the rubble, but it was still going to be tough going for Unity infantry, and the climb out would be even worse. The defenders had the advantage of the high ground, as well. They could barricade themselves in that little hole in the wreckage of the wall and fire down at the enemy.

Unfortunately, there was room for only two or three Valdekan soldiers in that hole. The armored bulk of a Caractacan would be too much. So Scalas shouldered his powergun and started down the uneven, unstable fan of debris that had sloughed off the shattered wall and down toward the crater bottom.

The first few clone soldiers were already clambering down the inside of the crater to his left. There were more behind them; more than he'd thought there would be after the slaughter before the wall. A ragged burst of cone-bore fire crackled past his helmet, and he dashed for what little cover there was.

The impact that had created the crater had come in from above, but at such an angle that it had punched a hole through the top edge of the wall before expanding to form the rest of the crater below. That had left a lip of crumbling steelcrete around the breach itself, some of which had fallen in during the subsequent artillery bombardment. One long, ragged section had dropped and embedded itself in the detritus just below the breach, and that was what Scalas plunged toward and quickly crouched behind as cone-bore shots spat grit and debris off the ground around and behind him.

Some men in Scalas's place might have been sickened by the slaughter that he had just witnessed and taken part in. Others might come to revel in it. There is, after all, a sense of power that comes with killing, and not all men can resist it. But Scalas had fifteen years of training and guidance in the Code—training that allowed him to shut down any emotional involvement in the fight. When he was in combat, he was a machine: cold, relentless, analytical. He killed those who presented a threat to himself, to his men, or to those he was tasked to protect, and he was merciful when sparing a life would not endanger those for whom he was responsible.

He was a warrior, not a butcher.

Yet even his practiced detachment was becoming shaky now that he was faced with these hordes of clones. There was something unnatural, inhuman about them, something that went far beyond the simple fact that they would all look exactly the same up close. They were a wave of replicated humanity, not a unit of individuals working together. Instead of each man finding his next piece of cover, moving to it, and firing on likely targets to cover his comrades' advance, these men moved more like... insects. Or perhaps flocking birds. Where the lead moved, all the rest followed, almost without thought. When the lead fired, the rest blazed away in the same direction.

It was almost as if none of them were really trained. Or really *men*, in the true sense of the word. They acted on instinct, not thought.

He understood then what Viloshen had meant when he'd called the clones "living dead."

But the enemy's bizarre behavior was a matter for analysis at another time. Regardless of their mindlessness, in these numbers they could easily overwhelm the defenders, simply by burying them under a tidal wave of bodies.

Scalas took a breath to steel himself, then rose above his cover and opened fire.

More of the Caractacans, along with some of the braver Valdekans, were scrambling down the slope behind him, taking up firing positions and adding their powergun and coilgun fire to his own, hammering bolts down into the mass of bodies pouring into the crater. Raskonesh skidded to a halt right next to him in a small avalanche of debris, already cramming more of the molecular grenades into the launcher. He snapped it shut and heaved it to his shoulder, and another chorus of faint *thumps* heralded the grenades' passage toward the enemy, followed by detonations that felt as though they might batter and bruise even Scalas in his armor, two hundred meters away. Then yet more fire came pouring down into the crater from the far side, the west side, where Soon's century had set in.

And still the clones came on. They scrambled over the pulped, crisped, and shredded remains of their dead, undaunted and uncountable.

The Caractacans and Valdekans, shoulder to shoulder, kept killing them. They just couldn't kill them fast enough.

The clones blazed away with their cone-bores, most not even bothering to aim. They pointed in the general direction of the defenders and held down their triggers. Given their numbers, it was enough. The air was as full of flying metal as it was of sun-hot copper plasma. Even through his helmet, Scalas imagined he could smell the ozone, the smoke, and the stink of bodies blasted apart and torn asunder.

Then a new noise entered the fray, a howling roar, though it was almost drowned out by the thunder of gunfire. And as it rose from behind them, a flash brighter than any of the 1cm or 1.5cm powergun bolts suddenly lit the entire crater, dispelling the pall of dust and smoke that hung over them and slapping the infantry down into the dust with a tooth-rattling shockwave.

Costigan.

His tank came gliding through the breach, his standard whipping from its wand, billowing dust and ash roiling up from its fans. His main gun fired again, the concussion battering not only the sides of the crater but anything within a hundred yards to either side.

Where those bolts touched, clones died by the dozens. Often there was nothing left that was recognizably human. Against the Unity armor, the Destrier's firepower had been impressive, but against infantry…

It was like the wrath of God.

With a seemingly unending, sky-cracking roll of thunder, Costigan's gunner fired again and again, traversing the turret from one side of the breach to the other, firing as fast as the powergun could cycle.

In minutes, it was all over. The outside of the breach was glowing and smoking, a hellscape of twisted, charred remains, heat mirage rippling above it and obscuring the no-man's land beyond. The tank gunner and the infantry ceased fire, simply because there was no longer anything left to shoot at.

The clones had just kept coming until they were all dead.

But even as the fight died down, Scalas became aware that not *all* the shooting had stopped. His augmented hearing inside his helmet picked up the sound of intense fire coming from somewhere off to the east. And someone was calling him over the comm.

"This is Cobb!" the squad sergeant bellowed, trying to make himself heard over the cacophony of battle on his end. "We need reinforcements, now! Breach at the junction with Section Nineteen!"

Scalas keyed his own comm. "This is Scalas," he said. "We're on the way. Where's Dunstan?"

"No idea," Cobb replied grimly. "If they're on the other side of the breach, they're not coming to reinforce us."

[11]

It was a struggle to get back up the slope, and another struggle to get through the narrow tunnels to Section Nineteen. The passages were jammed with wounded being hauled away toward casualty collection points and reinforcements trying to get to the breach. Including more than a few armored Caractacan Brothers. Scalas held his powergun's muzzle high as he pushed through the passageways, in order to avoid burning any of the less-armored Valdekan allies with the still-hot muzzle shroud.

The tunnels ran along the outside of the defensive wall, with sub-forts at the boundaries between sections. Hatches opened on the outside, allowing access to the smaller revetments or pillboxes set between the sub-forts. Often, men had to duck into those hatches to clear the way; the tunnels weren't wide enough for two-way traffic.

The noise ahead heralded a desperate fight. The thunder of powergun and hard-shot fire echoed down the tunnels in a continuous roar. He dreaded what he was going to find at the breach. Unless the wall had been broken completely, which he doubted—even over the noise of the earlier fight, they should have heard such a blast—this battle could see no rescue by one of Century XXXV's tanks. This would be a pure infantry fight, outnumbered as they'd never been before.

He came to the last turn, where the passageway zigged toward the next defensive position. And what he saw was a close-combat nightmare.

The far side of the defensive position was just *gone*. The corner of the revetment had been cracked open by a catastrophic impact, leaving a gap in the wall and a hole in the floor. Part of the ceiling, weakened by the collapse, had fallen in, leaving a stack of rubble at the breach. Bodies, both Valdekan and Caractacan, lay mangled on the floor just inside—some had died in the blast that had blown the hole open, but others had fallen to the small arms fire as the clones had tried to enter. Clone corpses were piled in the breach, forming a carpet that spread down the slope of debris that had sloughed down from the hole in the wall. The Unity troops were still pushing in, trying to get over the dead, firing long, wild bursts as they came. Cone-bore rounds were smacking off every hard surface in the pillbox, ricocheting around the inside of the hardened space with angry whines that Scalas would never even have heard if not for the enhanced hearing filters of his helmet, not over the painfully loud, crackling thunder of responding powergun fire.

He realized, as he dove to a knee behind the partially opened armored hatch, that there weren't any Valdekans left alive at this position. Only the heavier-armored Caractacans had survived, and only a handful of them at that. Cobb was still alive, on one knee behind the pile of debris that had fallen from the ceiling, firing into the swarming clones as fast as he could pull the trigger. That close, and with the targets packed that thick, there wasn't even really a need to use the sights. Cobb and the other survivors were just pointing and shooting.

Scalas fired as he moved forward, dumping the remains of the BR-18's drum into the charging clones with a strobing flash and roll of thunder that seemed intense enough to split the pillbox apart by sheer volume. The brilliant bolts did their job, ignoring the clones' flimsy armor and blowing charred holes through heads and vitals. With the intensified firepower pouring into the breach, the assaulting clones were pushed back, and Scalas advanced, though he still had to shelter behind a pile of blasted rubble halfway between the hatch and the breach.

Raskonesh was suddenly behind him, with Viloshen by his side. The warrant officer had ditched the grenade launcher, to Scalas's relief. Those grenades would have buried not only the clones but what remained of the Caractacans in the pulverized remains of the pillbox. Raskonesh was back to carrying his powergun instead, and he ducked out to fire on the clones while Scalas finished reloading.

He couldn't have gotten off more than a few shots before he was thrown violently backward with a loud *bang*, his helmet shattering. Even as Scalas returned fire, he was sure the Valdekan warrant officer was dead. Yet to his surprise, in between shots he heard what could only be a stream of vicious profanity in Eastern Satevic coming from behind him. It seemed that Raskonesh was alive after all.

"This is not going to end well, Centurion!" Cobb barked between shots. He had advanced with Scalas and Raskonesh. "If we try to hold here, we're going to be overrun!"

Scalas knew it. He just didn't have a solution yet. He had grenades on his belt, but there was a good risk that they'd be just as effective as Raskonesh's molecular grenades, but without the stand-off. He ripped off another magazine at the swarming bodies in the breach. The clones were forcing the defenders back and pushing inside the pillbox by sheer weight of numbers. It was going to be knife work before long. And then it would be all over but the screaming.

But Cobb hadn't been looking for ideas. He'd been announcing his intentions, in the way only Cobb could. The squad sergeant was suddenly on his feet, dumping the remainder of his magazine into the breach before vaulting over their meager cover and rushing toward the hole.

"Cobb!" Scalas bellowed. "Get back here!"

The senior squad sergeant gunned down a dozen clones in as many seconds, then took a knee beneath the growing rampart of corpses in the breach. "Get clear, Erekan!" he shouted over the comm. "And take any of the Valdekans who are still alive with you!"

Scalas knew what Cobb had in mind. He wanted to stop him. Wanted to run in there and drag the man who wasn't quite a friend, but was closer than a brother, back from the breach, to say that there had to be some other way. But he forced himself not to feel. Only to think. They would be out of powergun charges by the time they killed all the clones in the breach. Maybe even well before. And he knew that more clones would be moving in. They'd been thwarted by Costigan's tanks at the big crater, but the tanks couldn't stop them here.

"Damn it, Cobb!" he yelled as he picked Raskonesh off the floor by his gear and flung him with abnormal strength down the corridor, back toward Section Eighteen. "You can still get clear!"

"Just go, Erekan!" Cobb answered. He primed a grenade and tossed it over his shoulder, even as he was already pulling out a second. "Get out of here!"

Cobb had decided that the only way to stop the breach was to bring part of the wall down. It was going to take every grenade he had.

The calculation made sense. But the action might well be suicidal.

Scalas grabbed Viloshen by the load-bearing gear and propelled the old corporal down the corridor in front of him. "Fall back!" he shouted, his exterior speakers making his voice boom even over the noise of the fight behind them. "Move!"

The first grenade went off, the heavy *thud* of its detonation vibrating through the steelcrete. The next four followed in quick succession, and then there was no more gunfire behind them, only a catastrophic crash like the side of a mountain falling, and they were engulfed in billowing dust and smoke.

Scalas took a knee at the turn, pointing his powergun back the way they'd come. Clouds of grit blasted at them, hissing against his armor. He squinted against the flying debris instinctively, even though it would have to be moving a lot faster than that to even scratch his visor. Raskonesh and Viloshen were huddled behind him, and the passageway was packed with more of his armored Caractacan Brothers, weapons either at the ready or pointed at the ceiling.

The world had fallen suddenly silent and still. And even with his helmet's image enhancement, Scalas could see nothing in the choking clouds that filled the passageway. But he did not relax his guard. It was still possible that Cobb's gambit had failed, the breach had not collapsed, and they would find themselves facing more swarming clones in another few seconds.

But then the comm crackled with a strained voice.

"Can someone come back here and dig me out?" Cobb called.

Scalas let out a breath he hadn't realized he'd been holding. "Moving up," he called.

Digging Cobb out was a job for Caractacans. Even if he hadn't been one of theirs, the dust in the passageway was too thick for the Valdekans, most of whom were without enclosed helmets, to be able to breathe.

The squad sergeant had been buried up to his pauldrons in collapsed steelcrete. He was closer to the hatchway than he had been when Scalas had last seen him; he must have tossed all his grenades and sprinted for the exit. Self-sacrifice was honored within the Brotherhood, but none of the Brothers were suicidal. If sacrifice was called for, they would rise to the occasion, but if survival with honor was possible, they wouldn't throw their lives away.

Gauntleted hands carefully moved blocks of steelcrete away. "I don't know if this is such a good idea, Cobb," Kahane gibed. "If we shift too much of this, it might collapse the whole thing on the rest of us too. Then where would we be?"

"Just get this off me, Kahane," Cobb grunted. "There's a slab that's trying to crush my breastplate into a dinner plate."

Scalas worked alongside the others, with a few men posted to hold security, in case the cascade of debris slid aside to reveal more clones. Scalas had come to realize that he wasn't the only hardened Caractacan who was nonetheless disturbed by the clones' hivelike swarming and utter disregard for their own lives. It was deeply disquieting.

What could make a man act like that?

There were ancient horror stories floating around the galaxy, stories from even before the Qinglong Wars. Stories of mind control experiments, suicide cults, nightmare worlds with collectivist governments that brainwashed their people until they were little more than slaves in their minds as well as their bodies. And worse. Stories of alien environments and influences that had driven sapients mad. But as exaggerated as these stories had doubtlessly become across centuries of time and light-years of distance, none of the Brothers had ever encountered anything like this.

The slab that Cobb had been complaining about was at last uncovered, slowly and laboriously. It was huge; had he not been in armor, Cobb would certainly have been crushed to death.

"Careful," Scalas instructed. "Ovoyes, brace that side. Don't let it slip. The rest of you, get over here and push." He crouched down, bracing his boots against the pile, and grabbed Cobb's gauntlets. "Can you tell if that slab is the main one pinning you?"

"I think so," Cobb answered. His voice sounded even more strained than before. Even through his armor, the pressure had to be intense. The armor had a certain amount of flex, which kept it from shattering altogether in such situations, but also meant that the slab was surely compressing his ribs painfully.

"Well, hopefully I'm not about to rip your feet off," Scalas said. "Stand by. Now."

The Brothers heaved. The slab shifted. Scalas pulled.

Cobb slid forward a fraction of a meter, then caught.

"Push harder," Scalas instructed.

None of the Brothers complained. They just dug in and heaved. The pile of debris shifted dangerously, and Scalas held his breath as he pulled at Cobb's arms.

The squad sergeant slid forward, slowly and heavily. There was still a good deal of debris on top of him. But after four more heaves and pulls, he was free.

The Brothers holding up the slab let it go. Almost immediately, the debris pile shifted, and part of the ceiling started to crack.

"Out!" Scalas bellowed, getting a hand under Cobb's arm and lifting him off the floor. "Move! Before it comes down on all our heads!"

As the Caractacans dashed for the hatch, the cracks widened, and the entire structure creaked and groaned. They made it through the opening, dust sifting down around them, as the entire wall shook as if struck by a giant hammer.

"The bombardment's started again," Cobb gasped, as he leaned against the wall for a moment. "Thank you, gentlemen. I don't know how much longer I could have held out under there."

"We don't leave Brothers behind," was all Scalas said. He was vaguely uncomfortable. It was similar to the feeling he got when he talked to Costigan. He was already haunted by the nagging thought that Cobb should have been promoted to centurion by now—even before Scalas himself had been. And now he had survived thanks to the other man's self-sacrifice. If Cobb had been killed in the process... It was a painful thought, one that he didn't want to entertain.

Sometimes, in the quiet of the night when he couldn't escape such thoughts, he wondered if his misgivings about being promoted ahead of Cobb were selfish. If they were more about his own self-image. If he was worried it would all come out that he *shouldn't* have been promoted ahead of Cobb.

He didn't know.

But right then, he was just glad that Cobb was still alive. Too many others weren't.

He clapped Cobb on the pauldron and got an answering buffet in return. It was Cobb's signal that he was all right. Not to worry about him. But he didn't say anything.

Scalas knew that silence. He knew it from Venulia VI, where too many Brothers had died, all because the local commander had wanted the genocidal rebels wiped out without losing any of his own men. So, the man had deliberately understated the threat to the Caractacans, letting them do the fighting and the dying while he kept his own forces back and refused to commit them. They'd won. But they'd lost a lot of Brothers. And Cobb had been just as quiet then.

As Scalas was starting to turn back toward what was left of Section Eighteen, to determine just how many of his hundred men he had left, Cobb spoke. His voice was flat and weary and distant.

"I lost my powergun."

Scalas swallowed. He knew Cobb well enough to hear the pain behind those four words. It wasn't just about his weapon.

"There are many that no longer have wielders, Brother." It was all he could say. The Brotherhood stood for a certain stoicism in combat.

He felt Cobb's eyes on him, even through the visor. Then the squad sergeant nodded and heaved himself off the wall, straightening. Scalas studied him for a moment, then nodded in response and turned away.

Cobb would recover. As much as any of them ever did.

"Brother Legate," Scalas called, as the wall shook again. "The east flank is secure for the moment."

"Acknowledged," Kranjick's heavy voice replied. "Fall back to what hardened positions you can. It appears that the enemy has abandoned the assault and renewed the bombardment. Valdekan Command informs us that the next wave of starships is inbound from the L4 point. Valdekan armor will be moving to replace our tanks at the breach once the space-to-surface fire has passed. Centurion Costigan, withdraw your armor to a safe haven within the fortress."

Scalas checked that he was on the private command channel with Kranjick. It would not keep his words from the other centurions' ears, but it would keep the rest of the Brothers from hearing. "Sir, what happened to Centurion Dunstan and Century XXXIV? They weren't in position to help repel the clones at the breach."

"Dunstan is not answering his comms," Kranjick said coldly. "But Valdekan Command informs me that the *Sword of the Brotherhood* lifted and flew toward the far side of the spaceport shortly after the artillery bombardment began, apparently on 'special orders.'"

"What are they doing over there?" Costigan asked. "What 'special orders' did Dunstan get?"

"He received no special orders from me," Kranjick answered. "But apparently there was a second push made in that area not long ago, a push that's still going on, though the defenders appear to be holding for the moment."

"He's probably looking for Rehenek on his own," Soon replied acidly. "It seems Dunstan's contempt for the Code now extends to abandoning his position and disregarding orders in a grab for glory."

"Enough," Kranjick thundered. "Centurion Dunstan will have the opportunity to answer for his decision, should he survive. Until then, regroup your centuries and take shelter. I don't need to tell any of you that our armor will not withstand a direct hit from a starship's weapons."

Being under a space-to-surface bombardment is a terrible experience.

They were in the deepest parts of the defenses, fifty meters below the pillboxes, in the orbital fire bunkers, and still the pounding from above was rough enough to shake the ground under their feet. It wasn't the first time for Scalas, or for most of his century. But it was the first time for the ten newly minted Brothers who had joined just before departure.

No, not ten. Seven. Only seven were now left. One had died in the crater, before Costigan had intervened with his tanks. Two had died at Cobb's side, trying to fend off that swarm of suicidal clones in close quarters.

Cobb didn't talk about it. He proceeded as if he hadn't even noticed that his squad of twenty was now down to eight. But of course he'd noticed. Of course he felt the loss.

And Scalas knew Cobb well enough to know that he was thinking about more than just the men he'd lost. He was thinking about Dunstan.

He wasn't alone. Dunstan's desertion was weighing on all of them.

Kahane, for certain. He was trying to joke with his men, but Scalas could hear the brittle edge in his voice. Kahane was young, aggressive. And while he had lost far fewer than Cobb, he would be itching to take his rage out on Dunstan.

Kunn was… Kunn. Blank, impassive, good at giving directions, not so good at connecting with the men in his squad. Scalas had heard him asking his men about their wounds, their ammunition, their equipment. He'd even said a few things that might have been inspirational, coming from anyone else. Except that Scalas had been listening long enough to hear the same sentences, in the same order, three times. It was a speech that Kunn had memorized. Nothing more. Perhaps Scalas should speak to Kranjick about Kunn. The man was a good soldier, but he was no leader. And that could be a problem.

Solanus was sitting with his squad, looking upward toward the ceiling. He was the youngest squad sergeant in the century. Scalas stepped over and crouched beside him.

"How's your squad, Solanus?" He had his speakers pitched low, so that his voice wouldn't carry far.

Solanus started a little and looked at him. "They… uh…"

"Have you checked on the wounded?" Scalas prompted quietly. "Checked on the others, to make sure no one's wounded without realizing it? Checked ammunition stocks, equipment? Made sure that none of them are wavering?"

"I, um… I checked on ammunition. And the wounded. They're stable."

"Your squad needs to have confidence in you, Solanus. That means you have to *show* confidence. Sometimes that means taking the first place in the breach. And sometimes that means simply keeping busy, showing them you're not completely absorbed in your own fears and worries."

"Yes, Centurion," the younger man said formally.

"But they're not the ones who most need to see us at our best," Scalas continued. He inclined his head toward the huddled group of Valdekan soldiers at the end of the bunker, near the massive blast doors. "Our Brothers are all trained and hardened warriors. Their morale is the more robust for it. But the Valdekans, the people we're here to protect… they need to see that there is hope. That the Caractacan Brothers are here to help them."

"But we can't," Solanus whispered. "We can't save them. Can we, Centurion?"

Scalas shook his head slightly. "No, we can't," he admitted. "I did not say 'save.' But hope will give them the strength to survive. Let them despair at this juncture, and they will die for certain. Even if we must take Rehenek and leave the rest behind, with hope, some will survive. They will resist. Or even surrender. But either is better than being slaughtered in a rout." He stood up. "So stand up, stand tall, and let our Brothers and our allies see what a Caractacan squad sergeant is made of."

Solanus rose, squaring his shoulders under his armor. "Yes, Centurion."

Scalas clapped him on the shoulder, a hard smack of synthetic gauntlet on hardened armor plating, before moving on to Volscius. His "pragmatist" squad sergeant.

The man did not look at him. As well he might not. Scalas forced himself to check on Volscius's squad anyway. They were still his Brothers.

The ground shook and shuddered as the starships above rained down destruction.

———

Powergun bolts, HELs, and railgun rounds the size of groundcars hammered at the defenses, blasting glowing craters in the landscape and the wall. Fountains of dirt, ash, and smoke rose hundreds of meters into the atmosphere, where it was whipped into a frothing fury by the storms still raging from the passage of so much energy. Beams of near-light-speed particles and collimated light stabbed skyward in reply, punching through the clouds and adding to the storms' fury.

Unseen by the men underground, eleven of the twenty starships above were hit. Particle beams carved two into separate pieces that continued to fly, unpowered, off into the depths of the system. A high-energy laser penetrated straight through the hull of another, setting it spinning. Two more were struck by both HELs and particle beams, and the energy dump shattered them into thousands of spinning fragments.

The others lost reactor containment and detonated. Their radioactive particles would continue on their current trajectories, following the wreckage of their similarly stricken sister ships into the void.

The fight for Valdek went on, no matter how inevitable its end might be.

$$[\ 12\ ]$$

Captain Mor cursed as a world-shaking impact rocked the *Dauntless* on her landing jacks. The catastrophic noise reverberating through the hull that followed actually made him flinch. "Status!" he snapped.

It took a moment to get a reply. "The overhead hatch took a direct hit on one side," the damage control officer reported. "The shot penetrated, and debris fell into the silo."

"Damage report?" Mor found he was gripping the arms of his acceleration couch.

"Most of the debris seems to have fallen alongside the ship and missed the hull. We have minor hull damage in Sections Four, Six, and Seven. One of the spaceport umbilicals was destroyed. Umbilical Port Three is *gone*."

"Can we lift?" Mor asked, even as he called up the displays in a window on the side of the holo-tank.

"Provided the remains of the hatch can be moved out of the way. All ship's systems appear to be functional, though we'll have to run the reactor hotter to make up for the loss of the umbilical."

We would, except that we've been running hot ever since we set down. They'd never drawn the *Dauntless*'s primary reactor all the way down to standby, because they'd had no way of knowing when they might need to lift on short notice.

"Contact the Port Authority," Mor said. Port Authority in the fortress was controlled by the Valdekan military, and so was directly involved in the defense. "Ask if they can get that hatch out of the way, or if we're going to have to blast our way out to go support our infantry Brothers."

"Blasting out would likely do far more damage to the ship," the executive officer, Commander Fry pointed out. "If we do need to self-extricate, might I suggest a slightly more careful course of action? Like work crews?"

"Not the point, Fry!" Mor snapped.

"Caractacan Starship *Dauntless*, this is Valdekan Port Authority." The woman who appeared in the small comm window in the holo-tank was stiff-necked and formal, her blond hair drawn back severely behind her head. But she was quite attractive, despite the scowl that she probably thought made her look more professional. "Be advised, the protective hatch on your silo has been disabled, and we cannot open it remotely. Do not attempt to launch. Work crews are on their way."

"Acknowledged, Port Authority," Mor replied. "We are deploying our own work crews to assist."

The woman's frown deepened. "Starship *Dauntless*—"

Mor cut her off. "My Brothers are out there on the line, under fire, Port Authority," he said. "We need to be able to lift to support them. Time is pressing, and many hands make light work. I'm sending my work crews up. Have yours rendezvous with us as soon as they arrive. *Dauntless* out."

He cut the transmission, reached down, and punched the release on his harness. The ship rocked again as he swung his legs off the side of the acceleration couch.

"Captain?" Fry asked. "Are you really going to do that much good up there? Shouldn't you stay here, on the command deck?"

"I was turning a wrench while you were still in school, Fry," Mor replied. "I'm pretty sure I can still remember how to run a cutting torch and a winch." On the way to the lift, he called over his shoulder to the comm officer, "Contact Centurion Scalas and Brother Legate Kranjick. Inform them that we won't be able to lift to provide support or launch the dropships again for some time."

The comm officer replied without looking up. "We won't be the only ones. The *Vindicator* has been heavily damaged, and the *Boanerges* is as trapped as we are."

"Then we'd best get to work, shouldn't we?" Mor said.

———

"Acknowledged," Scalas called over the comm, almost at the same time that the heavy impacts of starship weapons stopped. Brother Quinias's transmission had been faint and broken through the weight of rock and fortifications, but Scalas had gotten the gist.

"Brothers," he said, his voice echoing through the bunker, "we're going to have to hold our positions for a while longer. The *Dauntless* is trapped in her landing pit and cannot launch the dropships to retrieve us. We could start back on foot, but Brother Legate Kranjick has decided that we will hold. If another assault comes before the Valdekan reinforcements arrive, we might be our allies' only hope."

Getting murmured acknowledgments from his squad sergeants, he started across the underground chamber toward Raskonesh. A new series of heavy impacts or explosions vibrated through the ground under his feet. But these seemed... lighter somehow, he thought, looking up. Not as much dust and grit was sifting down from the steelcrete ceiling.

"Artillery," Viloshen said as he approached, noting the movement of Scalas's helmet. "They must not be quite ready to launch next attack yet."

Raskonesh said something, which got a feral chuckle from most of the Valdekan soldiers gathered nearby.

"Maybe they saw how we chewed up last assault, and some

shiver of fear has even reached blank minds of *vrykolok*," Viloshen translated wryly.

"Maybe," Scalas replied coolly. He looked up again. He was not given to the chest-thumping that some men needed to get their morale up before a fight. He was colder, more calculating than that. "Somehow, I doubt whoever is directing these 'living dead men' is as mindlessly aggressive and loyal as they seem to be. The clone soldiers on the assault might not care, but I expect that their commander has recalculated, and is not in a hurry to waste quite so many of his resources."

Viloshen shook his head before even translating. "They have thrown thousands of them at us," he said. "They do not care about their soldiers' lives. If they even have lives."

"They are human, are they not?" a familiar voice asked through Caractacan helmet speakers. "They breathe, they bleed, they move themselves. They have lives."

"Father Corinus," Scalas said, turning to the familiar voice. The legio chaplain was clad, as always, in black armor, with a white cross above the star-and-crossed-rifles emblem of the Brotherhood. He carried no weapon, but he walked the battlefield without fear, nevertheless. He must have landed with Kranjick and the rest of his century. His armor was as dusty and scarred as all the rest.

Viloshen pointed at the wall, indicating the devastation beyond. "They swarm like insects, heedless of their own lives, and kill with as little conscience as wolves. How can they be human? They do not act like humans."

"And that is one of the great sins we look upon here," Father Corinus said, sitting down on an ammo crate. "Whatever tinkering made these men the way they are, it has robbed them of their very dignity, made them little more than cogs in a machine, instead of children of God." He shook his helmeted head sadly. "I weep for them as much as I weep for the devastation they have wreaked upon the Valdekan people."

Coming from a politician, the words might have been mere platitudes. Coming from Father Corinus, Scalas knew they were sincere. If there was any Caractacan who took his moral duty completely seriously, it was Father Corinus. And given that no man joined the Brotherhood without knowing that moral duty, that was saying something.

Nearby, Squad Sergeant Volscius spoke up even as Viloshen was still translating what Father Corinus had said to the Valdekans.

"Men?" Volscius scoffed. "How can you call those *things* 'men'? They are clones. Copies of human beings."

Scalas snapped around, ready to put his subordinate in his place, but Father Corinus replied mildly. "Copies?" he said. "Yes, I suppose they are, in a way. In the same way that an identical twin is a copy of his brother. But is a twin any less of a man because he shares a genetic code with his sibling? Is he a carbon copy, a ghostly echo? Or is he his own person?"

"That's different," Volscius insisted.

"Perhaps in origin," Father Corinus said. "I will not deny that the enemy must be doing terrible things to produce these clones. To play God, to artificially force life into one's desired template, all for that life to be used as an expendable pawn from birth... that is a great crime. But it does not make these men any less human. It only makes them the victims of someone else's manipulation."

"If they are human, then they still have free will, do they not, Father?" Kahane asked. Most of the men in the bunker had begun to gather around the priest as the discussion continued, even as the enemy artillery pounded at the defensive positions above them. "Then they must know what they're doing."

"I will not dispute that on some level, yes, they must know," Father Corinus said. "Nor do I dispute the necessity of killing them in combat. A man may understand his enemy, even have compassion for him, and still be required by the moral imperative of defending his home and his people to kill that enemy. I do not say that they are victims in order to argue that we must lie down before them. But the greater crime lies with whoever has brainwashed them, presumably from the first moment of their birth, and thrown their lives away in the pursuit of power."

Viloshen had been translating as Father Corinus spoke, and now Raskonesh spat and snarled something. "We have seen more of *vrykolok* than you have," Viloshen interpreted. "They are monsters, nothing more. We will kill them, all of them, wherever we find them."

"Even if they surrender?" Father Corinus asked mildly.

"They do not surrender," Viloshen said flatly, not even bothering to translate the question. "They do not know how."

"And if they do not, and they still present a threat," Father Corinus allowed, "then you truly have no other choice." He sighed. "And so I fear what this means," he added quietly. "What this war heralds."

Scalas couldn't see the older man's features behind the black casque of his helmet, but he knew the man's sorrowful expression. Father Corinus saw all men, ultimately, as brothers. Brothers estranged, to deadly extent, but brothers nevertheless. Yet he was a warrior's priest. War was his parish, but he saw war as all Caractacans should; as a sometimes-necessary evil. He would not preach nonviolence where such would leave the defenseless at the mercy of the aggressive and the cruel.

A heavy hand descended on Scalas's pauldron, and he turned to see the massive, armored frame of Brother Legate Kranjick looming over him. The legate was taking the time they had hunkered down under the bombardment to check on his legio. All of it.

Kranjick didn't say anything. He simply inclined his helmeted head toward the far corner of the bunker, near the tunnel leading to the next such shelter, where one of the overhead lights was out, and away from the group gathered around Father Corinus, debating the ethics of killing clones in job lots.

Scalas nodded and slipped away from the edge of the knot of battered, dusty survivors.

———

"Hold it!" Mor barked, his voice amplified by his helmet's comm. His armor was different from the infantry suits—sleeker, slimmer. A wider vision slit. It needed to protect him in case the hull was breached, not from close combat. It was still designed along similar lines, though. "Don't cut that yet! Connors hasn't secured the lines! You want to be the fumble-fingers who dropped half a ton of steel-crete on the *Dauntless*'s nose?"

He wasn't impressed with the Valdekan work crew that the Port Authority had sent him. They were nervous and hasty, and their urgency to get the job finished as quickly as possible had already nearly crippled the *Dauntless* with falling debris twice. They were scared, and they were sloppy.

Of course, as another rocket buzzed overhead to slam into a more distant part of the spaceport, he had to admit that he understood. These people had been under bombardment of some form or another for days on end, and more and more of the rocket artillery was getting through the spaceport's rapidly degrading network of point-defense lasers.

He'd probably be jumpy and trying to spend as little time in the open as possible if he was them, too. But understanding them didn't get the *Dauntless* freed from her damaged silo any quicker.

The damage to the clamshell meant that they needed to set up winches to pull the doors apart. These had been provided by the Valdekan work crews, who anchored the powerful motors with their big cable reels to the roof of the silo before deploying the lines to pry the damaged silo hatches apart. The anchoring had gone according to plan, mostly, but actually freeing the damaged hatches and getting them open was proving more difficult.

And the language barrier wasn't helping. Mor was doing a lot of pointing and makeshift sign language to get his directions across. He was still shouting and carrying on, in both Trade Cant and Latin, but it was mostly noise to the Valdekans. He thought wryly that it would have provided considerable entertainment to his own crew had the situation not been so dire.

Another pair of rocket projectiles roared overhead. The first went long, but the second impacted against another closed clamshell hatch only a few hundred meters away with a tooth-rattling *wham*. Fragments whickered through the air and came pelting down around them. Mor flinched just as much as the rest when a chunk of errant steelcrete smacked off the still-intact clamshell with a *bang* and fell into the silo. It *probably* wasn't going to do much more damage to the hull, but he lamented every impact on his beloved starship. This was no way for a ship to die, slowly crushed underground while she sat on her landing jacks.

"Connors, hurry up and get those last two lines secured and get tension on them," he snapped. "Our friend with the cutter there doesn't look like he's all that certain he should wait."

His crewman was already hard at work, trying to set the pitons that would anchor the lines to the jagged edge of the damaged hatch. The pitons were designed to punch into steelcrete and then practically weld themselves in the hole, nearly becoming a part of the material itself. But they needed to be placed right, especially given the damage that had already been inflicted on the hatch, or they wouldn't be able to keep the heavy, armored door from falling onto the starship below.

Connors got the first one placed, but as he tried to punch in the second piton, the steelcrete, already damaged, crumbled. Unfortunately, the Valdekan worker really didn't intend to wait. He already had the cutter running, and when yet another rocket salvo came in from the outer defenses, knocked out of the sky by laser hits, creating a rippling curtain of explosions only a few short kilometers away, he instinctively ducked and put his cutter to the hatch.

Mor started to dash across the uneven top of the silo, trying to stop the Valdekan, visions flashing through his mind of a half-ton of steelcrete falling and permanently disabling his ship. He reached out to grab the local and throw him away from the hatch when Connors yelled at him.

"Captain, we're set! Let him cut!"

Mor snatched his hand away just before seizing the worker, who was now looking up at him, wide-eyed behind his safety goggles.

"Go on," Mor said, waving at him to continue, convinced the man didn't understand a word. But the Valdekan set the cutter to the hatch and began expertly, if a little sloppily, cutting the damaged hatch free.

Mor looked out at the pall of smoke and dust that hung over the outer defenses. The infantry Brothers were out there, probably getting hammered by the bombardment, and they currently had only one ship that could even lift. The *Sword of the Brotherhood* wasn't even answering comms, so he had to assume she was even more badly damaged than the others.

We're coming, Brothers. We're coming as fast as we can.

Kranjick leaned against the wall under the burned-out ceiling light, unsealed his helmet, and pulled it off. Faced with his mentor's heavy-lidded, blank expression, Scalas did the same. If the Old Man wanted to talk face-to-face, he'd talk face-to-face.

Kranjick, as ever, looked kind of sleepy and bored. But Scalas knew the legate too well to ever believe that his seeming disinterest was anything but a façade. The Old Man saw more than anyone would ever expect.

"How are you holding up?" Kranjick asked, in that same heavy monotone he always used.

"I lost a lot of men," Scalas admitted.

Kranjick nodded slowly. "Yes. You did take a heavy hit, didn't you?" He continued to watch Scalas. "As I said, Dunstan will answer for it, in this life or the next."

"Do you know where he is?" Scalas asked.

"I have some idea of the general area. But let me worry about that. You worry about your men. Prepare for the next step in the fight." His expression did not alter a whit, but it seemed as if his gaze sharpened. "Do not let this drag you down, Erekan. You did not fail them—Dunstan did. And the same could have happened even if Dunstan had held his post. It is appointed to each man his time to die, and those men died defending others. 'No greater love,' remember?"

Scalas nodded, looking somewhere far away. "Yes," he replied. "'No greater love hath a man, than he lay down his life for his brother,'" he quoted. He met Kranjick's gaze again. "But if they did not need to die…"

"It does not matter if we see the needs or the causes. You know that. We do not see all ends. We cannot live on might-have-beens or should-haves. We can only act according to what is right, given what we know at the time. Those men who died today did that. And they stopped the assault. You can see that much good, at least."

Scalas nodded again, though reluctantly. He knew why Kranjick had sought him out, knew that he wanted to hold on to the resentment, particularly against Dunstan. Kranjick had led him through many battles as centurion, and knew his strengths and weaknesses. The Old Man knew what needed to be said, knew that his subordinate commanders sometimes needed that extra reminder to get their heads right for the fight.

"We will mourn the fallen when the time is right," Kranjick added. "Remember that. Remember that they died as Caractacans, in battle, facing their enemies. As any one of us might at any time. And then clear your mind so you can lead the rest of these men properly."

"I will, Brother Legate," Scalas said firmly.

Kranjick nodded, his face as impassive as ever. He heaved himself away from the wall and replaced his helmet. "Good. I think we should go join the discussion around Father Corinus for a moment, but then we need to start getting the men back up to the defensive positions, at least those that are still intact enough to withstand the bombardment. There will likely be another assault coming soon."

———

Mor hadn't realized how much he'd been sweating under his armor as he'd worked with the work crews to clear the silo doors. Only as he clambered back into his acceleration couch did he catch a whiff of himself and grimaced. He ignored the acrid smell as he quickly strapped himself in.

"Tell me we're ready to lift!" he demanded.

"We're ready to lift," Fry replied. "The hull damage won't slow us down, and aside from some backlash when that umbilical port got wiped out, all systems are intact. The *Vindicator*, *Challenger*, and *Boanerges* are also ready to lift, though the *Vindicator* indicates she's taken severe damage and is at roughly seventy-percent combat effective."

"Then we're lifting in five," Mor snapped, his hands dancing over the controls in his armrests. "Contact the ground force and tell them to be ready to move."

[13]

For the second time in only a few hours, four massive, spearhead-shaped starships rose once again into the Valdekan sky. This time they rose from within a pall of smoke and dust, riddled with the passage of rocket artillery and railgun rounds. But no sooner had the ships' noses risen above the levels of their silos than their own point defenses went to work, helping the Valdekan lasers clear the rockets, at least, out of the sky.

The thunder of their drives shook the ground for kilometers around as they accelerated up into the atmosphere. And then their powergun batteries opened fire.

Line-straight, blue-tinged lightning that made the Caractacan infantry powerguns seem like little more than sparks in comparison, lanced out, seeking the artillery emplacements that were still hammering the defenses and the starport. Vehicles detonated with actinic flashes as powerful plasma packets impacted, dumping thousands of ergs of energy into materials that simply weren't designed to hold up to them. In seconds, the incoming fire had slackened to almost nothing in the face of the power of the ships rising into the sky.

Tilting slightly, the starships drifted toward the battered section of defenses where the Avar Sector Legio had held the line. More powergun fire licked out, hammering at several assault columns that were already starting to crawl across no-man's land, blasting armor into glowing scrap and reducing men to their constituent atoms. And then the dropships, at least those that had survived relatively undamaged, launched and plummeted toward the inside of the wall on tails of roaring, blue-white fire.

———

The light strobing through the firing slits of the most intact surviving pillbox heralded deaths in the hundreds, if not the thousands. And yet Scalas couldn't help but feel relieved.

He turned to Raskonesh. "Some of the pressure should be off for a while. I expect the enemy commander will rethink matters after having two assaults destroyed in a matter of a few hours. We can even hope he doesn't have the assets left to launch a serious attack after this. At least not for a while."

Viloshen passed his words along to the Valdekan warrant officer, who grunted a reply.

"They have clones," Viloshen translated. "They will only grow more."

But Scalas shook his head as one of his dropships settled only a few dozen meters away, on the other side of the wall, its drive vibrating the floor beneath them. "Even if they can grow them in a matter of days, they still have to make the weapons and equipment too," he pointed out. "I can't guarantee that we've bought you a significant breather, but maybe we've bought a few extra hours."

Raskonesh suddenly smiled. If there was a certain brittleness, a bleakness in the expression, it could only be expected after what the man had been through. He held out his hand, and Scalas folded it in an armored gauntlet.

Raskonesh then said something in Eastern Satevic and motioned to Viloshen. The older man protested in the same language, but

Raskonesh held his ground. Scalas looked from one to the other, painfully aware that he was going to have to break away soon. The dropships were on the ground, and they had to move.

Viloshen, looking quite unhappy, turned to Scalas. "I am being reassigned," he said slowly. "I am being your interpreter now."

Scalas studied the man. "And you are not happy about this?"

"This is my unit," Viloshen explained. "I belong here. But Raskonesh says that they must protect old uncle, because I am too old to be here any longer."

Scalas looked at Raskonesh. The warrant officer's face was grave, and his eyes held little more than a distant hope—a hope that by sending Viloshen with the Caractacans, he might save at least one of his command.

Scalas couldn't bring himself to remind the man that going with the Caractacans was no guarantee of survival either. They weren't going where the fighting was lighter, after all.

Raskonesh clapped a hand against Viloshen's shoulder, speaking as he did so. His voice was simultaneously reassuring and gruff, even though Scalas couldn't understand the words.

"He says that you need interpreter," Viloshen translated reluctantly, "and that I should not worry so much about leaving. He says there will be plenty of opportunities to die for Valdek for all of us."

"I don't doubt he's right about that," Scalas replied drily. "Well, if you're coming, then we need to move. The dropships are here, and they can't linger. Sooner or later, those enemy starships will be back overhead."

Viloshen spoke rapidly to Raskonesh. His voice was earnest, and it was clear that the thought of leaving his unit pained him a great deal. But Raskonesh replied in the same reassuring tone, taking the corporal now by both shoulders. Finally Viloshen nodded, though he was tight-lipped and unhappy. He turned to Scalas and squared his shoulders under his dirty combat tunic.

"I am ready," he said.

"Good." Most of the century was already out on the open ground of the landing zone, jogging toward the cone-shaped dropships. "Let's go."

It took some doing to get back out into the open; part of the stairs leading down the inside of the wall had been obliterated by the bombardment. Scalas was confident that his armor's articulation would let him jump the rubble-choked gap without destroying his knees, but he wasn't so sure about Viloshen. Fortunately, some of the gear in the underside of their sustainment packs was carried for just such a purpose.

Scalas pulled free a rappelling cable and secured it to Viloshen's combat harness. "Hold on to this," he said, putting the cable in Viloshen's hands. "Otherwise this is going to get very uncomfortable, just before you fall out of your harness." There wasn't time to rig a seat, and it wasn't all that far to the ground, anyway. Far enough to break bones, but not enough to kill a man.

Viloshen looked momentarily confused, then looked down and nodded. He grabbed the cable, and Scalas braced himself against the wall and began to play it out. Viloshen must have rappelled at some point in his past, because he expertly put his feet against the side of the steps, eased out, and disappeared over the edge.

Scalas held the tension even as he watched the rest of his squads board their dropships. The squat, truncated-cone-shaped ships had opened their middle thirds like flower petals for rapid boarding. When the sides were folded down, the steps set into the inner sections stretched down to the ground, and armored forms were now swarming up those steps. The dropship pilots could be dimly seen in the cockpits above them, preparing for a rapid takeoff. Beneath them, the ground still smoked and steamed beneath the thrust bells, which were showing faint blue glows; the pilots were keeping the drives as hot as they could without cooking the men as they boarded.

The cable went slack, then was tugged twice. Viloshen was on the ground. Scalas triggered the tiny winch to reel it back in even as he started toward the gap in the steps. He cinched his slung powergun down tight to his back, got a running start, and leapt over the gaping hole in the stairs left by a projectile.

He landed hard, right on the edge of the crumbling steelcrete. If not for his armor, his knee might well have been crushed by the impact. As it was, he merely teetered on the edge before flinging his weight forward to regain his balance. Then he was running down the remaining steps, hitting the flats at a sprint, and heading for the drop-ship with *XXXII-A* in large red characters just below the cockpit.

He pounded up the steps and paused at the top, right in front of an empty acceleration couch. There were going to be quite a few of those, he realized. He keyed his comm on the century channel. "Squad sergeants, head count. Let me know when we're ready to lift."

As he spoke, he craned his neck to look up toward the sky. There was little to see; the storms were still roiling above, mixed with dust and smoke kicked up by the titanic impacts of starship weapons and massed artillery. But he knew, even without seeing, that there were more of those white, pyramidal ships coming. The enemy had plenty of them to throw at the defenders. Just the brief glimpse they'd gotten in space was enough to tell him that.

Time was running out. For the Valdekans, and for the Caractacans who had come to help them.

"First Squad, up," Kahane reported.

Cobb's voice came right on Kahane's. "Second Squad, up. I have Viloshen, as well." He sounded like a man walking through a graveyard.

"Third Squad."

"Fourth."

"Fifth Squad, up." Volscius managed to sound arch even giving such a simple report. But Scalas ignored the man's tone. He was stuck with Volscius, and just had to deal with it. At least until they got back to the Sector Keep.

Presuming any of them even made it off Valdek.

He threw himself into the acceleration couch in front of him and quickly strapped in. "Century XXXII, all go," he reported to the pilots.

"Good copy," came the reply. "Stand by for a rapid lift. Brother Legate Kranjick says we are going straight for the *Sword of the Brotherhood*'s last known location, so you had best replenish now."

The dropships weren't just insertion vehicles; they also carried considerable stores of food, water, air, medical supplies, and ammunition, all of which were available through dispensers next to the acceleration couches. Brother Lathan, the chief dropship pilot aboard the *Dauntless*, would have made certain they were topped off before launching again. So as the dropship's sides folded up and the rumble of the drive intensified, Scalas began filling his water and drawing fresh magazines from the dispenser just off his armrest. He had to hurry; dropships could take off with some considerable gees, and even with his armor's articulation, it would not be a good thing to have his arm hanging off the armrest when that happened.

Lathan had the countdown on the overheads, flashing in bright red lights. Scalas hastily stuffed the fresh magazines into his ammunition carriers, then braced himself for lift.

The rumble rose to a mind-shredding roar, and then he was squashed down into his couch as the dropship leapt for the sky on a brilliant column of blue-white fire.

Almost immediately, Lathan was tilting the dropship's nose over, pushing the lander's trajectory away from the wall and toward their target. Scalas felt the hard kick of acceleration ease more quickly than he'd expected, even as the drive maintained its throaty roar, and realized that Lathan was trying to stay low, balancing lift and forward thrust with the drive, a tricky maneuver in one of the ballistic craft. The dropships' only lift came from their drives. They had no wings or rotors.

He found himself tilted backward, the blood starting to flow to his head, as Lathan skimmed the dropship over the battered defenses and toward the spaceport. Scalas was all but blind; the dropships didn't have windows in the troop compartments, and Lathan was too busy flying to worry about piping his sensor feed to the displays that could fold down in front of the acceleration couches.

Scalas momentarily wondered how Viloshen was doing. He didn't know what exploits the older man might have experienced as a merchant spacer, but doubted that something like this was among them. Still, it was a big galaxy, and one never knew. He decided the old corporal would be able to adapt. He certainly hadn't seemed like the type to panic while they'd been on the wall.

The first sign that something was amiss was when the dropship started to rock in flight. Then it suddenly dropped precipitously before steadying again. Scalas could dimly hear what might have been the crackling thunder of powergun bolts or missile detonations outside the hull, just barely audible over the rumble of the dropship's drive.

"We're taking fire, Centurion," Lathan reported. "There appears to be a sizeable enemy force around the target landing zone. And that's not all."

Lathan paused as if uncertain how to say what came next. Scalas felt a tightness in his chest as he waited for the worse news.

"The target zone is right next to what appears to be a large impact site, Centurion," Lathan continued. "It's mostly obscured by smoke, dust, and weapons fire, but the size is consistent with the low-level crash of a starship."

Scalas's mouth was suddenly dry.

"It would appear, Centurion, that the *Sword of the Brotherhood* has been brought down by enemy fire." Lathan's voice was strained, and with good reason. Not only was he flying the dropship under difficult conditions, but one fifth of their ship strength appeared to have been destroyed.

"Is there any sign of Century XXXIV?" Scalas asked. They were talking on a private command circuit. None of the rest of the century was hearing this.

"If the intensity of weapons fire near the wreck is any indication, there are definitely survivors," Lathan reported. "But we cannot land close to them. The nearest safe LZ is nearly a kilometer away, directly south of the wreck. Anything closer is either obstructed or under too much fire."

"Understood," Scalas replied. "Set us down where you can, and we will proceed to the wreck on foot." He felt his guts twist a little at the thought. He was going to lose more men. "What does the terrain look like?"

"This section appears to have mostly been devoted to auxiliary support structures for the spaceport. Expect built-up—" Lathan stopped suddenly, and the dropship rocked hard to one side as a nearby explosion shook it like a leaf. When he spoke again, it sounded like he was talking through clenched teeth. "Expect built-up industrial areas, with a lot of debris and wreckage. It looks like when that ship hit, it spread a lot of pieces over the area."

It sounded like a nightmare to fight in, but Scalas was confident in his Brothers. They were well trained—far better trained than the clones—and being able to maneuver would give them an advantage they hadn't had while holding the static defenses on the wall.

"Opposition near the LZ?" he asked.

"Not as heavy as it appears to be near the wreck. Though that's not saying much. Stand by. Touchdown in one minute."

Scalas switched to the century's channel. It was as good a brief as he was going to get. "One minute to touchdown," he called. "We're landing approximately one kilometer south of what appears to be the wreckage of the *Sword of the Brotherhood*. We will land, debark, secure the LZ and then proceed to link up with whoever survives of Century XXXIV. Once we've secured our Brothers, we'll attempt to rendezvous with Commander Rehenek and fall back to the spaceport."

There was no time for further explanation. He felt a momentary weightlessness as Lathan dropped the lander straight toward the ground as fast as he could, trying to get below the firing arcs of any heavy weapons that might be out there. It was a standard combat drop, but it never got any more comfortable.

The landing jacks hit hard, the impact jarring even as the hydraulics absorbed some of the shock. Then the sides fell away, unfolding to reveal the landing zone around them, and Scalas was hitting the quick release on his harness.

Lathan's description hadn't done the industrial area justice. Directly ahead as Scalas stood was a fiercely burning tank farm, belching black petrochemical smoke from shattered holding tanks twice the size of the dropship. A tangle of pipes stretched out in all directions, some intact, others smashed and twisted into jagged webs of metal. To the north were dense grids of containers, vast machines dedicated to the spaceport's workings, and various outbuildings. And above all this loomed a dark shape, smashed and broken, wreathed in smoke, and yet still bearing enough of the outline to identify it as a Spear-class starship.

The *Sword of the Brotherhood.* What was left of her.

Scalas took all this in even as he plummeted down the steps and hit the ground running. He realized that the only reason Lathan had been able to pick this spot as a landing zone was because the outbuildings had already been flattened, either by artillery or orbital strikes. Ash puffed from beneath his armored boots as he jogged toward the far side of the LZ, dodging the jagged, snapped-off structural members and twisted, blasted sections of wall that still jutted from the ground. The dropship pilots had needed all their skill to steer around those ruins to find a place to land.

Unslinging his powergun, he headed straight for the dark shape of the wreck, already deploying his squads to the flanks. Through the drifting smoke, his enhanced vision could make out movement in the container yards ahead.

They had clones to fight. And if he was seeing things right, there were a lot of them.

[14]

Though Caractacan internal comms codes were supposed to be unbreakable, many of the centurions still preferred to use hand and arm signals where possible. Technology was a useful tool, but it was not infallible. That was one thing that every novice learned in his first year. Especially when he was tossed into a survival situation without half his armor's systems working.

Scalas pointed to Cobb and Solanus and signaled for them to set up a base of fire on the pile of rubble overlooking the nearest avenue through the container yard. To Kahane, Volscius, and Kunn, he indicated that they would move down the next avenue over, leapfrogging as they went. They could probably hold their position and run their ammunition stocks dry if that was what they were there to do—but it wasn't. The objective was to get to the wreck, not to kill clones.

"Lathan," he called, risking the comm. "Hold on the LZ as long as you can. We'll extract as many of Dunstan's men as possible and be heading back here as fast as we can. If you have to lift, just make sure you let me know beforehand." The Brothers on the ground would have to adjust on the fly if that happened. Scalas didn't really want to think about it.

"I'm deploying the defense guns, at least until the enemy starships get within low orbit," Lathan replied. "After that, we're going to have to run for shelter or risk getting pasted."

"Understood," Scalas said. "We'll be quick." *I hope.*

He jogged through the drifting smoke toward the nearest cover. That proved to be the one remaining wall of a wrecked outbuilding that was still smoking. Considering it appeared to have been made of vitrified concrete, that meant that whatever had hit it had been packing a *lot* of energy.

Of course, he reflected as he crouched behind the ruined wall and peered around it, there were plenty of weapons being utilized on Valdek that fit that description. He had been in some brutal fights in his time, but this was the worst he had ever seen. Even worse than the handful of times he'd gone up against the M'tait.

The lane ahead was clear for the moment. Smoke and dust clouded the air, cutting visibility to less than a hundred meters. Kunn and his squad ran past, ducking into the gap between two stacks of containers across the lane from where his own squad had halted. Kunn stood in the center of the gap as three of his men set in, covering down the lane. One held high, the other low, and the third leaned out beside the two of them, exposing himself somewhat more but putting a third powergun muzzle on the danger area. The fact that he was one of the MT-41 support gunners helped.

Kunn, standing ramrod straight behind the Brothers covering the cross lane, looked around to make sure that all angles were covered before signaling to Scalas that they were set. His motions were stiff and precise, as would be expected from Kunn. The man was a machine.

Scalas got up, brought his powergun to his shoulder, and glided out into the lane. Behind him, Kahane's squad followed, spaced out in a rough file, weapons trained on every gap and overhead that wasn't filled by a Caractacan. Target identification was going to be crucial over the next few minutes, as they were moving toward other Brothers, who were presently engaged with the enemy. They had to be absolutely certain what they were shooting at before they fired.

That was part of Brotherhood training as well.

As he moved down the lane, Scalas swung to cover each opening he passed, keeping his muzzle trained down cross-passages until another Brother moved up to replace him. With visibility as limited as it was, they could not afford to take chances. An enemy might appear within a few meters at any moment.

He reached an intersection, or what had once been one. It looked like a high-energy weapon had struck the top of the nearest container stack, blasting one container in half and knocking the entire stack into an avalanched heap across the lane. He quickly took a knee facing down the left-hand lane, while Volscius took his squad and set up on the opposite opening.

The roar and crackle of weapons fire filled the smoky air. There was quite a fight going on, but it was shrouded in dust and smoke and obscured behind piles of wreckage.

The eerie quiet of the lane was suddenly broken by the snarling thunderclaps of powergun fire. Someone in Volscius's squad had just opened fire.

With a glance to make sure that Kahane's squad was covering their sector, Scalas lifted his muzzle and turned, looking back toward Volscius's position. He couldn't see much, only the flashes of powergun bolts flickering into the murk beyond. Then a cone-bore round skipped off the ground not far from his boot with a nasty *buzz*, confirming that Volscius's men weren't shooting at shadows.

A moment later the lane was filled with projectiles, shredding the tattered whorls of smoke and dust, the sharp *cracks* of their passage muted by his helmet. Scalas threw himself behind cover. His armor could stand up to a lot, but that didn't mean that standing in the open under fire was a good idea.

Yet he knew they couldn't afford to get bogged down there. There were going to be a lot of clones between them and the wreck of the *Sword*, but there were also starships inbound, ready to rain destruction down on their heads. Time was short.

Taking a deep breath, he heaved himself to his feet, bellowed,

"On me!" and began to run forward, right into the teeth of the clone rifle fire.

A shot *spanged* off his pauldron, but didn't penetrate. He answered with a fast trio of powergun bolts.

As he neared Volscius's position, he could make out the dim shapes of clone troops in the murk. There were a lot of them, as he'd come to expect. But they weren't using fire and maneuver. They were simply rushing forward, firing from the hip, just like their assault on the breach back at the wall.

Volscius's support gunners opened fire with their MT-41s, and the bulky, heavy powerguns raked the oncoming mob of clones with almost continuous, blue-tinged beams of destruction. The clones fell as fast as they came, mowed down like grain, but they kept charging, kept shooting.

Scalas added his fire, dropping two more with as many shots, as he came abreast of Volscius, who was barricaded against a container, leaning out to fire on the mass of clones.

"We need to push through," Scalas said. "We can't stay here!"

"There are too many of them!" Volscius protested, his voice amplified by his helmet to be heard over the thunder of powergun fire. "Even if we kill one with every shot, they'll mow us down!"

Scalas shot three more, as fast as he could transition between targets. Heat was already starting to ripple off his barrel, though it was nothing compared to the support guns. That was what the MT-41s had the thick cooling sleeves for. "If we push forward, some of us die, but we get to the *Sword*," he said. "If we stay here, eventually we either get overrun anyway, or the starships kill us from the upper atmosphere. And I wasn't suggesting. Move!"

Scalas might have been justified hanging back to coordinate his men. But that was not the Caractacan way. Firing as fast as he could switch targets and cycle the trigger, he ducked out into the lane and ran for the next available cover, a narrow gap between containers. Two more cone-bore rounds skipped off his armor, and a third struck his breastplate almost dead center, staggering him, but then he was in the alcove, dumping the rest of his magazine into the mob of clones still milling beyond the stacks of smoking bodies that the support gunners had laid in windrows in the lane in front of him.

A sudden flickering, thunderous hurricane of powergun bolts tore into the flank of the clone unit, through the next lane over. It seemed that Cobb had moved the support by fire element up as soon as he'd heard the shooting.

A crackling voice speaking an unfamiliar language—or maybe a code—boomed out through the smoky alleyway. Almost instantly, the clones still standing started falling back behind a blizzard of gunfire. The Caractacans kept up their own fire, answering hypervelocity bullets with sun-hot plasma bolts.

Then the last of the clones disappeared into the smoke, and there were no more targets. The powergun fire slackened; the Brothers only shot at what they could see.

"Status reports!" Scalas barked.

The squad sergeants reported in. Volscius had taken some losses. Urien, Tommas, and Borgin were down. Fredrich had taken a bullet through a joint in his armor and was out of action, though he looked like he'd survive.

A lot of ammunition had been expended. And they still had a long way to go.

"Move up, and watch for flankers," Scalas instructed. He didn't know what that voice had been, but his suspicion that the clone cannon fodder had trained commanders was getting stronger. It was a horrific, inhuman way of waging war, but he supposed that if one viewed the clones as expendable, easily replaceable assets, it made a cruel kind of economic sense.

Ducking down the next lane, he led the way toward the *Sword*. The sounds of battle coming from the wreck were only getting more intense.

———

Scalas dashed for another half-destroyed hunk of machinery, the purpose of which was lost to time and the powergun bolt that had shattered it. Crouching in the lee of the warped and blackened metal, he peered out, his helmet's enhanced vision helping paint a picture of what he was looking at.

They had broken out of the container yard after only a few more sporadic clashes with clones. Each time, the clones themselves seemed almost mindlessly aggressive, yet they were completely obedient to the commands blasted out by some unseen loudspeaker. Scalas had yet to glimpse one of the commanders, but he'd already resolved to put a powergun bolt through the helmet of the first one he saw.

Most of the area surrounding the wreck of the *Sword of the Brotherhood* had been blasted to dust. It was apparent that there had been buildings here—the remnants of foundations were still clear among the rubble—but little now remained that stood more than knee-high. The destruction appeared to be the result of heavy ground fighting, rather than starship bombardment, since the whole yard wasn't a single, massive, vitrified pit of blackened glass.

The *Sword* had clearly come down at an angle, striking near the engine bells and then tipping over to hit the ground. The impact had burst the hull in several places, and there were even more gaping holes along her visible flank from weapons fire. The area around the reactor was still glowing, and was no doubt ferociously hot, both in terms of thermal energy and hard radiation, even if the emergency dump had kept most of the contamination down. Without an emergency shutdown, there wouldn't have been a starship left at all. Or much of the surrounding landscape, for that matter.

The crash had thrown up a humped berm of debris, and the survivors appeared to be using that for cover. Ferocious powergun fire was blasting out from the crater rim, looking like an intense lightning storm at ground level, centered around the wreck of the *Sword.*

And the defenders certainly had no shortage of targets.

The ground around the crash site was swarming with clones and Unity fighting vehicles. The angular tanks that the Brotherhood had fought at the breach were closing in, even as hundreds of infantry fired on the defenders from almost every direction.

Kahane leaned out from behind Scalas and scanned the open ground between them and the wreckage. He whistled. "That's going to be interesting."

Scalas watched a platoon of tanks rumble past, apparently oblivious to the now grayish-brown armored forms hidden in the dust and ruins. He was wracking his brain, trying to think of a plan. They had three less-than-intact centuries, and there were thousands of clones out there on the four hundred meters of open ground between them and the remains of Century XXXIV. The Brothers could do a lot of damage, that was for certain; but could they win through to their beleaguered brothers and get back out, without getting slaughtered to a man?

A voice rumbled over the comm. "Costigan, this is Kranjick. Report your position."

Costigan's reply followed—a set of numbered coordinates.

At the touch of a few keys set into his gauntlet, Scalas brought up a faint overlay map in his visor, pinpointing the cavalry century's position relative to his own.

"We have been slowed by obstacles and dense structures," Costigan continued. "We should have line of sight on the crash site within the next five minutes."

"I need your tanks to go hull-down to provide direct fire support," Kranjick said. "There are enough enemy vehicles out on the open ground between our last covered and concealed positions and the crash site that I do not want to risk a direct attack. I've identified a covered route that should allow the infantry centuries to cross to the crater, provided your vehicles can keep the enemy occupied."

Even as Kranjick said it, Scalas's helmet overlay flashed with an indicator that showed him the path that might provide enough cover to cross to the beleaguered defenders. It would be extremely risky, but if the tanks could keep the enemy's attention…

"Acknowledged," Costigan replied. "Any chance of direct support from the starships?"

"Not yet," Kranjick said. "It's obvious that the enemy in this vicinity can present enough massed fire to bring down a Spear-class. I want to thin them out a bit before we risk losing another of our starships."

"Confirmed," Costigan said, a note of resignation in his voice. Scalas understood the other man's misgivings. The starships packed far more firepower than Costigan's tanks, especially the *Challenger*. But losing the *Sword of the Brotherhood* had already placed them at a severe disadvantage, making the surviving ships that much more precious. It was a delicate balance that the Brother Legate had to strike, and Scalas admitted to himself that he was glad the decision didn't lie on his own shoulders.

"Infantry centurions," Kranjick called, "begin to converge on my position, but keep behind cover. Engage only if necessary. Once Century XXXV's vehicles are in position, we will move. This is going to be a dead sprint through enemy fire, gentlemen. When I say go, you move hard, you move fast, and you do not hesitate. Understood?"

"Yes, sir," Soon replied. Scalas added his own acknowledgment, then turned away from the fight around the wreck to brief his squad sergeants.

That was when the whole world split asunder.

The flash could have blinded anyone looking directly at it. Even turned away, Scalas's visor dimmed to compensate. The thunderclap was a physical blow that almost knocked him off balance. Flying grit hissed against his armor.

He and Kahane turned back toward the wreck, only to see a scene of utter devastation.

A faintly glowing furrow had been blasted through the middle of what had once been a formation of Unity tanks. Most of those tanks were now burning wreckage, and the rest weren't moving. Either they had taken damage that wasn't immediately apparent, or their crews had been shocked into immobility by the magnitude of the blast.

A second blast raved through the dust, a little farther away. Fortunately this one wasn't as bright as the first, though Scalas's visor still nearly blacked out to compensate for it. The concussion, however, was nearly as intense, and the wave of high-velocity grit just as brutal.

"Those are starship powerguns," Kahane said. "Got to be."

Scalas agreed. But they seemed to be coming from the wreck...

With a sudden sharp *crack*, a brilliant flash darted upward from the crater rim, near the crash site.

Scalas suddenly understood.

"They managed to dismount a shipboard powergun and fire it," he said, faintly amazed at the combination of audacity and desperation needed to try such a stunt. "And I think it just failed."

Kranjick must have reached the same conclusion, though he didn't comment on it. "All infantry centuries, that's our opening," he said. "Go, go, go!"

There wasn't time to fine-tune who would go where. They had to move fast to take advantage of the sudden lull in the fight. Even the seemingly mindless clones appeared to have been stunned by the twin heavy-caliber powergun blasts.

Now that the hard-shot fire had died away to nearly nothing, the Brotherhood powerguns from the crater blazed away as intensely as before. No, not quite; there was nothing coming from the vicinity of that last flash.

"By squads, fighting wedge, on me!" Scalas snapped over the century comm. Then he was moving, ducking out from behind the wrecked machinery and running for the next hummock in the dusty, windswept ground.

It was not a straight-line sprint. Even after the twin shocks of those massive powergun bolts, that would have been suicide. At least some of the clones would have recovered by the time they covered four hundred meters, no matter how hard they ran. So the Caractacans moved forward in short dashes, moving from furrow in the ground to unidentifiable debris to wrecked vehicle, their armor shifting shades to make them dim shadows flitting through the smoke and dust.

Dravot had pushed hard to get in front and take point, but Scalas was right behind him. The haze thickened as the debris thrown up into the atmosphere by the powergun blasts began to settle. It wasn't enough to cover their sprint, but nor was it so bad that they couldn't see where they were going.

That crackling, amplified voice speaking that unfamiliar language roared out over the battlefield once more, audible even over the rolling thunder of powergun bolts. It sounded angry, strident, and Scalas was struck by the sense that the voice was having to push the clones harder than before. Maybe they weren't quite as mindless as they appeared. Maybe a sharp enough shock could actually break them, make them huddle in cover and not want to move.

But considering it had taken two shipboard powergun bolts from point-blank range to even begin to do that, he wasn't hopeful that this was a weakness that could be leveraged anytime soon.

Movement ahead caught his eye. Dravot must have seen it too, as he swung his powergun to his shoulder, fired, then ducked flat as cone-bore rifle fire buzzed through the air like a squadron of flesh-tearing insects.

They were still seventy meters from the crash site, and cover was thin. They couldn't afford to get bogged down. Scalas dashed forward, firing as he went, smacking clones off their feet with blue-tinged lightning bolts as they became visible. It looked like the ragged remains of a platoon was hunkered down in the lee of a wrecked tank, one that appeared to have gotten dangerously close to breaking through to the crash site before its turret had been taken off by an HV missile. The clones were spraying gunfire wildly at anything that moved, and it seemed to Scalas they were confused and scared.

They also died quickly. Especially when Geroges hit the ground a few meters behind Scalas and opened fire with his MT-41. A long, ravening burst that crackled and thundered like sheet lightning. It tore the clones apart.

Then Scalas and Dravot were forging up the crumbling outer slope of the crater. "Friendlies, friendlies!" Scalas was broadcasting over his comm. It would be the height of stupidity to get that far and get his head blown off by a friendly powergun because he failed to communicate.

As he crested the crater rim, he found Caractacan Brothers and a few Valdekans lining the rim to either side of him, their powerguns aimed over the heaped dirt and debris, watching for clones. Several more were stationed above, toward what was left of the *Sword*'s nose cone. "More are coming through," he said to the nearest man, a squad sergeant by the rank insignia on his pauldrons. "Where is Centurion Dunstan?"

The squad sergeant pointed toward the crushed bow of the *Sword of the Brotherhood*. "In the command post, against the hull," he said. "Coordinating the defense."

Of course he is.

Scalas didn't express aloud his contempt for a centurion who "coordinated" from a command post behind the fighting. He would never speak ill of another centurion in front of that centurion's subordinates. Or his own, for that matter.

"Brother Legate Kranjick is behind me," he said. "When he gets here, tell him where the command post is." Without another word, he stalked down the slope of the crater, in the direction the Century XXXIV squad sergeant had pointed.

The crash site was a nightmare. The smashed remains of the stricken starship loomed overhead, casting dark shadows over the crater, blocking out half the cloudy, dusty sky. The crater floor was loose, all crumbling dirt and shattered steelcrete, and made for treacherous footing. Dead and wounded lay amid the debris, and there were far too few men up on the crater rim, crouched behind powerguns and firing back at the clones that swarmed around the wreck. Scalas wondered just how many had survived the crash.

He watched Dravot looking around as they crossed the crater floor. While the armor disguised the younger Brother's expression, the man's carriage alone communicated the anger that built within him. Scalas's own thoughts echoed what he had no doubt was going through the other Caractacan's mind. He was remembering the dead from Cobb's squad too.

The command post was little more than a hole in the stricken starship's flank, where Dunstan was crouched behind some twisted hull plating along with the *Sword of the Brotherhood*'s executive officer and a couple of Valdekan officers. The spot was elevated above the crater rim, which would have allowed Dunstan a better view of the battlefield had there been less smoke in the air.

Scalas lengthened his strides as they neared the command post. He didn't want Dravot to get there ahead of him.

But Dravot was fast. "Traitor!" he snarled as he clambered up onto the curved bit of outer hull right at Scalas's side. "Deserter!" He lunged at Dunstan, and Scalas had to grab his arm. *"Coward!"*

Scalas yanked Dravot back with a heave. The younger Brother didn't even look at him; his visor was locked on Dunstan like a targeted powergun.

"How many died, Dunstan?" Dravot demanded. *"How many Brothers died because you left your post?"*

"Enough," said a rumbling voice behind them.

Kranjick had moved quickly as well. As he heaved his bulk up onto the warped and smashed plating, Scalas saw that his armor was newly scored by several deflected cone-bore rounds. He straightened, towering over Scalas and Dravot both, and stared at Dunstan.

"This disaster had best be worth it, Centurion Dunstan," he said, his voice flat and heavy. "Where is Commander Rehenek?"

Dunstan shook his head. "He was here, but he pulled out just before we arrived. It is my belief that this force was diverted here expressly to kill or capture him once the enemy figured out that he was here. They were on approach as he left, which was why we were shot down. If he hadn't retreated…"

"Enough," Kranjick repeated. "I don't want to hear your excuses for disobeying orders, lying to our allies, presumably lying to your men—I can think of no other reason your century would have unquestioningly followed you on this folly—deserting your post, and getting your ship destroyed and many of your men killed. You *will* answer for it. But now is neither the time nor the place. Squad Sergeant Yen!"

"Squad Sergeant Yen is dead, sir," one of the Caractacans standing below reported. "Squad Sergeant Rokoff is the only squad sergeant still alive in the century, sir."

Kranjick's helmet turned toward Dunstan like a weapons turret. "Squad Sergeant Rokoff!" he bellowed, his armor's amplification sending the call echoing across the crater.

The same squad sergeant who had greeted Scalas and Dravot as they'd climbed over the crater rim turned and strode over to the command post. "Yes, Brother Legate?" he asked, stiffening to attention.

"Brother Dunstan stands relieved for cause," Kranjick said. "You are now brevet centurion of what remains of Century XXXIV. Begin assembling your men for evac."

Rokoff saluted, lifting his powergun, muzzle up, in front of his visor. "We don't have many left, sir," he said. "Twenty percent of First Squad died when that powergun blew up."

"They bought you time," Kranjick said. "Their sacrifice will not go unremembered. Now, quickly. Before the enemy regroups."

Scalas was about to ask about how they would reboard the dropships with enemy tanks still roving the open ground beyond when a deep, ground-shaking rumble answered his question. With heavy, thunderous roars, the *Boanerges, Dauntless,* and *Challenger* appeared overhead, leaning forward, their drives both propelling them toward the enemy and holding them off the ground. Powergun bolts flashed down into formations of armored vehicles and beyond, deep into the dust-shrouded reaches of the spaceport's support yards and the smashed defenses beyond.

Kranjick was looking at Scalas as if he had heard the question that had gone unsaid. "One ship, unsupported and unready, flying into a prepared enemy, was shot down. Three ships, ready to fight and on the heels of the kind of disruption those dead men created by dismounting one of the *Sword*'s powerguns, are another matter entirely.

"Now hurry and assemble your men. We will need to lift before the enemy manages to regain their equilibrium. Our hunt for Commander Rehenek will require further preparation and planning. I am tired of rushing about, one step behind."

[15]

As the centurions assembled with General-Regent Rehenek in the Valdekan command center once more, the room felt suddenly far from the battle. The lights flickered occasionally as the latest starship fly-by pounded the fortress from above, and a continual low, thumping rumble of the bombardment penetrated the thick walls, but it was nothing like what they had just departed. Yet the Brothers themselves had brought the battle with them. They were covered in dust and soot, and they stank of ozone, smoke, and less wholesome odors. They smelled like combat.

"Yes," the General-Regent said wearily, "Amra is gone from the fortress. I became aware of my son's new mission only a few moments ago, after I could no longer recall him." The old man looked more than tired. He looked deeply weary in a way that went beyond time and age. He was tired in his soul, weighed down by the destruction being wreaked upon his people and now by the personal strain of seeing his son, whom he probably thought of as his world's last hope, throwing himself into the thick of battle, seemingly trying to get himself killed.

Scalas had no son, and never would. He was sworn to the Brotherhood for life. He could not truly understand the fears that were part and parcel of seeing one's own flesh and blood go into harm's way. But he had lost brothers in arms, and he knew the weight of command. So he could understand well enough.

With a wince of pain, the elder Rehenek steered his exoskeleton toward the briefing theater where he had first revealed just what they were up against. Kranjick and the centurions followed him. Brevet Centurion Rokoff seemed slightly hesitant, as if he still wasn't certain that he belonged here, but Rehenek didn't seem to have noticed the change in personnel.

Then again, none of them had doffed their helmets, so he had no way of noticing, unless he spotted the different markings on Rokoff's pauldrons.

Inside the briefing room, a holo was already up. It depicted what appeared to be the entirety of Gorakovati and the country around it, including the settlements and towns all over the shoulders of the towering volcano. It also showed several pulsing red malignancies, most of them centered around population centers. One of the largest was around the planetary defense fortress itself. Another was some four hundred kilometers away, on the other side of the mountain. A thin blue thread ran from the fortress, around the side of the mountain, toward that more distant red blotch.

The General-Regent pointed, and that same red stain pulsed brightly. "Recent signals intelligence has pinpointed that position as a groundside command post. My son believes that our remaining ground-based defenses make low orbit too dangerous, and since the distance to the Lagrange points makes direct command-and-control from there unfeasible, this so-called 'Galactic Unity' has landed a starship there, and is using it as a command center."

Kranjick nodded slowly. "And he's going to attack it."

It wasn't a question, but the General-Regent nodded in response, nevertheless. "He hopes to disrupt their attacks enough that we can regain some initiative." The heaviness in his voice spoke of his despair. The General-Regent knew, clear down to his bones, that Valdek was lost. Even if his son succeeded, the old man's spirit was already broken. He was hanging on to life through sheer stubbornness, to try to give his son a chance to escape.

The Duchess stepped into the theater. She said nothing as she stepped to her husband's side. The message was clear: whatever was to come, they would face it together. Equally clear was the fact that there was increasingly little that anyone in the command center could do. The defenders were set in, and they would stand or fall in place. Every resource the Valdekans had remaining inside the fortress was committed. They could not even reinforce a sector if it began to collapse, not without opening another hole for the seemingly endless swarms of clones to take advantage of.

The elder Rehenek looked up at Kranjick's visor. "He has a head start," he said, "but he's going around the shoulder of the volcano. I know that Caractacan armor is proof against vacuum. If you could go *over* the mountain, you might be able to catch up with him before he makes contact with the enemy."

"Do you wish us to prevent him from assaulting the command ship?" Kranjick asked quietly. His voice was as low and monotone as ever, but Scalas knew his mentor well enough to tell that he was somewhat conflicted about the request. They were being asked to convince a man *not* to fight for his planet and his people. It would be a bitter pill to swallow, and Scalas knew that were he on the receiving end of such a request, he would refuse.

"Getting him off this world is the only hope a Valdekan resistance has left," the Duchess said. "Explain that to him. Explain that unless he finds allies and returns with enough of a fleet to finally defeat these abominations, then all is truly lost. Destroying one grounded starship won't change that." She held out a data chip. "Show him this. It is a last message from me. He will obey his mother."

Kranjick took the chip gravely. "I will do as you ask, madam."

"I have drawn back a company of Valdekan First Force commandos to accompany you," the General-Regent said. "Along with what combat vehicles we still have left that we can spare. I fear they are few. Any of the commandos who survive must go with you when you leave the planet. They will form the core of my son's resistance force. The vehicles are mostly tracked or wheeled, but they should be able to negotiate most of the mountain, provided you don't go right through the caldera."

Scalas was frowning a little, and he would have expected Kranjick to be doing the same behind his visor were he not entirely familiar with his superior officer's near-constant expressionlessness.

"If time is so pressing, we will do a short-range lift by ship," Kranjick said. "That means we will also have better fire support once we manage to rendezvous with the commander."

But the General-Regent shook his head and tapped another control. The holo zoomed out until it showed the entire planet. One formation of Unity starships was moving away toward the L4 point. A second, larger formation, with dozens of ships surrounding a mammoth dreadnaught of unfamiliar design, was on an approach vector to the planet.

"Our remaining scanning capability is severely limited," the Duchess said quietly, "but it is clear that this dreadnaught carries far more firepower than we can hope to match. We might survive for a while inside the fortifications, but anything in the air will not. You will have a greater chance of going undetected—and therefore avoiding an orbital strike—if you go overland."

"But if we are cut off from our ships on the other side of the volcano, then we won't be able to get your son and his troops off-world," Soon pointed out. "And then the entire effort will be for nothing."

"That is why you must not tarry," said the General-Regent. "As my wife said, we can hold out here for a time. That monstrosity will eventually batter through our defenses, but not immediately. Trust me, Centurion: I will not allow your ships to be destroyed on the ground if I can help it."

That all the Valdekan defenders would likely be dead if that happened went unsaid.

A flashing light drew every eye to the room's control panel.

Rehenek clumped his exoskeleton over to it, pressed a key, and spoke briefly in Eastern Satevic. He frowned at the reply, then said what sounded like an affirmative before turning back to the holo.

A comms window opened up in midair. It showed a man with longish hair and a full beard. His olive skin was lined but still hale, his pale eyes bright. He wore a coat with shoulder boards and a tall collar heavy with gold braid. He was immediately recognizable from the first message Rehenek had played for them. Geretesk Vakolo was making contact again.

"Hello, Bozhidar, old friend," Vakolo said. There was a strange lilt to his Trade Cant, but Scalas couldn't place it. "Isn't it time to end this?"

"'Friend?'" Rehenek spat. "Is this how Sparatans show 'friendship'? You have wrecked my world, slaughtered my people…"

"As my message made clear when our forces arrived, Bozhidar," Vakolo said calmly, "the goal ahead of us is far too important to let sentimentality stand in our way. I warned you what resistance to the Unity would cost, and still you chose to resist. You went into this war with both eyes open. Do not attempt to say otherwise."

Rehenek stood firm. "I have nothing more to say to you that I have not already said with laser, railgun, particle beam, and powergun."

The bearded man sighed, rather like a disappointed father. "You will not surrender? Not even seeing that your last fortress is on the brink of failure, and my forces are legion beyond numbering? See reason, Bozhidar."

Instead of answering, Rehenek barked what might have been a curse in Eastern Satevic, and aimed an unmistakable command back at the control panel.

But the window did not close. The bearded man leaned closer.

"Unfortunate," he said coldly. "The Unity will not be stopped. Galactic civilization can never progress while all its peoples still live scattered and leaderless, focused only on their own small, petty concerns. I had hoped that you would see sense and submit. Instead, the Unity will be built upon your bones." His eyes shifted. "I would warn you, Caractacans, to depart, but your kind will ultimately have no place in the order that is to come. Your deaths on this world should serve as a message to your comrades. I might consider letting one of you live, though, to send back to your headquarters. So that the rest of your dying order will know what awaits them."

Only then did the comm channel cut out.

Rehenek turned to the control panel. His face was pale, and for a brief instant, Scalas could see just how shaken the old man was. And no wonder—how many shocks of impending doom could one man withstand?

Rehenek spoke urgently to whatever comm tech was on the other side of the panel's intercom. When the conversation was finished, the General-Regent looked at his wife, stark fear in his eyes. "The tech says that he tried to cut the connection, and failed." He spoke in Trade Cant, apparently for the benefit of the Caractacans. His voice was low and haunted. "Geretesk was in complete control of our comm systems."

"Is it possible that his people on the ground got a virus into your systems?" Costigan asked.

The General-Regent shook his head. "The techs are looking for one, but comm security has been paramount since the war began. It should have been detected." He shook his head again, his eyes haunted. "No, it was as if he simply reached down and took control."

Scalas knew of no way that was possible without some kind of virus attack, but he realized that the fear and the strain of the last weeks—being forced to watch one's defenses crumble under a never-ending onslaught—would make even the most hardheaded of rationalists start to see unnatural power in their enemy.

He suddenly thought of the inhuman, swarming behavior of the clones on the battlefield, and a shudder went through him. Perhaps there was more to the Valdekans' fears than just the grinding strain of shell-shock and the seeming inevitability of defeat. There was something strange, something disquieting on a deep, fundamental level about the so-called "Galactic Unity's" forces. And he had no doubt that this was by design.

The General-Regent looked at Kranjick. "There is something different about him," he said hoarsely. "That is not the Geretesk Vakolo I knew in the Tyrus Cluster. He has changed, somehow. Geretesk was a hero of his people, and with good reason. But now…" He stared at nothing for a long moment. "We were of an age, all those years ago. But he seems young, hale. Whereas I…" He gestured at the contraption that kept him upright. "And I never heard of a man who survived a M'tait borer who came out of it stronger."

"He was hit with a borer?" Scalas asked in some disbelief. He'd seen the damage the wicked M'tait weapons could do. A borer was a near-miracle of micro-engineering, a projectile that slowed just before it hit, then slowly tore its way through the victim's flesh. It was designed to avoid vital organs for some time, prolonging the agony of the victim's death for as long as possible. And it wasn't even the cruelest of M'tait weapons.

Rehenek nodded gravely. "I saw him just before they lifted him off the asteroid. They had managed to seal his suit, but there was blood all over his leg. It had gone in his foot, you see." Every Caractacan, hardened combatants though they were, winced a little at that. An entry wound in the foot would give the borer the most time to slowly shred its victim from the inside. It was not a pretty way to die. "That was the last I saw of him. They told me that he had been taken back to Sparat for treatment. Well… that was the last I saw of him until a few weeks ago."

The floor beneath their feet shuddered. It was slight, but given the great mass of reinforced steelcrete and solid stone that formed the fortress, it portended something far, far worse.

A tinny voice reported from the control panel. Rehenek answered, then turned to the holo, which zoomed back in to highlight the fortress. A billowing mushroom cloud was rising above an emplacement on the upper tier, near the steeper slope of the volcano.

"That was Particle Cannon Five," Rehenek said. "That dreadnaught just hit it with an X-ray laser. Through the atmosphere, the dust, and the smoke. And they aren't even to high orbit yet."

Kranjick glanced at Scalas. That was not good news. Whatever that dreadnaught was packing, it was far more powerful than anything the Caractacans had heard of before. And to be able to target such a small target from that distance…

Kranjick studied the holo-tank. "Can you display the dreadnaught's trajectory?" he asked.

Rehenek frowned, apparently nonplussed by the question. Perhaps he expected the Caractacans would get moving at once rather than continue to ask questions. But he nodded and touched a series of keys.

A gossamer, glowing golden line traced out from the holographic dreadnaught, passed close to the planet, and curved around it.

Kranjick said nothing, but a few voices murmured quietly at the altitude where the ship's trajectory curved around its lowest point.

"Low orbital insertion," Soon said quietly.

"And if it's entering orbit, then there's our window," Kranjick said. He looked down at Rehenek. "I understand your concerns, General-Regent. But you have said it yourself: Valdek is ready to fall. Should I leave my ships here and this fortress fall to the enemy while we are in transit, then it's all over. The war, the Valdekan resistance, Caractacan assistance… all of it." He pointed to the holo. "If that ship enters low orbit, then we will have roughly a thirty-minute window while it's below the horizon to launch and get over the mountain. From there, we can rendezvous with the commander, get him aboard, and get off the planet."

He laid a heavy hand on the old man's shoulder. Rehenek was no longer looking at him, but staring at the holo-tank, his face weary and haunted. "I gave you my word that we would see him off this planet. This is the best way I can do that."

Rokoff's stance looked a little uncertain. He looked back and forth between the two older men, as if he was wondering why his superior wasn't just laying down the law. But Scalas knew. If Kranjick didn't persuade Rehenek of the wisdom of this course of action, the General-Regent could give orders to prevent the ships from getting launch clearance.

After a long pause, Rehenek bowed his head. "I suppose," he said, his voice barely more than a whisper, "that I had hoped to see my son one more time before I die. But you are right, Legate. Go. Prepare your ships. And may the Universe be on your side."

————

The landing silo shuddered and shook with the pounding the fortress was taking from above. Deep, thrumming vibrations heralded the Valdekan return fire. They were taking a beating, but they weren't giving up. Scalas was impressed. These were a tough, stubborn people. They would go down—their eventual defeat was now impossible to stave off—but they would keep fighting until they no longer had the means left to do so.

And they would do whatever they could to buy time for the Caractacans to get their core resistance force off-world. Their sacrifice would be remembered for ages. He hoped. But first the Brothers had to make it off world with the younger Rehenek.

The thought of what would happen to the survivors once resistance finally collapsed was haunting. He doubted that the harrowing of Valdek would end when the guns fell silent. Again, the sense of inhumanity and alien strangeness that clung to the Unity's clone forces sent a crawling shiver up his spine.

His men, those who were left, were finalizing their own loading. It wasn't just his own century in the troop bay, either; Valdekans were coming with them, and the survivors from Century XXXIV, including Dunstan, had been spread out among the four remaining ships. The Valdekans had offered supplies as well, including more powergun ammunition, and the Caractacans had accepted gratefully. Their numbers were severely depleted, but more firepower would be welcome where they were going.

Scalas's eyes found Dunstan, sitting with about half a squad of his remaining century, his centurion markings still on his pauldrons. He didn't look nearly as dirty as the rest of the men of the century, and the sight set Scalas's jaw a little. The disgraced centurion would have been in a holding cell aboard the *Boanerges* if they didn't need every Brother for the fight to come.

Spotting Viloshen and Cobb talking to another man in the green and black of the Valdekan commandos, Scalas walked over to join them.

Viloshen turned. "Centurion, this is Warrant Officer Atelevek. He commands company of First Force commandos. He will be with us on trip over mountain."

Atelevek was a younger man with a flat, pugnacious face and small, mean-looking eyes. He seemed to wear a permanent grimace on his face, a cruel one, his mouth slightly twisted by a vicious scar that had nearly taken one of his eyes. He looked at Scalas dully, without the borderline awe that some of the other Valdekan troops had displayed. There was something predatory about the man—like a sullen brutality was just waiting for an opportunity to be let loose. Scalas had met such men before, including in the Vitorian Commandos, and had always been wary of them.

In fact, he had always had a contingency plan in mind to kill such men before they could do too much damage.

Of course, it was possible that he was judging too much by Atelevek's appearance. The man might just be ugly. Brother Simonum, whom he had trained with, and who had departed to the Poran Sector Legio many years before, had been the ugliest man Scalas had ever met, and had also been one of the most staunch, honorable friends he had ever known. But when Atelevek looked at the centurion's outstretched hand, sneered, and then shook it with such a perfunctory manner that it was almost an insult, Scalas suspected that he wasn't judging the man harshly enough.

"Our launch window should be opening soon," Scalas said coolly. "We should start getting equipment secured and strapping in."

Viloshen translated his words, and Atelevek looked at Scalas as if he was insulted to have been told that. Scalas kept his expression carefully neutral. He would not let this man see that his attitude had succeeded in irritating a Caractacan centurion.

Atelevek then said something in a careless tone to Viloshen, waved at him casually, and walked away toward the dropships that had been detailed to carry the Valdekan ground troops.

Viloshen watched the warrant officer go, then glanced sidelong at Scalas. Scalas did not meet his eye, but as he watched Atelevek warily, he asked the question the old corporal was obviously waiting for.

"Will he be a problem?"

Viloshen shook his head. "I do not think so. He will follow his orders."

"Do you know him?" Scalas asked.

Viloshen shook his head again. "No. But he is First Force commando. There is selection process."

Scalas watched Atelevek's back. "Perhaps." He had certainly seen murderers and conscienceless killers slip through selection courses before. He'd also seen some men become such *after* selection. He resolved to keep an eye on Atelevek, as much as he could. "Get to your dropship and strap in," he said. "We're leaving soon, and I need my interpreter."

Viloshen nodded resignedly, and followed Kahane toward First Squad's lander.

Scalas found his own couch, dogged down his helmet, and strapped in. He brought up his holo display in front of his visor. It displayed the curve of the planet and the location of the spaceport. The enemy starships coursed above, the fearsome dreadnaught at their center, still firing on the fortress, but nearing the horizon.

Soon, the enemy would be below that horizon. Then they would launch.

[16]

THE MASSIVE GALACTIC UNITY DREADNAUGHT WAS OF A RADICALLY different design from the swarms of blunt, angular, pyramidal ships that formed its escort. It out-massed them by an order of magnitude at least, and resembled a monstrous, eight-sided ziggurat, slightly flattened on two flanks. Its mountainous hull bristled with HEL emitters, powergun turrets, and missile banks.

Its enormous drives, each thrust bell nearly large enough to swallow one of the smaller Unity starships, were currently pointed along its line of travel, glowing a brilliant blue, slowing the enormous ship so that Valdek's gravity could swing it into low orbit. Yet its weapons still rained destruction down on the planet's surface, flickering lines of plasma and coherent radiation stabbing down into the storm-wracked and dust-laden atmosphere, aimed with inhuman precision at targets the naked eye could never resolve.

Return fire was barely visible, just faint glowing pulses of superheated air and dust as beams punched skyward through the roiling atmosphere, but many of these shots were nevertheless finding their targets. One Unity cruiser of the brutal white pyramid variety took a direct hit from a particle beam that carved off a fifty-meter chunk of its flank. Outgassing and sublimating metal started the ship tumbling, and an HEL strike a moment later snapped the ship's spine in half. Out of control, it tumbled along its previous course, pulling ahead of the decelerating formation. It would continue on an unstable orbit until it eventually struck the atmosphere several years hence.

A brilliant point of light appeared on the dreadnaught's flank, as another HEL beam struck. But this beam did not punch through. It merely created a glowing bright greenish dot on the huge ship's hull, growing then fading as the beam cut out. A few kilometers away, a similar beam punched through a cruiser's reactor, detonating it in an actinic flash. And when the faint, bluish line of a particle beam reached up from the planet below and struck the dreadnaught dead on… it had no effect either. Less than a meter from the hull, the beam broke up into coruscating curtains of blue and green light. It never actually touched the hull.

The fire control techs on the ground had to see how ineffectual their fire was against this behemoth. Not that it mattered what they saw or didn't see. A second later far more powerful beam weapons momentarily linked the leviathan with the groundside weapons that had dared fire on it. X-ray lasers blasted the HEL and the particle beam cannon into glowing dust in a fraction of a second.

Finally reaching its ideal velocity and altitude, the great ship's drives cut out, and it rotated to bring still more of its weapons to bear on the surface.

The Unity's dreadnaught had entered low orbit over Valdek.

Mor lay on his couch, feeling every shudder and vibration that ran through his ship from the surrounding silo, his fingers poised just off the controls in his armrest, his eyes fixed on the holo-tank. He had zoomed the tank out so that it now framed most of the planet, with the positions of the spaceport and the enemy dreadnaught brightly marked. A great deal of other information was displayed as well, but none was as vital as the relative positions of the Brotherhood ships to the Unity's heavy hitter.

The clamshell doors above the ship were still closed. It would take them a few moments to open—provided they didn't take a hit like before—but the Port Authority had ruled that all silo doors were to remain shut during orbital bombardment. Mor chafed at the extra time it would take to launch, but he had to admit that a direct hit on the silo while the doors were open would not end well.

The dreadnaught was nearing the horizon. They would have to be careful not to lift too high too soon; if they weren't careful, their starships could easily rise above the dreadnaught's horizon and into the arc of its weapons. And they would be helpless if they had to face it. Mor had seen the data; he knew that the groundside weapons hadn't even scratched that thing. He had to remind himself that their mission wasn't to knock it out, but to evade it. As soon as they rendezvoused with Commander Rehenek, they would get off the planet and out of the system.

A warning chime sounded, and a wider view window opened in the holo-tank, showing more of local space around the planet. Swarms of blood-red symbols were moving, descending on the planet from the Lagrange points. There were hundreds of them. It looked like most of the Unity fleet was closing in on the planet, now that the dreadnaught had entered the fray.

The Brothers had less time than they'd hoped.

A countdown suddenly appeared in the top of the tank, starting at twenty seconds. The dreadnaught had just passed below the horizon, and the clamshell doors were starting to open.

"I don't need to tell you that we need to fly fast and low, gentlemen," Captain Trakse said over the comm. "I take it everyone has seen the incoming vampires?"

"Vampires" was an old, old code phrase for hostile ships.

Acknowledgments came in from the *Vindicator* and the *Challenger*. Mor added his own. "From the Brother-Legate," Trakse added before signing off, "'Fly fast, fight hard, and God go with us.'"

Then there was no more time. The doors were open, the count-down was nearly at an end. Mor tapped keys on his armrest, bringing the drives from standby to lit, feeling the rumble through his bones. He took a deep breath, letting himself feel his ship for a moment, the massive structure of metal alloy and composite becoming an extension of his body. Then he keyed the intercom.

"I suggest you keep your teeth together, Brothers," he called. "This is going to get rough."

The countdown hit zero, and Mor throttled the engines up, their thrust quickly exceeding the weight of the ship and starting it skyward. The throaty roar of the engines vibrated through every fiber of the ship's structure, and blue-white flame splashed against the hardened steelcrete below them, vapor billowing as the automatic systems in the silo fought to keep the internal temperatures down. The *Dauntless* rose quickly out of a roiling cloud of steam and smoke, weirdly underlit by the sun-hot blast of her engines.

As soon as they were clear of the silo, Mor throttled up further. A heavy, invisible hand crushed him into his acceleration couch as the ship hurtled skyward at nearly six gees. There would be some damage to the spaceport below—that kind of high-energy lift wasn't usually encouraged around established installations, since low-altitude, full-power drive plumes tended to blast molten craters in the landscape—but time was pressing, and the fortress was probably doomed anyway. The Valdekans themselves were out of the way; they'd had plenty of warning to take shelter.

He started the axial tilt early, while still barely a few hundred meters above the ground. They had to keep their trajectory relatively flat, so he was maneuvering tightly. Soon they were blasting across the slope of Gorakovati, the *Boanerges* and the *Challenger* keeping pace on one flank, the *Vindicator* on the other, like bullets fired at the towering peak.

As Mor fought to breathe and keep from being overwhelmed by the task of keeping his ship steady, he reflected that this was not an inapt simile. The *Dauntless* had a pair of radiators that might be easily mistaken for fins, but they had limited to no aerodynamic utility. She was effectively a missile. Mor was flying by brute force of drives, thrusters, and gyros.

It was going to make deceleration interesting.

The sky behind the four ships was torn asunder as every remaining battery in the fortress opened fire on every Unity target they could find, throwing a storm of destruction skyward to cover for the four starships flying fast and low over the peak of the shield volcano.

The swirling storms, smoke, and dust hadn't dispersed from around the fortress for days, and as the *Dauntless* rose higher, ferocious winds buffeted her, threatening to throw her higher, ram her sideways into one of her sister ships, or suck her down to smash her wreckage against the mountainside, barely three kilometers below. Lightning flickered and flashed around the ship in the plain visual window that he opened. It was, perhaps, less detailed and informative than the holographic representation that was supposed to be the flight display, but Mor preferred it, if only to momentarily glance at it. He liked to *see* what he was flying through, even when, as now, he was largely flying on instruments.

The *Dauntless* burst out of the clouds a third of the way up the volcano's side, and was briefly surrounded by multiple layers of towering clouds that wreathed the peak of Gorakovati in a tumultuous riot of black, white, and gray. The clouds were lit by flickering, brilliant flashes of lightning, both natural and manmade, and the dark blue of the sky, fading to indigo at its zenith, peeked through the gaps in the overlapping storms high above.

It was a breathtaking view, but one that Mor could not afford to linger on. He was too busy fighting to keep the ship on course, struggling against the tortured jet stream around the higher elevations of the volcanic peak that threatened to snatch her from his control. And then they were plunging into another flat, wind-whipped storm that wreathed the upper elevations of the mountain, and the visual feed dropped to a few meters of hazy gray, lit only occasionally by a distant flicker of lightning.

When they broke out once again, they were nearly in the stratosphere, above the highest clouds, yet the mountaintop still loomed above them. Mor hadn't truly appreciated the sheer size of the volcano until then. The four ships hurtled higher into the thinning air, and by the time they were curving over the caldera, the last of the storms was nearly a kilometer below.

The caldera was a vast bowl of bare, naked rock, far too high for plant life or even snow. In fact, a glance below revealed that it was, in fact, a network of overlapping craters. Apparently the volcano's eruptions had never come at exactly the same spot over the millions of years of its growth.

"We're still in the clear," Fry reported in a strained, grunting voice, though Mor hadn't asked. It had been understood that if any Unity ships had been within range and above the horizon at that point, they could be engaged. Passing over the caldera was the high point of the starships' trajectories. It was also where they were most vulnerable. "Some of the closer ships coming from L2 have opened fire, but between the distance and our countermeasures, they're still hitting wide."

Mor saw that fact vividly illustrated a moment later, as a kinetic kill munition struck the caldera below them with a flash. Shortly thereafter, the impact spot started to glow a dull orange; it seemed the magma was a lot closer to the surface in the caldera than he'd thought.

"We might be able to hit one with a powergun bolt," Fry mused.

"Negative," Mor replied. "We can't afford the time or the added attention. Let them think we're transports trying to flee before the fortress inevitably falls."

Their planned landing zone was coming up fast, even as they plunged through another storm. This one seemed almost gentle in comparison to what they'd gone through on the way up. Mor guessed that was because they were almost three hundred kilometers from the impact zone where orbital and ground fire were still dumping megajoules of waste energy into the atmosphere. It was still powerful, though, and still dangerous.

Then it was time. "Stand by for maneuvering!" Mor grunted, a moment before he hauled back on the controls.

The gee forces intensified as he hauled the *Dauntless*'s nose toward the sky, flattening the Brothers deeper into the carefully padded couches. In seconds, the ship was effectively flying sideways, her nose up, her main drives pointed at the ground below, air resistance helping to slow her hypersonic forward rush. He kept tilting her back until she was angled nearly thirty degrees from vertical, her nose pointed slightly back toward the towering peak of Gorakovati behind her, her engines roaring and blazing to help arrest her forward momentum even as she dropped toward the forests and meadows below.

A powergun bolt thundered through the air, missing the ship by meters. "Well, we've spotted that grounded command ship," Fry reported. "And it's spotted us. It's still over two hundred kilometers east, but we're taking fire. And they might be scrambling transatmospheric fighters shortly."

"Target and engage as needed," Mor ordered, fighting to keep the ship steady. A wrong move at that altitude and they were all dead.

"The *Boanerges* has been hit!" Fry reported.

Mor checked the display. The *Boanerges* did appear to have taken a direct hit from either a powergun bolt or a high-energy laser. There was a wound in her hull, and she was struggling to keep upright on her drives.

The *Challenger* returned fire. The big, Sarissa-class ship wasn't just the cav carrier. She was considerably larger than the more common Caractacan Spear-class, and had power and batteries to match. A furious storm of blue-white lightning flickered from her guns, replying to the intensifying powergun fire coming from the east. At the same moment, the Unity fighters appeared, compact, wedge-shaped darts with stubby, forward-swept wings. They were coming fast, outrunning sluggish sound and already firing green-tinged powergun bolts. The *Vindicator* and the *Dauntless* both sent brilliant streaks of plasma flashing away toward the enemy in reply.

Fighters had little use in space, which was why the Brotherhood rarely used them, preferring their starships for close support when possible. But in certain circumstances, they still had a niche to fill, and the Unity had apparently come prepared.

There were those who would scoff at the idea that single- or double-seat fighters, with considerably lesser powerplants and weapons, could possibly present a serious threat to a combat starship, a behemoth capable of reaching out and striking another ship with annihilating force from across a planetary orbit. But Mor was not one of them. He knew that sheer numbers could count for a lot, and while an individual fighter might not have the punch to severely damage or destroy one of the Caractacan ships, the entire squadron that was flying toward them at the moment could.

The *Dauntless*'s point defense lasers lashed out, and the lead fighter exploded violently, scattering glowing wreckage across the blue-tinged forest below and starting several fires across nearly three kilometers. At the same time, a spray of 3cm powergun bolts hammered against the ship's hull, and the damage control officer started calling out reports.

"Hull breach in Section Four, losing power in ventral thruster hub Sixteen," he reported. "Direct hit on Bay Three's hatch." He paused. "Hatch is damaged, but still operational."

In the time it had taken him to report, four more Unity fighters had been swatted out of the sky by the *Dauntless* alone. The *Vindicator* had taken more, and the *Challenger* was reaping a swath of destruction through any formation that dared get close to her bulk. The survivors flashed past with a roar of sound and a scattered burst of powergun bolts, and then they were diving close to the deck, skimming the trees and racing away, already banking to come at the descending starships from a different angle.

But by the time they were in position for another pass, the *Boan-*

erges was nearly to the ground, though she was still shaky, wavering slightly as her drives and thrusters pulsed unsteadily. Mor frowned; she must have been hit harder than he'd thought. Her batteries had been all but silent during the last few moments of airborne violence.

They were descending toward a valley on the shoulder of the mountain. A jagged ridge of ancient, tree-swathed lava that was probably once a rivulet from a particularly massive eruption had already masked the wounded *Boanerges* from the Unity command ship. In fact, it appeared that the *Challenger* was the only Caractacan ship still with line of sight on it, as none of the rest were taking fire from starship weapons any longer. They only had to worry about the fighters that were coming around at the end of the valley, where the land dropped off in a sheer cliff nearly half a kilometer high.

The fighter pilots seemed to be as suicidally dedicated—or indoctrinated—as the ground troops that the infantry centuries had engaged. They came in without hesitation, low and fast, their supersonic shockwaves battering the trees below them, spraying brilliant powergun fire at the silvery ships that descended toward the woods on columns of fire.

Mor couldn't see Fry from his couch, but he could imagine his tactical officer's squinting frown. He could also imagine what was coming next, and he wasn't wrong.

The *Dauntless* opened fire on the fighters with her main powergun batteries.

The blue-white lightning was powerful enough that even a near-miss threw the lead fighter out of control, sending it spinning into the mountainside, where it exploded in a drawn-out, rolling fireball. That same bolt impaled a second fighter, which was suddenly just *gone*, vanished in a brilliant, actinic flash. A second bolt took out three fighters at once; they had been holding close formation, and the explosion of the middle ship's demise from a direct hit engulfed the other two.

The last few kept coming, straight into a blinding wall of powergun fire from the *Vindicator*, *Dauntless*, and *Challenger*. Only a faint scattering of glowing debris survived to finally strike the ground.

The *Boanerges* was down, nearly hidden in clouds of vapor as her onboard cooling systems tried to bring the ground and the surrounding atmosphere down to livable temperatures. The other three ships descended in a protective triangle around the damaged ship.

Given the sheer weight of a starship, it would seem unwise to land on anything but a prepared and reinforced platform, but it had been discovered, centuries before, that the blazing thermonuclear fury of the ship's drive had a tendency to vitrify the soil beneath it, fusing any manner of planetary surface into rock solid enough to support the ship. However, it still required no small amount of skill to safely set a starship down on unprepared ground.

Mor was eyeing the landing zone carefully, deftly drifting the *Dauntless* back and forth, trying to level out his chosen landing spot. He had heard about a starship tipping over after landing on ground that was slightly too steeply angled. That would likely not be survivable.

When he was satisfied that he had burned a mostly flat pad of fused mineral into the ground, Mor gingerly settled the *Dauntless* toward the surface. Her massive landing jacks lowered, coolant vapor pouring from their ports and raising a billowing, blinding cloud around her hull. Then they touched, the massive hydraulics compressing under the weight, and they were down.

"Touchdown," he announced over the intercom. "I suggest you gentlemen get moving, while we do what we can to get the *Boanerges* back in action."

[17]

DEPLOYING DROPSHIPS WHILE ON THE GROUND WASN'T COMMON
practice, but neither was it unheard of. The starships had been
designed for the possibility, and the Brotherhood trained for the task.
There were times where an actual launch simply presented too high a
risk that the landers would simply be shot out of the sky.

The landers had been rotated as soon as the starships touched
down so that they were no longer pointed out the hatches, but had
their noses aimed up at the sky. When the hatches opened, armatures
moved the landers outside the ships, dangling them from super-
strong cables that were clamped into housings at their noses. The
dropships hung in the air, swinging slightly, then the cables slowly let
out, lowering them toward the ground at a sedate, stable pace and
setting them down lightly. Scalas imagined that the dropships' pilots
were as thankful as he had been to make a soft landing, considering
the bone-jarring shock that was usually a combat touchdown.

Scalas hit his harness release and got up. Kranjick had sent the
assembly signal as soon as the *Boanerges* had set down, and Scalas
had seen enough on the way down to know just how little time they
had. "On me," he barked, snatching his BR-18 out of its cradle and
starting down the ramp.

The landing zone remained oppressively hot. His armor did a respectable job of moderating its internal temperature, but he could see the air rippling between still-roiling clouds of coolant vapor, and could feel the heat of the fused soil beneath his boots. As he jogged toward the *Boanerges*, his century was on his heels. The Valdekans were holding back for now, as their battle suits weren't quite as high-quality as the Caractacan armor, so they would need a few more minutes before they were able to brave the hostile environment that was a starship's landing zone.

Kranjick was standing at the ramp of his personal dropship, towering over every other Brother in sight. The howl of Costigan's vehicles could be heard as the remainder of Century XXXV made its way through the clouds of fog from the grounded *Challenger*.

"Board the sleds as they come," Kranjick ordered, his voice booming out over the LZ. "Costigan's tanks will lead out, with the sleds and the assault guns in the rear. We have a tentative contact point where we should be able to get the commander on comms."

"Do we have his general location?" Scalas asked over the comms.

Kranjick's visor turned, and he seemed to look straight at Scalas through the coolant murk. "A *general* one, yes. We were able to get some fragmentary comm contact with him while in flight, but only enough to give us a cardinal direction and approximate distance." That was no surprise; there had been far too much energy flying around for comms to have gone unaffected. "It was enough to determine where we need to go to try again."

The first of the sleds appeared through the mists, a flattened ovoid hovering on a roaring air cushion. Its turret was set far forward, with the troop compartment in the rear. The driver brought it to an easy halt, swinging the vehicle around on its fans to present the rear troop hatch to the infantry Brothers.

Scalas looked back at Cobb and Kahane, who were closest, and pointed. The squad sergeants started getting their men on board.

Kunn and Volscius directed their squads as well, both keeping their distance from Scalas. Kunn might have glanced over at him once or twice, but was otherwise wrapped up in the workings of his own squad. Volscius didn't look at Scalas even once, or at any of the other squad sergeants for that matter.

What are you thinking of doing? Scalas wondered as he watched Volscius. He knew it was not a good sign that he didn't trust his own squad sergeant, but there had been something off about his lone "pragmatist" ever since Dunstan's desertion. Volscius had looked up to Dunstan, had agreed with him about the need to make the Code more "flexible." And now… Scalas might have thought that the cost of Dunstan's hubris would have had a sobering effect on his subordinate, but instead Volscius had withdrawn from the rest of the century —except for those few in his squad whom he had groomed to his way of thinking. His brief words with the others had been clipped, formal, and laden with an undertone of resentment.

Scalas would have to keep an eye on him.

The rest of the combat sleds, along with the handful of comparatively blocky Valdekan infantry fighting vehicles, gathered around the battered *Boanerges*, and the men boarded. Kahane was standing on the ramp of the first sled, watching him, but Scalas waved at the man to tell the driver to wait. As the centurion, Scalas would be the last one to board, and the first one off in combat.

But he also had another reason to wait. This needed to be addressed.

"Squad Sergeant Volscius," he called.

Volscius paused at the ramp of his own sled, then stiffly turned and marched over to Scalas.

"I'm detaching Diego, Marsdan, and Farlander from your squad," Scalas told him. "Tell them to report to Squad Sergeant Cobb."

Volscius stiffened. "May I ask why you're taking from my squad?" He had tried to keep his voice flat and formal, but there was a note of petulance in it that Scalas didn't like.

"That should be self-evident," Scalas replied. "Cobb took the heaviest losses on the wall. Your squad took the lightest. So Cobb gets some of your men." He stared at Volscius for a moment. "Why else would I pick yours?"

"Because of my friendship with Centurion Dunstan," Volscius said defiantly. "I know that the rest of the century considers him dishonored."

Scalas wished that his visor was transparent, so that Volscius could see the scowl of contempt that crossed his face. "And if the rest of us took honor as lightly as you and Dunstan, then you would have a reason to suspect my motives," he said coldly. "Tell those three to report to Squad Sergeant Cobb and get to your vehicle."

For a moment Volscius neither moved nor replied. Then, almost choking on the words, he muttered a quick, "Yes, Centurion," before turning on his heel and stalking away.

Yes, I definitely need to watch him. Kunn perhaps should not have been promoted simply because he lacked the charisma of a leader, but Volscius was dangerous.

Something made him turn, and he could have sworn that Kranjick was watching him. But he might have only imagined it.

He turned and jogged up the ramp of his own sled, ducking his head and swinging onto a combat seat. "All in," he called to the driver, and the troop door swung shut.

A few minutes later, the vehicles were heading uphill toward the crest of the gigantic ridge that loomed over the landing zone. The fans howled and roared, and the tanks occasionally had to force their way through the trees, sending blue-fronded trunks falling away with a crash, a hundred years of growth succumbing in seconds to a hundred tons of metal and composite driven by irresistible force.

The clock was ticking, and every man in the convoy knew it.

———

Scalas joined Kranjick and Costigan on the ridgeline. Their armor had turned a vague grayish-blue, blending in with the rocks and the few stunted, wind-swept trees that clung to the top of the ridgeline. The three centurions crouched beneath the limbs of a hoary old pseudo-conifer that had been bent almost double by the wind over the years, its roots splitting rocks as it held on against the fury of the mountain's storms.

Scalas lifted his magnifiers to his visor. The forested slope stretched away below them for some distance before reaching the cleared farmland and plains of the flatter lowlands. With enough magnification, he could even see the ominous, squat silhouette of the grounded Unity command ship just outside a small city in the distance. It appeared to be a larger version of the standard cruisers they had fought in space, but thicker in beam and, if he was looking at it right, five-sided instead of four.

But the command ship didn't hold his attention for long. There was a lot of activity on the plain. Two large formations of armored vehicles were trundling through the fields, sending up great plumes of dust behind their tracks, and more transatmospheric fighters were spooling up for launch, with another flight just now arriving from somewhere off to the south.

"They sure don't lack for numbers, do they?" Costigan muttered.

"No, they do not," Kranjick agreed. "One has to wonder where they're getting all the material. How long has this been in the offing, to grow this many clones and build this much war machinery?"

"We still don't know how long it takes to grow the clones," Scalas pointed out. "If they've discovered a way to accelerate growth, as the Valdekans believe…"

"Does it matter?" Soon asked as he joined them. "They're here, in numbers that no one has ever seen before. I think we'd better see the mission through before we worry about the implications of cloning tech."

The column of vehicles had halted about two hundred meters

below them, hidden from the enemy by the bulk of the ridge, turrets turned skyward and searching for fighters.

"Soon is right," Kranjick said. "Time enough for speculation and planning once we're off-planet and far away from this system." He tapped his gauntlet, tying his armor's comm unit in with his vehicle's. "Commander Rehenek, this is Brother Legate Kranjick of the Caractacan Brotherhood. Your General-Regent sent us to find you. Please respond."

There was a long pause. Faint static hissed over the comm channels. Given the amount of disruption, radiation, and stray energy in the atmosphere, it was actually somewhat surprising that it wasn't far worse.

"This is Commander Rehenek," a voice replied in faintly accented Trade Cant. "Stand by for rendezvous coordinates."

Scalas bristled a little at the young man's tone. They were here as allies, not subordinates. But he forced himself to calm his thoughts. Humility was a virtue to a Caractacan Brother. As was patience.

Rehenek rattled off a series of numbers, and the Brothers quickly calculated the position he had given. They would have to cross the ridge and descend about halfway down the mountain, through the woods, to reach the rendezvous. Worse—one of the enemy's armored columns below was moving almost straight toward the rendezvous coordinates.

There was nothing for it, though.

Kranjick tapped several controls on his gauntlet, and a holographic representation of the ridgeline appeared in the centurions' visors. He traced a glowing line to show their planned route. "There appears to be a saddle here," he said, indicating a notch in the ridge. Whatever geologic catastrophe had created the gap in the massive rivulet of lava was long lost to time. "We should be able to get through without skylining the vehicles on top of the ridgeline. From there, we can move relatively quickly to the rendezvous point." Which, upon closer examination, was another hanging valley, not unlike the one where the starships had landed.

Kranjick suddenly looked up sharply. Scalas followed his gaze and saw a cluster of dark dots, high and coming in fast. Another air attack.

Kranjick slapped another key, and the holo vanished. "Get to your vehicles," he ordered. "Time is flying."

The armored officers scrambled back down the slope and ran to their designated sleds. As soon as Scalas was aboard, his driver pulled the troop door shut and revved the fans, getting the vehicle ready to move. The sense of urgency was palpable.

The first of the angular Unity fighters flitted overhead, followed a moment later by the rolling *boom* of its supersonic shockwave. The rest of the flight followed in a tight wedge. Powergun turrets tracked the enemy ships, but the gunners held their fire. The sleds and tanks had much the same chameleonic coating as the infantry armor, and though it was scarred, there was still a chance that they might blend into the mountainside.

Of course, the starships would still be targets, but even grounded, they could still put up a ferocious fight as long as their reactors were hot. And they *would* still be hot, that deep in hostile territory, grounded or not.

But then one of the Valdekan IFVs opened fire, and any hope that the vehicle column might go unnoticed was lost.

To the gunner's credit, at least it was a good shot. A 3cm powergun bolt punched into the last fighter's engine, and the ship exploded, its burning wreckage plunging down toward the forest in a fiery arc.

At that point, there was no sense in anyone else holding back. Every vehicle in the column with line of sight on the aircraft opened fire, and a veritable blizzard of blue- and green-tinged lightning blazed up out of the woods. The enemy fighters had begun to scatter like frightened birds the moment the first ship blew up, but they had been caught flat-footed, and six more of them were swatted out of the sky in mere seconds. Three exploded instantly as high-energy plasma packets struck their powerplants. One took a trio of bolts across its wing root and seemed to fold in half before spinning down toward the mountainside. It hit with a thunderous explosion, the roiling fireball of its demise setting nearby trees ablaze. Another took a hit in the nose and flipped end over end before going into a flat spin and falling toward the ground. Yet another showed no smoke, no wound where it had been hit, but simply rolled over and plummeted toward the ground. The pilot must have been killed.

They had not killed the entire formation, however, and the survivors were now diving for the treetops and banking sharply to come around for an attack run.

One stayed too high and it simply vanished in a white flash, struck by a starship's 20cm powergun bolt. There was hardly any debris to be seen in the aftermath of that catastrophic hit. The rest stayed low, skimming the terrain and rushing at the column, powergun fire spitting from their wing roots.

The Valdekan IFV that had started the fight died spectacularly, its turret blown off and greenish fire blazing from its upper deck as its ammunition supplies detonated. A Caractacan tank avenged the Valdekan vehicle a moment later, a 1cm powergun bolt blowing the fighter's angular cockpit canopy to molten shards and reducing the pilot to a headless chunk of charred meat. The fighter bored into the ridgeline above the column, impacting with enough force to shake the ground beneath the vehicles.

The Valdekan vehicles' camouflage wasn't as effective as the Caractacan vehicles' chameleonic coatings, and they suffered for it. By the time the fighters swept overhead and disappeared over the ridgeline, three of the five Valdekan armored vehicles were burning. Only one of the Caractacan tanks had been hit, but it was hit badly; smoke poured from it as three of its six-man crew bailed out and ran to the nearest sled. The rest of the crew was presumably dead.

"Keep moving," Kranjick's dispassionate voice commanded over the comm. "If they come back, best not to provide them with sitting targets."

Costigan's tanks started driving ahead once more, heading for the saddle, ten kilometers up the ridge. Turrets continued to turn, powergun barrels elevated toward the partly cloudy sky, scanners searching for the enemy. But the fighters didn't reappear.

It seemed that the Unity commander valued his fighters more than his clones' lives. From the looks of things, the clones were cheap. Transatmospheric fighters were expensive.

The column forged ahead, climbing the mountain slope and driving through the dark, bluish trees, ramming massive trunks down where needed.

"I'm hoping those clone tanks can't make this kind of headway," Kahane commented as the holo showed a trunk nearly a meter in diameter getting cracked in half. "Those tanks we fought at the breach didn't seem to have nearly the weight or power that ours do."

"Cheap vehicles, mass-produced for massed assaults," Scalas agreed. "But they'll find a way through, sooner or later. They can always use their main guns to knock the trees out of the way if they have to."

"I hadn't thought of that," Kahane said. "I guess if they've got munitions to spare…"

Scalas looked across the troop compartment. "Torgan! Keep that HVM launcher close. I think we might end up needing it."

The younger Brother nodded and clapped the tube with a gauntleted hand. "I never let it get far, Centurion. Quirinus might steal it if I did."

Sitting across from him, Quirinus scoffed. "I don't want to lug that heavy thing. I'll let *you* carry it, *then* steal it when there's a really juicy target."

Torgan shook his head in mock sorrow. "Do you hear that, Centurion? Stealing from another Brother!"

Scalas just nodded. The banter was a good sign, but there was a brittleness to it, the jokes slightly forced. The men were trying to keep their spirits up with levity, but they weren't really feeling it. The fact that Torgan and Quirinus's byplay only drew a handful of grim chuckles said that much. Even so, Scalas wasn't worried. Caractacan

Brothers were no regular soldiers. They were warriors of the highest degree, and no matter how low their spirits, they would fight the hordes of clones as fiercely and as staunchly as if they were fresh and rested, facing a handful of ragtag pirates.

Discipline, honor, and courage didn't rely on feelings. And discipline, honor, and courage were what made a Caractacan Brother.

[18]

The sky remained clear as the column started down the slope. *Mostly* clear—through gaps in the trees, the distant specks of aircraft or transatmospheric fighters could still be seen circling above the distant command ship. But they were keeping their distance, at least for the moment.

Scalas suddenly imagined the command ship opening fire on the column with its primary weapons, and felt his chest tighten. They would be hard to detect at this distance, especially masked by trees and terrain from time to time, but a single heavy bombardment missile could conceivably wipe the entire column off the face of the planet. Or a handful of 20cm powergun bolts. Yet the command ship stayed quiescent, and they were soon down among the fingers and draws along the side of the ridge.

In another hour, with the sun dipping toward the horizon, blazing briefly through gaps in the clouds, the column reached the hanging valley. Another ridge masked them from the command ship and all but the highest of the aircraft circling above it.

As they came out of the trees, Costigan's tanks spread out, their turrets swinging freely to cover every centimeter of open ground. Bluish grass grew on the banks of a clear, rushing stream. The valley appeared deserted to the naked eye, but not to the vehicles' advanced sensor suites.

"Commander Rehenek," Kranjick called out. "The tanks are mine. You have nothing to fear from us."

A moment later, a figure stepped out of the trees on the far side of the valley, in the very spot where the sensor suites had pinpointed the reinforced company of Valdekan troops and their vehicles hiding under camouflaged netting. The commander's vehicles were very unlike the bulky vehicles that Atelevek had brought; these were narrow and articulated in the center, with small powergun turrets fore and aft. With their separately suspended wheels, they appeared to have been purpose-built for use in mountains and forests.

As soon as Scalas's driver brought his sled to a halt, Scalas banged on the hatch, which dutifully lowered. The infantry Brothers piled out, weapons ready, moving a little gingerly from having been crammed into the cramped rear compartment for the last few hours. Scalas straightened, feeling his back pop, then strode toward where Kranjick was climbing out of his own sled. It still amazed him that the older man could show no discomfort even after folding his considerable bulk into such a small space for so long.

As the Brothers set in their perimeter, Kranjick led his centurions across the narrow stream to meet Rehenek.

Commander Amra Rehenek was a short man, shorter than his father, and slightly built. Even so, there was an intensity, a vibrancy about him, that was palpable even through the deep weariness that showed on his face. He wore a combat suit similar to those worn by Atelevek's commandos, and he held his helmet under his arm, his powergun slung over his shoulder.

Kranjick came to a halt a few paces from the young commander, looking down at him with his own helmet still in place and his BR-18 in his hands. Rehenek looked up at him, a faint squint around his pale eyes, and ran his free hand through his lank, dark hair.

"You are the Caractacan legate?" he asked.

"Yes," Kranjick rumbled. "Your father asked us to find you."

"Good," Rehenek said briskly. "If your men are half as good as their reputation, I could certainly use your help. The enemy has a considerable force gathered around the command ship, and it's going to be a hard target to get to."

Kranjick shook his head. "That is not our mission, Commander. We were specifically asked to get you and as many of your men as possible off-world, to rally support for the liberation of Valdek." He held out the data chip. "Your mother sent this."

Rehenek's eyes flashed and his jaw worked, but he stepped forward after a moment and took the chip. He pocketed it without looking at it. "I know what it says," he said bitterly. "'Run, save yourself, Valdek is lost.' Well, I don't believe it."

"Whether or not you want to believe it is immaterial, Commander," Kranjick said. "Facts are facts. Look around you. Your mother and father coordinate a defense that is slowly being whittled away, in the last standing planetary defense fortress on this world. You are attempting to assault a grounded battlecruiser—and presumably at least a division of troops and armor—with a reinforced company. And you may not know it yet, but a dreadnaught of a size that has not been seen in living memory has entered orbit in the last few hours. Valdek is lost. And our launch window to get you off is closing swiftly."

"Valdek is not lost until these *vrykolok* march over the bones of the last of its defenders!" Rehenek snapped. "You would have me abandon my people, run off to the stars some distant safe haven while they suffer under the boots of these abominations? Never! My place is here. If that means I die in Valdek's defense, then so be it." He straightened and squared his shoulders. "I am going to take that command ship or die in the attempt. Either you can come with me, or you can leave while your launch window is still open."

Kranjick did not budge. "We gave your father our word."

"And that means nothing to me," Rehenek retorted. "My father is wounded, and though my mother is strong, I am her weakness. Of course they wish me to leave. But my duty is here."

"Is it your duty to kill any hope that is left to your people, boy?" Kranjick ground out relentlessly. "To fight gloriously and die, leaving no one to lead them except their new overlords? No one to rally a liberation fleet, thus leaving them under the boots of the *vrykolok*, as you call them, for Heaven knows how long?" He took a step closer. "You are no common soldier, boy. You are a leader, and will soon be a head of state. You have responsibilities that extend beyond your own glory."

As if it had been orchestrated, at that moment the comm chimed. "*Challenger* to Brother Legate Kranjick."

Kranjick did not move, but simply answered, "Send it."

"We thought you should know, sir, that we just lost all contact with the fortress," Captain Hwung-Tsi reported.

Kranjick switched to external speakers, his vision slit still locked on Rehenek's face. "Say again, Captain," he said heavily.

"I say again," Hwung-Tsi repeated, slowly and loudly, probably thinking that the comms were bad, "we have lost all comm contact with the fortress."

Rehenek's expression was frozen. He didn't move a muscle. Kranjick said nothing more for a moment, letting this news sink in.

"Brother Legate?" Hwung-Tsi called out. "Did you copy?"

"Yes, Captain," Kranjick said. "Is it possible that it is simply a comm disruption, given the storms we went through on the flight over the mountain?"

"Doubtful, sir," Hwung-Tsi replied. "We had decent comms until a few minutes ago. They did report that the dreadnaught appeared to be deorbiting and descending toward the fortress itself. That was one of the last exchanges we had with anyone in the fortress."

"Acknowledged. Do you have a current read on the dreadnaught?"

"Negative. It's over the horizon, on the other side of the mountain. The attack group coming from L2 appears to be entering low orbit, however, and there might be another group coming in from L3."

"Copy that, Captain. Keep me informed if you detect anything else." Kranjick closed the circuit.

Rehenek wasn't looking at Kranjick anymore, or at any of the Caractacans. His eyes were far away. This news was clearly a shock, and Scalas wondered just how many shocks a man had to face before he went numb to it all. Valdek had been hammered by an unprecedented war for weeks now; he couldn't imagine what all the young man had seen since the "Galactic Unity" had first entered the system.

"There is nothing left, Commander," Kranjick said softly. "If your world is to have any hope of liberation, you need to leave it."

Rehenek brought his gaze back to the present and focused on Kranjick. There was nothing but bitterness and rage in his eyes. "I thought it went against your Caractacan Code to flee before an enemy," he sneered.

Kranjick took a step forward at that, and Rehenek recoiled despite his bravado.

"Flee?" Kranjick growled, his helmet's speakers making his deep voice even harsher than it already was. "If you do not truly understand the difference between flight and strategic retreat, boy, then I wonder if perhaps your people wouldn't be better off if you killed yourself in a pointless assault on an asset that, given the presence of the dreadnaught overhead, is clearly no longer vital anyway."

This was the closest to a display of temper Scalas had ever seen from the Brother Legate.

Kranjick took a deep breath and spoke in a quieter tone. "I know your rage, boy," he said. "I know the sense of helplessness, knowing that all is lost, and that you must leave with the enemy undefeated. I was on Pontakus IX. I was on the retreat from Meretreya."

Scalas couldn't help himself; he looked over at Costigan. The other centurion's visor turned toward him, and though Scalas couldn't see his friend's face, he could see surprise in his body language that mirrored his own. Kranjick had been on Pontakus IX? That was fifty years ago. How old *was* Brother Legate Kranjick?

"I could have stood and fought, and inevitably died," Kranjick continued. "It would have satisfied the demands of honor and glory. But in so doing, we would have left the handful of Brothers who remained at Chalchais understrength, to be ultimately overrun. As it was, we were just barely enough to hold the line once we returned. Had we held to our pride, held the line, and died, then we would have failed our responsibility to our Brothers.

"There is a fine line between honor and duty. Sometimes it seems that duty is nothing more than a justification for abandoning honor. But duty *must* come first. And your duty now is to your people. You cannot help them by throwing yourself at that command ship.

"Those men in the woods are relying on you, Commander. The survivors in the cities are relying on you. Even if you were not hereditary head of state, you are now, to my knowledge, the only senior Valdekan military officer still at large. You can throw your life and those of your men away, or you can come with us and have some hope of organizing an off-world resistance and, perhaps, eventually, rally enough allies to liberate your planet from this so-called 'Galactic Unity.'"

Another, older Valdekan had come out of the trees after Kranjick had broadcast Hwung-Tsi's transmission. He stood just behind Rehenek, barrel-chested and pugnacious, with a scarred, battered face that looked like it had picked up more than a few new wounds since the war had started. He now spoke in rapid Satevic to Rehenek, who answered in the same language, the same strain of bitterness in his voice. But the older man glanced up at Kranjick and spoke even more urgently, gesturing toward the command ship and the flatlands below, where the Unity forces were pushing forward.

"That is Major Zorek," Viloshen said quietly at Scalas's elbow. Scalas hadn't even noticed that the old corporal had come with him. "He is arguing that your legate is right, and that we must either decide now, or go to their forward operating base. The enemy is getting too close to stay here."

Rehenek turned back to Kranjick, anger and resentment still burning in his eyes. "It seems that my executive officer agrees with you, Legate. I am still not convinced. But he makes a good point: we need to move to a more defensible position if we are going to plan our next move, whatever it may be." He pointed uphill. "We have set up our forward base in some old lava tubes higher up the mountain." He looked around at the blowers and the bigger IFVs. "I think that we can fit most of your vehicles under cover. The caves are very large."

Scalas could imagine. Everything about Gorakovati was oversized.

"We'll try to find a route that your tanks can negotiate without too much trouble," Rehenek finished. As he turned back toward his men and their vehicles, he added, "Try to keep up. The enemy will not leave us alone for long now that they know we are up here— thanks to the pyrotechnics on your approach."

Scalas scowled a little as he turned back toward his sled, and he was glad that his visor hid his expression from both Rehenek and Kranjick. He was sure his old mentor's expression was placid as always, almost bored. The man's imperturbability was infuriating to some, but it was a trait he'd tried to pass on to his men, including Scalas. "Never let any man get under your skin," he'd said more than once. "Patience is the only way a warrior keeps his head, and keeping your head is the only way you'll survive a tough fight, much less survive with your honor intact."

Scalas waved at Viloshen to get back to the vehicle, then followed after him. But not without a glance at the eastern sky. Was that an aircraft, or only a bird?

Were there even any birds left on this war-blasted world?

———

It was getting dark by the time they reached the lava tubes. The entrances were actually lower down than Scalas had expected, and nearly hidden by trees. It took a moment to see that not all of the trees were actually growing there; the Valdekans had cut some down and hauled them up to thicken the grove. The Valdekans pulled some of these out of the way to allow the vehicles through, and soon they were passing defensive emplacements set back just inside the entrance. Heavy powerguns, autocannons, and HV missile launchers were mounted on tripods and carriages behind parapets built of quickset steelcrete and rock. Anyone trying to force their way into the caves would have a tough fight on their hands.

The tanks and sleds roared and howled, the noise battering the dismounted troops in the enclosed space. Scalas pitied the Valdekan troops who had to be out there without the hearing protection built into the Caractacan Brothers' helmets. He and the rest of the infantry Brothers stayed in their sleds until the vehicles were parked along the walls of the cave, their noses pointed back toward the entrance, along with their turrets, their noisy fans shut down.

A glowing symbol appeared in his visor. Kranjick was calling assembly. Scalas gave his squad sergeants quick instructions: let the men get some rest, but be ready to move out in a minute or less. It was standard Brotherhood procedure for a temporary security halt in hostile territory. Then he was heading deeper into the cave, jogging past vibrating tanks and combat sleds toward the deep bunker where Rehenek had set up his field headquarters.

That headquarters proved to be almost as heavily barricaded as the entrance; clearly the Valdekans were prepared to mount a defense in depth if they were found. But the command post itself consisted of little more than two heavy comm units and a single portable holo-tank, which was currently displaying Gorakovati and its much smaller neighboring mountain, the name of which Scalas didn't know.

Rehenek was leaning over the holo-tank but looked up as the Caractacans approached. He seemed more composed now, and there was a certain air of resignation about him, though still mixed with a certain resentment.

"Major Zorek has convinced me that you are right," he said to Kranjick. "It's a bitter thing to swallow, but yes, Valdek is lost unless we can gather enough force to overwhelm this 'Galactic Unity.'" He sighed. "I will not thank you for taking me away from my world and my people in their time of need, but I can recognize the strategic necessity of it.

"However, I will not go as a helpless refugee aboard a Caractacan ship. From what I know, you don't have enough space aboard your remaining starships for all of my men and our equipment anyway. We have somewhat more than a reinforced company—it's more like an understrength battalion. And I will not leave *this* behind for the *vrykolok*."

He pointed to the holo, which zoomed in on the smaller mountain. A tracery of lines began to show what looked like a large and extensive installation in or on the mountain itself. The view zoomed in further, revealing a starship landing silo built right into the peak of the mountain. A big one. A *very* big one.

The ship inside was a massive, towering cylinder with a thick ring wrapped around her hull amidships and huge, tapered engines at the base.

"What is that?" Soon asked.

"That," Rehenek said with a note of satisfaction, "is the most powerful ship we have. One of the *last* ships we have," he added, some bitterness creeping back in. "Unfortunately, we didn't have him crewed and ready to launch by the time the rest of our fleet was destroyed, and my father did not wish to see him destroyed for nothing." He paused, with a small frown, as if his father's logic had suddenly clicked in his mind now that he could apply it to the current situation. He shook his head a little. "That is the *Pride of Valdek*, a Triamic Hegemony Astrana-class dreadnaught."

Costigan let out a little whistle. "How did you end up with one of those?"

"He was stationed here while Valdek was a protectorate of the Triamic Hegemony. When the Hegemony collapsed…"

"They just left it here?" Soon asked.

"The crew was of the Hagrash Pack," Rehenek explained. "Their pack-home was destroyed."

Scalas couldn't suppress a bit of a wince. One of the horror stories that had made it out of the triamic worlds after the Hegemony's collapse had been the genocide of entire packs. Hagrash had been one of the worst hit. And something about the pack culture of the triamic race had led the survivors to suicide once word reached them.

"They were good enough to swallow poison instead of flying the ship into the sun," Rehenek said dryly. "Our people cleaned him up and have worked to maintain him ever since."

"Even so," Kranjick said, "that ship must be almost two centuries old."

"Older than that," Rehenek said. "But I've been assured that he will still fly, and still has working weapons." He stared determinedly at Kranjick. "I will come with you, Legate, but in my own flagship. If my new task is to find allies to free my world, I will not do it as a refugee and a beggar aboard someone else's ship."

Kranjick nodded. "Very well, Commander. We happen to have some of your spacers with us, if they can be of assistance. They returned with us from the wreck of the *Mekadik*."

"They are welcome," Rehenek said. "The dreadnaught's crew is presently extremely small, based on the last reports I had."

"How quickly can the ship launch once we get there?"

"It will take some time, even with additional spacers," Rehenek admitted. "At least two hours. And there's an enemy unit not far away from the mountain that we will have to get past."

"And in the meantime, they'll be massing for an attack here on Gorakovati," Kranjick said. "We don't have much time."

"No, we do not," Rehenek agreed. "My men will be ready to move in thirty minutes. Can your men be ready in that time?"

Kranjick looked down at him. "My men are ready to move now."

Rehenek might have looked slightly chastened as he nodded.

[19]

Under cover of darkness, the combined column of Caractacan and Valdekan fighting vehicles rumbled out of the lava tube and turned north, toward the mountain where the *Pride of Valdek* waited. Scalas watched the holo display in the troop compartment, thinking that he had spent entirely too much time lately in the back of a combat sled. The cramped quarters aside, he wanted to be able to stick his head out and *see*, to be able to run and fight and maneuver, instead of feeling like cargo in a truck.

The holo showed the glowing threat indicators of a pair of Unity fighters flying overhead, but he couldn't hear the distant scream of their engines over the pitched howl of the sled's fans. He just watched, his eyes riveted to the blood-red darts on the display.

The two transatmospheric fighters were skirting the higher slopes of the mountain, circling off to the northwest. They seemed to be flying a search pattern. Scalas wanted to point them out, but he knew that everyone else in the command elements was watching the same holo display and seeing the same craft, and they were well aware of the threat they represented.

A remote sensor drone, launched from one of the starships, was providing the bulk of the sensor data keeping the holo updated. It was a tiny craft, hopefully too small to be noticed by the fighters. But of course the ships on the ground were far too large to go unremarked, either by the ships in orbit or the fighters circling above, even if they hadn't been seen landing.

"We have just been painted by a targeting scan," Captain Trakse announced over the comm. "The orbitals are still clear at the moment; it appears they have not deployed their ships to cover the entirety of the planet yet. But the drone is picking up a major launch from the direction of the command ship. At least two wings of transatmospheric fighters are coming this way." The holo zoomed out to show a cloud of crimson advancing quickly from the east. "We are launching to provide direct support. I suggest that you gentlemen get to that mountain as quickly as possible."

"Is the *Boanerges* ready to launch?" Kranjick asked.

"We've gotten her weapons back online," Trakse replied. "She's not spaceworthy, though—the damage taken in that last attack was too extensive. We wouldn't be able to get out-system without major groundside work. The plan at the moment is to provide top cover for the column en route to the target installation, then land, evacuate the ship, and rendezvous with you to lift with the dreadnaught."

"Understood," Kranjick said. "Godspeed."

"And to you as well, Brother Legate," Captain Trakse said. "Be advised, one of the enemy ground formations has penetrated nearly ten kilometers into the forest, about five kilometers from your planned line of march at this moment. They're moving slowly, but they are making headway."

Scalas peered at the holo display. Sure enough, a blob of red was pushing into the woods and the rougher terrain of the mountains. The Unity vehicles were definitely having a harder time of it; they didn't have the maneuverability of Rehenek's mountain terrain vehicles or the sheer power of the Caractacan blowers. But as always they had the advantage of numbers, as well as that same unsettling, single-minded persistence that the clones had displayed from the moment the Caractacans first engaged them.

The display didn't show infantry patrols—which meant the Unity forces might be a lot closer than they appeared, if they'd pushed their foot-mobile forces out ahead of the vehicles. Infantry would be a lot harder for the sensor drone to spot, being smaller targets even in their swarming mobs, and better concealed by the trees and the terrain.

Once again, he wished that he was out on the ground, on his feet. The requirements of speed made it impractical—they could cover a lot more distance a lot more quickly in the vehicles—and he understood that.

But he didn't have to like it.

———

The *Dauntless* leapt for the sky, keeping close beside the wounded *Boanerges*. Mor had shifted the holo display so that the wider situational view was now in its own window, off to the side. He was facing a closer-in, nose-cone view from the *Dauntless* herself. He needed to be even more "one with his ship" than usual for the maneuvers ahead.

The four ships rose on tails of fire made even more brilliant by the darkness of early night. They spread out as they climbed, turning toward the oncoming fighters and roaring at them at blistering velocity, passing the speed of sound in seconds. The hammering shockwaves of their passage blasted the mountainside below, making the trees bend and sway violently, some being nearly flattened to the ground.

The oncoming fighters opened fire on the starships as soon as they rose above the ridgelines, and the starships answered. Thunder rolled in a continuous, crashing roar as destruction flickered back and forth between the opposing formations, powergun fire turning the sky into a curtain of blue- and green-tinged light.

Entire flights of fighters were blasted to glowing wreckage by single 20cm powergun bolts. Answering 3cm bolts seemed like ineffectual pinpricks by comparison, but enough hits could bring down even one of the silvery behemoths streaking across the sky.

The *Boanerges* had pulled ahead of the other three ships, and as such was the focus of more of the enemy fire. Still, although bolts peppered her hull where her ECM systems hadn't been able to spoof the enemy targeting scanners, those systems were largely successful, creating an intense hash of electromagnetic noise, invisible to the naked eye, that filled the atmosphere around the ships and the fighters alike. When the weapons employed against you were as deadly as powerguns and HELs, the best defense was not to get hit in the first place. And when the weapons fire moved at the better part of the speed of light, the only way to do that was to make the enemy shoot at ghosts and shadows.

While the two formations started several hundred kilometers apart, they closed within minutes, the starships plunging through the center of the fighter formations. Nearly a dozen fighters exploded in a brief few instants, but fire also gouted from the flank of the *Boanerges*. A burst of powergun fire had found a hole in her already compromised defenses and punched deep into her hull.

Then they were kilometers past each other once more, racing away at a combined velocity many times the speed of sound. Compared to the speeds they'd be reaching in space combat, the fighters and starships alike were moving cripplingly slowly—but this close to a planetary surface, at such close engagement ranges, it was still nearly too fast to think.

Mor punched the thrusters and pulled on the main drives' thrust vectoring, dragging the *Dauntless*'s nose around to circle back toward the fighters. More powergun and laser fire reached for the starships from below as they came entirely too close to the grounded command ship. A few blue-white stabs of light flashed back down from the *Dauntless*—Fry, grunting under the gee forces of the turn, had swiveled the starship's powergun turrets to return fire—but Mor was too tightly focused on flying the hurtling missile that was his ship to see if the commander had hit anything.

The fighter formations had similarly split and banked hard to either flank, trying to come around and reengage the starships before the big, fast-moving craft could come around. It was ultimately futile, as the starships' weapons were far more mobile than the fixed-forward powerguns mounted on the wings of the fighters.

Mor found himself facing a formation of nearly an entire wing of fighters. The *Vindicator* was just off his starboard side, but under the circumstances, that seemed somewhat less than comforting. There were just too many of the enemy fighters, no matter how many they'd already blasted out of the sky.

Mor glanced at the wider display. They had to finish this quickly; the nearest formation of Unity starships in orbit would be over the horizon in a matter of minutes, and the closer they got, the fewer maneuvering options he had. He didn't dare climb too high, lest the *Dauntless* be targeted by orbiting starships and fighters at the same time.

He very nearly flinched at the sudden deep *ka-chunk*s of missile launches. Fry's call of "Missiles away" came rather too late.

"Missiles?" Mor grunted. Those were anti-starship weapons, carrying enough punch to knock a battlecruiser out of the sky from long range. They hadn't been designed for anti-fighter fire.

But Fry knew what he was about. The missile engines ignited with roars heard through the ship's hull, barely a few meters away, and leapt away. Less than a second later, both of them detonated, very nearly right in the middle of the fighter formation.

The double, sun-bright detonations would have blinded anyone looking at them, and the nearest fighters simply disappeared in the bright flashes.

It was the shockwaves, however, that did the most damage.

The twin explosions were so intense that they created a vacuum at the point of detonation, forcing the atmosphere away in nearly solid spheres at substantial mach numbers. When those twin shock-waves hit the Unity fighters, they sent them spinning out of control if they didn't crush them into scrap immediately. White-painted, wedge-shaped darts went tumbling wildly, some already breaking up, others colliding with their wingmates in fiery conflagrations that nevertheless seemed dim compared to the incandescent fury of the missile warheads.

The *Dauntless* and *Vindicator* hit the shockwave a split second after the explosions, unable to avoid the superheated blast wave. The massive starships shook and rattled like leaves in a stiff wind, but Mor clenched his teeth and sent his fingers dancing over the controls, fighting to keep from striking the wrong key or control as the ship threatened to spin out of control. He imagined he could actually *feel* the rise in hull temperature as they bored through the still-dispersing fireballs.

The sky felt strangely calm once they were through. Mor released a breath he hadn't realized he'd been holding. "A little more warning would be appreciated next time, Fry!" he called.

"Sorry," the weapons officer replied, sounding almost as breath-less. "It was a stroke of genius, and there wasn't time."

Mor was about to retort acidly, but held his peace as he began to bring the *Dauntless* around in a wide arc to come to the aid of the *Boanerges* and the *Challenger*. Fry's action had been risky, and they might very well all have died… but he had, in the end, cleared out their entire opposition with one shot. Mor would have to remember that move if they ever found themselves in a similar situation again.

"Make sure you log what you did, so next time we've got some advance warning," he said.

Then he had to concentrate on flying. The *Boanerges* was in trouble.

———

The *Boanerges* had a tighter turning radius than the far bigger *Challenger*, and so had found herself facing the second wing of fighters nearly alone. It was more an illusion than anything else; the firing arcs and ranges of the starships' weapons made dispersion at these altitudes and distances nearly irrelevant, but that didn't negate the fact that the *Boanerges*, being closer, momentarily became the sole target for nearly a hundred Unity transatmospheric fighters.

Even as the distance to the enemy closed and her onboard powergun turrets ravaged the formation ahead of her, each bolt blasting as many as three or four fighters out of the air, the fighters' lighter weapons hammered at her hull, tearing glowing wounds in her plating. Follow-on bolts penetrated more deeply, blasting into the inner hull and striking more vital systems. One powergun turret was sheared away altogether. The starship's ECM defenses were almost pointless against that volume of fire from such close range. With such a blizzard of plasma tearing through the sky, aiming didn't matter; some of it couldn't help but hit.

The ammo feed for the destroyed powergun shut down automatically, preventing a catastrophic explosion. Chain reactions had been known to tear ships into subatomic bits in the past. Even so, the impact nearly made the ship spin out of control; only Captain Trakse's skill kept her on a steady course.

Her remaining powergun was still spitting bolts, her point-defense lasers were scoring less spectacular kills, and the *Challenger*'s full batteries were tearing the fighter formation to shreds. But even as the *Dauntless* and *Vindicator* added their own fire, swatting the remaining fighters out of the air with brilliant explosions that momentarily lit the forest below through the growing pall of smoke from fires set by earlier crashes, it was clear that the *Boanerges* was in serious trouble.

Engine power was dropping in the Number Two drive. The hull was breached in too many places to count. Several of the main maneuvering thrusters were holed, fused chunks of scrap, and others had been blasted completely off the hull. Trakse was in a serious fight just to maintain control. He had to lift the nose to try to bring the ship to a hover to stabilize her, and when the *Challenger* swept past, her supersonic shockwave threatened to throw the *Boanerges* against the mountainside.

But Trakse hung on. Struggling mightily against the ship's degrading handling, he slowly started to bring the *Boanerges* down.

———

Mor watched the *Boanerges*'s descent helplessly, even as he brought the *Dauntless*'s nose up and throttled back, not quite hovering over the mountain, but slowing significantly from the headlong velocity of the fight. Fry was still engaged, blasting powergun bolts at the armored formation creeping its way up the mountainside toward the friendly column's line of march, but his line of fire would be cut off shortly, because the *Boanerges* was drifting directly toward that formation. Already she was starting to take fire from tanks and assault guns, though thankfully the Unity ground vehicles didn't seem to be armed with powerguns. Even so, the faint flickers of muzzle blasts and the snap and shudder of impacts against the star-ship's hull were evident in the holo-tank.

Only in the last few moments had Mor realized what Trakse was up to. It appeared that part of the *Boanerges*'s landing gear had been hit, and was not lowering. There was no good way to land the ship. So dropships had begun to blast away from her ports, presumably with the bulk of the ship's crew aboard.

And Trakse... he was going to get the last bit of fight out of his ship that he could.

The *Boanerges* dipped lower, her drive flames flickering, and began to drift directly over the Unity formation. Mor couldn't help but imagine that being under a starship's main drives at that distance must be very close to being in hell.

At least for a moment.

Vehicles burned and detonated under the assault of sun-hot

plasma and hard radiation. Ground fire intensified as the rest of the Unity forces realized what was happening and tried desperately to bring the starship down before it cooked them all. Explosions rippled along the starship's hull, and she shuddered. Then a white-hot fireball gouted from her midsection and broke her spine.

Trakse lost all control.

The *Boanerges* twisted in midair, her drives stuttered, and then she was tipping over. No, not tipping. She was *thrown* violently aside by a thrust imbalance, and she impacted the center of the Unity formation with the force of a falling mountain.

The resulting explosion lit the side of Gorakovati as bright as day. A sheet of white fire leapt skyward as the reactor safety dump went off. The shockwave blasted trees to splinters and swept most of that Unity spearhead into oblivion.

Along with Trakse himself, and anyone else who had remained aboard.

Swallowing the sudden lump in his throat, Mor steered the *Dauntless* toward the buried installation. There was nothing more they could do for the *Boanerges* or Captain Trakse. The dropships had punched out and flown toward the same destination.

It had been the plan to leave the *Boanerges* behind all along, and yet Mor had been harboring a hope that somehow they could get the wounded ship off the planet, get her repaired enough in the outer system, and then get away. That hope was now dashed. And only three of the five Caractacan ships were left.

To make matters worse, a warning chime sounded. Mor had expected it. The first formation of Unity starships was due to crest the horizon at any moment. But when he looked up at the red indicators in the holo-tank, his blood ran cold.

The Unity cruisers were indeed over the horizon. Not by far, yet, and they would have considerable difficulty targeting at that angle and so close to the mountain. But they weren't the cause of Mor's concern.

The dreadnaught was there too, soaring over the peak of Gorakovati, following a very similar flight path to the one the Caractacan ships had taken not long ago.

———

The infantry had been able to watch the feeds from the starships, though somewhat sporadically, during the aerial battle. So the ground element saw the dreadnaught coming. Scalas hoped that the Valdekans, already battered by defeat after defeat, wouldn't simply break in panic at the sight, but then he remembered that the Valdekan vehicles didn't get these information feeds. A small mercy, perhaps.

Viloshen was staring at the display though, and Scalas could see the man's near-despair through his translucent visor. If the dreadnaught was here now, there was little doubt that it had destroyed the last standing planetary defense fortress—and had done so in a matter of minutes. Facing that behemoth with only three starships and a column of tanks, tracked fighting vehicles, and combat sleds... they would stand no chance at all.

Scalas knew he had to say something. "We can still make it," was all he managed. "We're almost there, and it will take even that monstrosity time to blast through the thousands of tons of rock over the *Pride of Valdek.*"

"What about our other ships?" Torgan asked. For the first time, there was a note of uncertainty, almost fear, in his voice.

"If that ship's as big as Rehenek's holo made it out to be," Scalas answered, "we can send the other ships ahead as soon as we're inside. We'll all fit aboard the *Pride.*"

He didn't know for sure if they believed him or not. He wasn't sure if *he* believed it. All signs pointed to that Unity dreadnaught having accomplished in minutes what entire squadrons of starships and regiments of troops hadn't managed in days. But while there was even the merest hope, Kranjick wouldn't give up. And he would not allow his men to, either.

Of course, the column hadn't stopped just because the fury of battle raged overhead; time was pressing. And the death of the *Boanerges* had cleared the way. The smoking, flame-lit crater that was the *Boanerges*'s final resting place was still most of four kilometers down the slope, but the shock of the impact had flattened trees clear to their position. It was taking some extra maneuvering to get some of the tracked vehicles over or around the blow-downs, but they were still making headway, their passage lit by growing forest fires and the brilliant blue-white flames of the remaining starships' drives.

The holo display jumped and fuzzed a little. Scalas expected that was due to the nearness of the drive flames and the intense ECM battle going on as the Unity starships got higher in the sky. Orbital weaponry began to hammer the mountainside, laser pulses, powergun bolts, and kinetic munitions sending pulverized rock and smashed trees flying high into the sky.

"There's a relatively clear ridgeline ahead that leads to the installation entrance," Kranjick called over the comm. He must have been in direct contact with Rehenek. "Full speed, cross the gap, and we'll be under cover." He paused. When he spoke again, there was an unfamiliar tone in his heavy voice. Was it sorrow? Despair? "*Challenger, Dauntless, Vindicator.* Launch immediately and get away from the planet. Linger on the edge of the system if you will, but *someone* must get away from here and back to the Avar Sector Keep. If we succeed and launch with the *Pride*, then we'll rendezvous and return together. If not… honor our names."

There was an even longer pause before Mor replied. "As you command, Brother Legate." His voice was slightly choked, heavy with grief. Not only for those who had fallen, and might still fall, but for being ordered away from the battle, Scalas suspected.

"It is not flight to obey the orders of your superiors, Captain," Kranjick said. "Your honor is intact."

"Yes, Brother Legate," Mor replied.

A moment later, a small green light blinked in the corner of Scalas's visor. He answered the private call from Mor.

"You had best get to that ship and do whatever menial tasks it takes to get it off the ground, Brother," Mor said, his voice thick. "This ship is empty enough as it is."

"We'll make it, Brecan," Scalas assured him. "If God is willing."

"God willing," Mor replied, his voice thick. "Go with Him."

"And you as well," Scalas answered. "I'll see you on the other side. One way or another."

[20]

REHENEK MUST HAVE CALLED AHEAD, BECAUSE THE GATES WERE already rolling back as the lead vehicles approached the installation's entrance across a long causeway that bridged the valley between the ridgeline and the solitary peak that housed the ancient dreadnaught. Given the fact that the installation was buried in the mountain, Scalas had expected the entrance to be camouflaged. Instead, the gate was simply a massive, arched tunnel leading into the mountainside, covered over in gray metal. There was a sign in white lettering over the entrance, but it was in Eastern Satevic, so Scalas couldn't read it, and he didn't bother to ask Viloshen. He had more pressing concerns.

Then they were rolling into the echoing tunnel that had been bored into the mountainside, and the outside darkness gave way to lights set into the rocky ceiling. These lights were both dim and green, for an obvious reason: to protect the installation's defenders' night vision. But as they moved deeper into the tunnel, the lighting slowly brightened to a brilliant white.

Rehenek's vehicles led the way nearly a kilometer underground before coming to a halt in a large vehicle hangar that was only about a quarter full of wheeled and tracked vehicles. The Valdekans didn't seem to use ground effect vehicles much.

Kranjick was out of his sled almost before it had stopped moving, and Scalas stepped off the ramp of his own before it had touched the ground. Rehenek was already ahead of the Caractacans, making for a nearby elevator, a clutch of his commandos in tow.

The Brother Legate didn't seem to rush, and yet somehow he closed the distance in only a few strides. A man in a Valdekan service uniform was hurrying toward them. He saluted Rehenek and gave what was unmistakably a status report. Rehenek replied briskly before turning to the Caractacans.

"Commander Schukhin is the installation commander. He tells me that the *Pride*'s reactor is hot, and has been since the first strikes began. He does not, however, have an operational crew. Captain Horvaset and your remaining spacers should be enough to fly him, but likely not enough to fight him efficiently."

"Is the ship crewed enough to lift?" Kranjick asked.

Rehenek grimaced. "He has always had a skeleton crew at best. The *Pride* was never the front-line ship of the fleet, and outfitting him with modern weapons that we could support has proved more difficult than anticipated. Some of my father's advisors had strongly recommended abandoning him and making him a monument instead. I expect that once the war started and the fleet was destroyed, all but the most vital personnel were reassigned to more immediately useful posts."

"But the installation is still manned, obviously," Soon pointed out.

"Because it's still an asset, and one of the last remaining to us," Rehenek said grimly. "I cannot say much more than that. Hopefully the spacers you brought from the *Mekadik* can fill out the crew, but they'll have to familiarize themselves with its control layout." He turned to Schukhin and asked a question, then quickly issued an order before adding, "The survivors from your ship made it to the lower pads. They, and our spacers, are on their way up toward the ship itself."

Schukhin wasn't finished, though. His voice was urgent as he spoke quickly, pointing back toward the gates and the causeway.

Rehenek's face turned grimmer, if that was possible. "In addition, there are ground forces even now advancing on the installation's entrance. They have taken the defenders under fire from the shuttles, and are crossing the causeway. The defenders have them under fire, but are not stopping them."

Kranjick keyed his comm. "I need two squads. Volunteers only. Gather at the command sled in five minutes. We will need heavy weapons and a heavy demolition charge." Rehenek frowned at that, then his eyes widened as he realized what Kranjick had in mind. "Everyone else, proceed to the upper levels and prepare to assist in getting the ship ready to lift." He turned to Rehenek, lifting his head as he saluted the younger man. "Prepare the ship. We will buy what time we can. Contact me on comms just before you lift, and we will rejoin you."

Rehenek returned the salute, his face unreadable. But Scalas thought he saw a flicker of something in his eyes as Kranjick cut the salute. Was it respect? Confusion that a man who didn't know him as anything but a package to be escorted would be so willing to throw himself into the teeth of an enemy attack to buy him time?

Such confusion was not unknown, when outsiders first encountered the Brotherhood's Code and what it meant.

Kranjick looked at Scalas, Soon, Costigan, and Rokoff. "Centurions, get your men above and ready to lift. Lend what help you can." He turned and started back toward the command sled with long strides.

"Brother Legate," Scalas began, turning to follow. He caught up quickly, and Kranjick stopped, turning toward him and putting a heavy hand on his shoulder.

"No, Erekan," he said quietly, before Scalas could utter a word. "If I don't make it back in time to lift, you are acting legate. Both of us cannot go down there, and I have the advantage of rank." There might have been a faint smile in his voice, though his heavy, immobile face was hidden by his visor. "Get the men boarded and make sure you and they are doing everything possible to help Horvaset and the spacers. If we can get back to you in time, we will, but do not hesitate to lift if we cannot."

Scalas felt his throat tighten as he looked up at the Brother Legate, realizing just how much of a father this big, slow-speaking man had become to him. He didn't want to be acting legate. If Kranjick was going down there to make a last stand, Scalas wanted to be by his side.

I'm not the one to lead the legio. I'm not that leader. I'm not a good enough strategist. I don't have the charisma.

I'm no Michael Kranjick.

But almost two decades of discipline spoke for him. "Yes, Brother Legate." His voice sounded choked in his own ears.

Kranjick now put both hands on Scalas's shoulders. "Every man has his time, Erekan," he said. "A time to die. A time to say goodbye to his mentors and stand in their place. Perhaps this is that time. Perhaps it is not. Let it be as God wills it." He clapped Scalas on the arm, an impact that would have been bruising if not for his armor. "Now, we both have work to do, and time is pressing. Do your duty, Acting Legate."

Scalas saluted. "Yes, Brother Legate."

There was nothing more to say.

———

Michael Kranjick had been living on borrowed time for fifty years. He felt every one of them as he jogged down the tunnel toward the entrance to the mountain installation, hearing the thunder of weapons fire echoing down the passage toward him. The heavy demolition charge that he and Kratzke had pulled out of one of the combat sleds weighed him down and made every joint ache.

As he'd expected, he'd gotten quite a bit more than two squads worth of volunteers. It was not the Caractacan way to shrink from a fight, much less one so desperate and vital. In fact, he was slightly disappointed that he hadn't had to turn the entire legio away. The bulk of his men wanted to go, but the handful who hadn't stepped forward made him wonder if he had truly done all he could to lead his Brothers, almost his sons, down the right path.

But it was too late for such regrets. Together with thirty Brothers, he trotted toward what could very well be the last fight of his life.

Trite thinking, old man. Every *fight could be the last of your life. It's in God's hands. It's always been in His hands.*

Still, the weight of the demolition charge clenched in one gauntlet had a certain finality to it.

The charge was a last-ditch measure. They wouldn't set it off until it seemed that all was lost. But it was there, as ominous as the faint rumble of the distant dreadnaught's drives, dimly audible even over the sounds of the desperate fight ahead.

The lights were turning dim and green as they proceeded, and the Caractacan armor darkened along with them. They were armored shadows, specters clumping through the stone passage toward the fight.

The gates had been shut after the vehicles entered, but the Unity forces outside were clearly hammering at them with everything they had; heavy ordnance had already blasted several gaps in the barrier. Intense flashes flickered through the holes, momentarily lighting up the darkened tunnel and filling it with a deafeningly reverberating thunder.

Kranjick and Kratzke moved to the gate and set the demolition charge down. The other men flowed past them, splitting to move to the bunker entrances on either side of the gate and reinforce the beleaguered Valdekan defenders.

Peering through the nearest hole, Kranjick assessed the situation as best he could.

The shuttles hovered on their thrusters at the far end of the causeway, dancing in and out of the cover of the ridgeline as they took the bunkers and the gate under fire from above, while a company-sized force advanced by fire and maneuver across the causeway itself. Even as he looked, a pair of HV missiles slammed out from one of the shuttles, and he had to duck as one punched through the compromised gate above his head, showering him and Kratzke with debris.

He quickly turned his attention to prepping the demolition charge. It was a short priming sequence, followed by syncing the initiation system to a remote control in his gauntlet. Now they could seal the tunnel as they retreated back toward the *Pride*.

As he turned toward the nearest bunker entrance, another HV missile hit the gate only a few meters in front of him. For a brief moment, the world went black as he was thrown backward, landing heavily on his back with a crash. Only the padding inside his armor saved him from serious injury, and his visor's display flickered from the shock.

He rolled over in the cloud of dust and smoke and heaved himself up off the ground. Fragmentation had severed his powergun's sling, and he had to scramble over to pick it up, checking it over quickly to make sure it was still operational. Bright scars had been scored in the metal, but it appeared to be intact. Then he looked toward the gate.

The missile had punched a man-sized hole in the barrier, and it had cracked enough of the rest that a chunk nearly three meters tall fell away with a crash, barely missing the demolition charge as it struck the floor. The gate was completely compromised. The defenders' fire was the only thing keeping the enemy out.

The nearest enemy soldiers were now less than two hundred meters away. There was little cover on the causeway, but they were still advancing cautiously, rushing forward in short dashes before dropping prone or to a knee and opening fire. They were making up for the lack of cover by sheer volume of fire.

And these weren't the same barely trained, cheaply equipped clones they had fought at the fortress. They were fully armored, with strange, faceted helmets, and they moved like elite soldiers and carried powerguns and HV missile launchers.

And there was something else.

A single figure stalked forward in the middle of the formation, making no effort to take cover. It was not as quick as the shock troopers making their short dashes, but its bulk was unmistakable. Power armor was rare, because its disadvantages often outweighed its advantages. It wasn't as flexible or maneuverable as articulated battle armor, it presented a very large target, and it was heavy. But it was actually well-suited for this sort of assault, for one reason: it could soak up an unholy amount of punishment, and could carry a *lot* of firepower.

This one looked like it was one of the heavier suits, the kind that was even proof against powergun fire, though it was of a design that Kranjick wasn't familiar with. Instead of having a helmet, its entire torso and head were a single, vaguely egg-shaped plastron of armor —decreasing its vulnerability to precision shots. And the quad-barrel powergun on its shoulder was spitting green-tinged lighting fast enough that it looked like a single, continuous beam of destruction sweeping across the defenses.

Kranjick returned fire, peppering the front of the power armor's plastron with a tight grouping of six bolts even as he analyzed the overall situation and tried to think of a plan short of simply falling back and detonating the demolition charge. Because as he looked at the firepower the shuttles, the advancing assault troops, and that power-armored figure could bring to bear... he started to think the original plan wasn't going to be enough.

The power-armored monster staggered as Kranjick's fire sublimated metal and composite off the front of the plastron, but it didn't stop. As Kranjick ducked back, a return burst of hypervelocity plasma chewed into the metal and steelcrete above his head, blasting a deep, smoking furrow in the remains of the gate with a crackling roar of thunder.

The Caractacan Brothers had brought a couple of HV missile launchers, and one of them suddenly blasted from the left-hand bunker, aimed at the shuttles. But a chin-mounted point-defense laser crackled and detonated the missile in midair, still short by nearly twenty meters. The armored shuttle was rocked by the force of the explosion, but nothing more. And then four more HVMs slammed into the bunker, which went silent.

In the meantime, the assault force had bounded forward another fifty meters.

"Scalas, Kranjick," he sent over the comm between rapid shots, hoping his transmission would reach through the installation's internal relays, which they had synced with on the way down. "Status."

"We are aboard, but it will still take some time to get the ship ready to lift, sir," Scalas replied.

That decided it. He had to find a way to hurt the Unity forces, drive them back. Simply collapsing the tunnel would hold them precisely as long as it would take them to blast through the rubble. And that wouldn't be long enough.

Kranjick swung out from behind cover again and dropped a charging Unity soldier with a headshot. The faceted helmet exploded into glowing shards, along with most of the skull beneath it, and the armored body fell. Another burst from the power-armored figure's quad-barrel forced Kranjick back a moment before another trio of HVMs from the shuttles brought more fragments of rock and steel-crete down around him.

"If we get closer, the shuttles won't be able to fire on us without killing them," Kratzke pointed out between shots from where he was barricaded on the other side of the hole.

"Presuming they're more solicitous of their soldiers' lives than they've shown themselves to be so far," Kranjick agreed. He shot another charging shocktrooper and watched as a long burst from an MT-41 tore through two more. They were whittling down the attackers, but not quickly enough.

Although the left-hand bunker had fallen silent—the HVMs must have killed or incapacitated everyone inside—the fire from the right-hand bunker was only intensifying. Kranjick and Kratzke remained pinned down in the entryway, hunkered behind the largest remaining sections of the gate.

Kranjick hammered another trio of bolts at the power-armored figure, which had slowed. His aim was good, and he knew he was chipping away at the center of that plastron. But even knocking that monstrosity out wouldn't keep the shuttles from simply pounding the resistance to dust and ash with missiles. And that wasn't even accounting for the enemy dreadnaught, now visible as it dipped lower in the sky on columns of fire.

The man in the power armor suddenly broke into a lumbering run. The thinning of his forward armor under the Caractacans' hammering must have finally started to alarm him, and now he was trying to close the distance as quickly as possible, fire blazing from his quad-barrel as he came. The power armor looked heavy and unwieldy, but the length of its stride meant that he quickly outpaced the men in unaugmented combat armor, pounding toward the gaps in the gate.

Kranjick held his ground as a storm of powergun fire tore the air apart around him. He dumped the rest of his magazine into that chest plastron as fast as he could pull the trigger. A ravening bolt pierced his knee, exploding the joint in a blast of melted armor and super-heated tissues, and he fell—only to heave himself up on his remaining knee and keep firing. But when another bolt blew his pauldron off and shot mind-numbing pain through his side, he crumpled and lost his grip on his powergun.

The massive armored figure charged closer.

Gritting his teeth against the pain, Kranjick forced himself to grab his powergun again. Bracing it with his almost useless right arm, he shoved himself up to lean against the cover of the shattered gate. Kratzke's fire had fallen silent, but he didn't have time to look. If he had, he would have seen the other Brother flat on his back, a smoking hole through his helmet. Instead he faced the charging behemoth of metal and composite, got his shaking sights back on the glowing wound in the front armor, and opened fire again.

One bolt got through. The armored figure staggered. Its momentum carried it forward as it fell, and it plowed into the ground with a crash.

Kranjick crawled out through the gap in the gate, dragging himself toward the fallen power armor. The defenders' last fusillade of fire tore into the wedge of armored shock troops rushing forward, and then another HVM struck the last remaining bunker. The bunker vanished in a flash and a billowing cloud of dust. Fragments of rock and metal rained down on the ground before the gate.

Kranjick reached the power armor. He had hoped to turn that quad-barrel against the shuttles. But the weapon was bent and useless, crushed by the impact of the suit when it fell. The mini-HVM launcher mounted to the other shoulder, however, looked like it might be operational. The powergun would be better—he'd seen the shuttles swat a full-sized HVM out of the air—but this was what he had, and he would fight until his last breath.

"Kratzke," he rasped over the comm, still unaware that the other man was dead. "Get clear."

He gave Kratzke a few moments that the man was well past being able to use, and then he tapped the fateful control on his gauntlet.

The demolition charge was a molecular explosive. A charge half its size could vaporize a Destrier tank and knock out an armored man standing nearly three hundred meters away.

Brother Legate Kranjick was less than half that distance from the charge when it detonated.

When he came to, he tasted blood. He couldn't see anything, and for a moment, he thought he'd been blinded. He knew he wasn't dead; he was in far too much pain. Only after a moment did he realize that the mountainside was shrouded in dust.

The gateway behind him was gone. A chunk of the mountain that must have weighed more than a starship had slumped down to cover the gate and what was left of the bunkers.

And his legs.

He was buried in boulders up to his waist.

It didn't matter. He knew he was dying. Whispering a final prayer for forgiveness for all his sins, and for protection over those he had left behind, he pried the mini-HVM launcher free of its mount. The launcher hadn't been built to be mounted on the power armor, so it still had an external trigger, with a mechanism built into the mount to activate it. It also had iron sights.

He twisted it around, searching for the shuttles. They were drifting forward, no longer flying evasively now that the bunkers' fire had been silenced, their drives roaring with deep growls that vibrated in his chest. The battle-armored troops were advancing carefully, their weapons up, ready to quickly crush any further resistance.

Kranjick waited. He had no other choice; he couldn't move. Even if he hadn't been half buried, he was certain that every bone in his legs had been shattered.

Slowly the enemy troops advanced, apparently convinced they had eliminated the defenses and assessing how to get through the landslide.

That was close enough. Kranjick triggered all four of the mini-HV missiles at the nearest shuttle, aiming for the directional thruster in its thick, stubby wing.

The shuttle veered suddenly, and its point-defense laser took out one of the little missiles. The second shuttle got another one. The other two slammed into the tilt-thruster and detonated.

The drive exploded, flipping the shuttle over and sending it spinning to a fiery death on the mountainside below, taking out the landing pads in the process. The shockwave rocked the closest shuttle, but it held its fire. The clone soldiers were too close.

Kranjick dropped the launcher and found his powergun. It was still in one piece, having been shielded from the blast by his body. He opened fire, using the hulk of the dead power armor as cover, and dropped six Unity soldiers in as many shots. They returned fire, blasting superheated bits of armor into his visor as they advanced.

Kranjick felt his strength waning. He knew he was bleeding to death.

He shot another Unity soldier through the angular chest plate, and then his weapon was empty, the grip giving him its warning vibration through his gauntlet. He dropped the magazine and reached for another one, but his belt was buried in rubble.

In the pause as he dug for a reload, the masked Unity troops intensified their fire, and five of them dashed around on the flank. Three powergun bolts struck Brother Legate Michael Kranjick at once, piercing his armor and blowing charred holes through his torso.

He was no longer moving when the lead trooper stepped up and put a final bolt through his helmet.

[21]

THE *PRIDE OF VALDEK*'S COMMAND DECK WAS STRANGE TO THE Caractacans' eyes. It had been designed for the triamic, who had been taller and longer-limbed than most humans, and the colors were all slightly off, as the triamic had seen deeper into the ultraviolet. The displays had been reprogrammed to show all their data in Eastern Satevic, but that was just as much gibberish to the Caractacans as the triamic languages.

What required no translation, however, was the scene projected in the holo-tank. The feeds were coming from defensive casements higher up the mountain, near the silo doors, so it was blurry, but it was enough to see most of Kranjick's last stand. The image shook and the view of the mountainside was obscured by dust and smoke when the demolition charge went off, but as the dust settled, they could see the shuttle get shot down and then the powergun fire start up again. Someone down there was still fighting, and somehow, Scalas knew it was Kranjick. The Brother Legate was less a man and more a force of nature. Or that was how most of his men viewed him.

Then the last of the weapons fire died away, and the enemy continued to converge on the wreckage of the gates.

It was over.

Scalas felt a hollow feeling in his gut. He wanted nothing else but to run back down there and fight. But he had his duty. And he had given Kranjick his word.

It's just you now. You're on your own.

It wasn't just that Kranjick had left what was left of the legio in his hands. It was that Kranjick had left *him*. The man had been Scalas's mentor. More than that—his second father. The man who knew more than he ever would. The man he could always ask for advice. Now that man's support was gone.

There were other experienced Brothers, of course. And there were the Elders. But none of them would ever be—*could* ever be—what Kranjick had been.

Beside him, Rehenek was watching the holo-tank as well. "I had hoped they would hold out longer," he muttered acidly.

Scalas turned on him. Rehenek had spoken in Trade Cant, which meant he had intended his words for Caractacan ears. Scalas grabbed Rehenek by the armored collar of his battlesuit and dragged him around to face him.

Rehenek's helmet was off, but Scalas had left his on. The indicators in his visor helped him coordinate his men, especially now that he was acting legate. The armored prow of his visor nearly touched Rehenek's nose.

"Brother Legate Kranjick and thirty more Caractacan Brothers just died to buy *you* more time," he growled. "You are the mission, but I am warning you: show some respect, or keep your teeth together."

For a moment, Rehenek's face went white, and rage blazed in his eyes. But then the fires subsided, and he nodded apologetically.

"Forgive me, Centurion. The strain led me to forget myself. The sacrifice of all the Caractacans who have died here will be enshrined in the memories of all Valdekans henceforth. I will be sure of it."

Scalas let go with a sharp nod. He distrusted most such speeches; they usually came from politicians, most of whom were dishonest and insincere. But Rehenek had a reputation as a warrior and a fierce fighter. Perhaps he was sincere.

"We *could* have used more time, however," Rehenek added. "Captain Horvaset?"

Horvaset was in her element, the alien controls notwithstanding. She'd reached the command deck minutes after Rehenek and Scalas, and had gone to work with barely a word to acknowledge even Rehenek. She didn't even take her eyes off the displays as she spoke over her shoulder. "The engines are about seventy-five percent of the way through their startup sequence." She spoke in Trade Cant for the benefit of the Caractacans on the command deck. "The reactor is at eighty percent, and full checks for launch will take about another hour."

"We don't have another hour," Rehenek said. "At most we have thirty minutes before that monstrosity of a ship is overhead."

Horvaset spared a dark-eyed glance over her shoulder. A cold, brittle half-smile quirked the corner of her mouth. "Which is why we're taking as many shortcuts as we can, Commander. But space-flight is dangerous enough as it is; if we miss a step and a system doesn't work as it's supposed to, it could very well kill us all."

"And that dreadnaught *will* kill us all if we are still stuck on the ground when it arrives," Rehenek growled. "We may just have to take our chances, Captain."

"And if we 'take our chances' and turn into a monatomic smear on the mountainside, then we still fail in our mission." Horvaset turned back to her displays. "Trust me, if it's at all possible to get us off the ground sooner, I'll get us off the ground sooner."

Rehenek's fists were clenched and his face was set, but he merely stared at the holo-tank. Scalas did the same. He had the rudimentary spacer training that all Caractacans received during their novitiate, but he was a ground fighter, and the triamic designs were completely foreign to him. The holo-tank was the only thing on the command deck that he understood.

The ground force at the gateway appeared to have halted. Kranjick's last stand had gutted them, and they were now faced with tons of rock between them and the main entrance to the installation. The landing pads below *might* have offered a way into an airmobile assault force, but the crashed shuttle had obliterated two of them, and the third was damaged enough to be unviable. The installation was effectively sealed off.

But the main threat was still the enormous starship that kept descending at a slow, stately pace down the slopes of Gorakovati, its sun-hot drive plumes so wide that one of the Spear-class ships could have vanished into it. Even as it descended, its batteries had already opened fire. Lances of green-white powergun bolts hammered at every emplacement on the mountainside, and intense HEL beams turned solid rock into flowing lava.

"Are there any other defenses still operational on the mountain?" Scalas asked.

"I doubt we have anything that could touch that," Rehenek muttered, but he looked over at the small side screen where the comms were still open with Commander Schukhin.

"Most of the anti-air batteries have been destroyed," Schukhin replied. Viloshen was next to Scalas, murmuring the translation. "The heavier batteries are buried deeper, including the main particle beam cannon, but we don't have the personnel to man them. And even if we did, the missiles can't accelerate fast enough to avoid the kind of point defenses a ship that size can bring to bear. Besides, I doubt that any of them could harm that thing, seeing as it appears to have shrugged off the fortress's ground-to-space fire."

"Where are the central fire controls for the particle beam cannon?" Scalas asked.

"On the fifteenth level," Viloshen translated, after relaying the question to Schukhin. "But…"

Scalas had already started for the elevator. "We might be able to keep that dreadnaught busy long enough to finish getting the *Pride* ready to launch," he said. "First Squad, on me! Viloshen, you too. I'll need someone to translate the controls."

He strode into the *Pride*'s central elevator, a strange half-sphere arrangement that seemed a bit wasteful of space, dogging his helmet back down as he went. When he turned around and the doors shut, he saw that Rehenek, his own battlesuit helmet under his arm, had come with them.

"What are you doing?" Scalas asked.

"The same thing you are," Rehenek snorted. "Buying time."

Scalas shook his head. "No, the mission is to get you off-planet and out-system. You're the package. If you go down in the guts of this place, then we've failed."

Rehenek's face was hard, his lips compressed in a thin line, as he shook his head in response. "You are speaking to the General-Regent of Valdek, aboard a Valdekan ship. It's not your decision to make, Acting Legate. It's mine. Your Legate gave his life to buy us time, as did my father. And seeing as my father fought on the front lines with us until he was so badly wounded that he had to be put in a medical exoskeleton and confined to the last standing planetary defense fortress, I myself could hardly do less." He grinned like a death's head as the elevator started down. "Besides, with me along, the *Pride* is less likely to lift without you. Shouldn't that be a good thing?"

"Not if we fail," Scalas muttered.

"Then we should not fail," Rehenek said, donning his helmet. "We are alike, you and I. Your legate sacrificed himself to buy us time. So did my father. We cannot help but follow in our mentors' footsteps."

Scalas studied the shorter man as they descended. Rehenek seemed composed, relaxed. But there was a brittleness to his demeanor that suggested that the recently-promoted General-Regent of a conquered world was barely keeping himself under control. He'd experienced too much defeat in the past few weeks.

Scalas only hoped that he could maintain his own control, at least until they got off-world.

Or died.

The elevator hissed to a halt, and Scalas looked up at the deck indicator, then over at Viloshen in frustration. The old corporal nodded; it was the right deck. Scalas strode out, his boots ringing on the steel decking, with Rehenek half a stride behind him. The airlocks and the massive docking bays were directly ahead, with the gantries leading into the silo beyond. All around them the impacts of weapons fire from outside shuddered through the very bones of the mountain.

Most of the survivors of Century XXXII's First Squad were already waiting on the far side of the gantry, their armor scarred and blackened, weapons held ready, though if they needed to use them, the odds were that all was lost anyway. The rest were coming out of the *Pride* behind Scalas and Rehenek. All told, only fourteen of the twenty men of First Squad were left. Still, it was better than some of his other squads. Much better than Cobb's.

Rehenek, speaking rapidly into his comm in Eastern Satevic, led out, breaking into a run as he moved down the curving tunnel that stretched all the way around the massive silo that housed the *Pride of Valdek*. The Caractacans followed, keeping up easily despite the days of fighting behind them. Caractacan Brothers had to keep at their peak, and Rehenek, exhausted by weeks of combat, certainly wasn't running at a pace that any Caractacan would call *fast*.

About halfway around the circle, Rehenek stopped at a large, round, armored door in the rock wall. He barked a hoarse query into the comm, then quickly put the entry code into a pad beside the door as Schukhin rattled it off. A light lit and a series of beeps sounded, but the door didn't move. Schukhin said something else and Rehenek put his eye to a retinal scanner with a curse. The light blinked out and the door slid open, rolling back into a recess in the rock, and in the short passageway beyond, lights flickered to life, revealing another door. The Valdekans took security for their weapons systems seriously.

Rehenek had to go through much the same process to get that door open, though apparently with a different code. The room on the other side was small, containing nothing but three consoles and a holo-tank. The consoles lit up as they entered, and Rehenek moved to the right-hand one.

"What do you need me to do?" Scalas asked.

Rehenek pointed to the center console. "Targeting controls. All I need you to do is aim." He turned to his chosen control panel and resumed speaking to Schukhin, asking quick, pointed questions. Schukhin's replies sounded increasingly hesitant, and Rehenek was starting to get acerbic.

Scalas spared a curious glance at Viloshen, who had followed them in. Most of the rest of the squad was outside, holding security on the passages to either side, just in case. "He is talking to Commander Schukhin about venting secondary reactor into particle beam cannon's firing chamber," Viloshen said quietly.

Scalas turned to stare at Rehenek, who tapped at the controls as he spoke. "That thing shrugged off high-energy lasers and particle beams—well, I'd like to see it shrug off an entire reactor's worth of plasma."

"Will the weapon even handle it?" Scalas asked. He sat at the targeting console and brought up the target acquisition program. There was no time to argue about it; whatever they were going to do, it needed to be done soon.

Another faint shudder passed through the mass of the mountain. Considering how much rock there was between them and the outside...

"I'm overriding several safeties and supercharging the coolant system," Rehenek said, his fingers dancing over the controls. "At least, I hope that's what I'm doing." He barked another query at Schukhin, who replied with a faint quaver in his voice. "We'll probably only get one shot. I want it to count."

"And emitter will probably explode on that one shot, anyway," Viloshen muttered. He was leaning over Scalas's shoulder at that point, helping him with the unfamiliar, Eastern Satevic-labeled controls.

Together, the two of them got the targeting solution set in, and the particle beam emitter pointed at the enormous hull of the dreadnaught, which was hovering overhead, its own beam weapons relentlessly burning away the mass of rock and debris that Kranjick had collapsed across the entrance. The whole mountain shook under the bombardment.

A voice suddenly broke into their comms. The signal sending it had to be extremely powerful to penetrate into the mountain, not to mention break through the encryption.

"I know you're still alive in there, Son of Rehenek," Vakolo's voice said coldly, echoing in every comm. "You have the chance to remedy your father's mistake. Surrender, join Valdek to the Galactic Unity, and your people will be spared considerable... unpleasantness. This has already gone on far too long. I had meant for your world to stand next to Sparat, one of the jewels of the New Order. Instead, you and your hidebound, narrow-minded parents have forced me to hammer Valdek into submission, doing damage that will take years to repair. End it now. I do not wish to further make an example of your planet."

Rehenek didn't reply, but continued to work feverishly at the console. "Are we targeted?" he asked Scalas.

"Ready when you are," Scalas replied. "Provided you're not about to turn us all into radioactive slag."

"I hope not," Rehenek said. He stabbed a key.

Far below them, the Number Two reactor opened one of its emergency shunts. Sun-hot plasma raced through a magnetized tunnel, a tunnel that was supposed to vent directly into the sky above the mountain. But some creative rerouting had instead directed the plasma toward the primary particle beam cannon's spherical firing chamber. The chamber would ionize the reaction mass for the shot, which would then be accelerated by powerful electromagnets through the main vertical shaft before being directed toward its target by the emitter rising out of its armored and camouflaged revetment on the peak, just below the hidden silo doors. Rehenek's bypasses managed to hold the reactor plasma for a fraction of a second before the chamber's mechanisms melted down.

It was just enough time for the shot. A torrent of plasma was accelerated to nearly the speed of light and spewed out of the emitter in a brilliant, eye-searing beam of white-hot devastation. The beam struck the dreadnaught's electromagnetic shielding, which coruscated wildly with curtains of multi-colored light before failing. A crater was bored into the thick ship's plating, punching through and doing serious damage, killing hundreds of clones, before the pilot threw more power to the engines and partially cut in the Bergenholm, flinging the dreadnaught thousands of meters up and out of the line of fire.

Scalas and Rehenek straightened from their consoles at the same time. There would be no follow-up shot. The particle beam cannon was utterly destroyed. The shaft was now little more than a lava tube lined with radioactive slag. The emitter, as Viloshen had predicted, had exploded, leaving a glowing crater beneath a rising mushroom cloud on the mountaintop.

"Come on," Rehenek urged. "We've bought a little time. Hopefully it's enough."

The Caractacans needed no urging. Together, the little knot of men ran back toward the gangway and the ship.

The rock was vibrating under their feet, punctuated by faint shudders as the distant enemy dreadnaught continued firing, though its targeting had to be a fuzz of radiation and thermal blooms by now. It had been damaged, but the leviathan was far from dead.

"The silo doors are opening," Rehenek gasped as they ran through the entryway and down the short, enclosed gangway leading to the massive cylinder of the *Pride*. Commander Schukhin and the last remnants of his skeleton crew were a few paces ahead of them. Through the transparency, light filtered down from above, wan and orange through the dust and debris in the sky.

They rushed aboard, and Rehenek called the command deck. "Captain Horvaset!"

"Are you aboard, Commander? We're ready for launch."

"That was faster than you made it sound," Rehenek said as they pounded onto the cavernous hangar deck.

"I didn't say we're ready for a *safe* launch, Commander," Horvaset said tartly. "I suggest you hurry and find an acceleration couch. Though you might not feel it anyway, as we're activating the Bergenholm in fifteen seconds and launching a few seconds after that."

Scalas broke in. "Why do I suddenly get the feeling you're not talking about just reducing our inertia to accelerate more quickly out of the silo?" He was breathing hard; the entire squad was making for the center of the hangar, hoping to get to a compartment with acceleration couches. Even with the Bergenholm on, if it wasn't turned to zero mass—which had its own problems in an atmosphere—enough gees could still crush a man.

"Probably because I'm not, Centurion," Horvaset said. "That dreadnaught is already closing again, and already firing on the silo doors. If we cross one of those beams, even inertialess the energy dump could still kill us. So we're going to outrun the beams." She sounded distracted. "Hurry up and strap in, gentlemen. We're going to have to time this precisely."

Rehenek was muttering what could only be a chorus of vicious profanities under his breath as they raced into the elevator and started up. The lift seemed agonizingly slow, even though Scalas knew it actually moved more quickly than the *Dauntless*'s elevators.

When the doors swept open, they dashed out into the circular corridor two decks above the hangar. Rehenek pointed, and they sprinted into an empty crew compartment. It appeared to be working quarters for the hangar deck crew, but there were enough couches for the understrength squad. The men ran for the acceleration couches and threw themselves down just as Horvaset announced, "Five seconds."

There wasn't enough time to strap in. They could only throw themselves flat and hope for the best.

The *Pride of Valdek* went tachyonic *inside* the mountain.

———

A sudden flash blasted out of the top of the mountain. For a brief second, there was a tunnel of pure vacuum from the bottom of the silo to the top of the atmosphere. The superheated shockwave blasted away from that tunnel by the ship's passage formed a nearly solid wall of sun-hot air that scoured the eastern slope of Gorakovati down to bedrock. The wave slammed into the Unity dreadnaught, staggering even that behemoth for a moment. Its pilot fought to keep the mountainous starship stable, and almost succeeded.

But the *Pride of Valdek*'s launch hadn't just bored a hole in the atmosphere; the starship's sudden, explosive departure had blown the silo apart, cracking the mountain asunder and sending most of the peak flying, thousands of tons of molten, rocky shrapnel moving faster than the speed of sound. Three boulders nearly the size of starships themselves flew at the dreadnaught, and had anyone been on the ground to watch, it must have looked like they would knock the gigantic ship out of the sky.

Yet damaged as it was, the dreadnaught's defenses were still hard to penetrate. Particle beams, high-energy lasers, and powerguns quickly cut the fragments of mountain down to much smaller rocks. They rained against the hardened hull, punching through in a few places; some hammered through the wound left by that single, desperate particle beam shot, doing even more damage. But although the ship staggered in the air, its drives laboring to keep it up, it was still intact.

Smoking, the dreadnaught limped off to the west, over the volcano and away from the roaring hurricane of tortured air left by the *Pride of Valdek*'s escape.

[22]

"Are we still alive?" Kahane croaked.

"If you can ask that question, then the answer is yes," Scalas rasped.

Even the absence of gravity didn't alleviate the aches in his body. That launch had put every hard drop he'd ever done to shame. He was surprised that the passage through the atmosphere at superluminal speed hadn't simply crushed the *Pride* altogether, but the triamic had built well. Even so, the shock and heat had been transferred through the hull, and it had felt like the starship had been shaking itself apart as the temperature had spiked painfully.

As he drifted up from the acceleration couch, he looked around. The lights were on, so there was still power. He checked his visor's indicators; they still had air, though the temperature was still dangerously high.

"All Centurions, report status," he called over the legio comm.

One by one, the others reported in. The numbers from Costigan, Soon, and Pa'u—who had taken over Century XXX after Kranjick's and Kratzke's deaths—were sobering. Nearly a third of the five hundred men who had deployed to Valdek were gone.

"Century XXXIV, forty-two, all okay," Dunstan called.

Scalas's eyes narrowed. Did Dunstan really think he could simply step back into control of his century with Kranjick dead? Did he have that much disrespect for the fallen Brother Legate's orders?

"Rokoff, report," he snapped.

There was an uneasy pause. Scalas felt the eyes of the rest of Kahane's squad on him.

"Acting Centurion Rokoff, report," he repeated.

"Century XXXIV, forty-two, all okay," Rokoff reported nervously.

"All centurions to the command deck," Scalas ordered. There was a great deal to discuss.

Rehenek was already pulling himself toward the elevator, using the handholds set into the deck, bulkheads, and overhead. Scalas was soon right behind him. The elevator was still working, though it made some strange noises as they swept toward the command deck. Scalas wondered just how much had been shaken loose in those horrifying first few kilometers of the launch.

At the command deck, Scalas and Rehenek swam out. Horvaset and most of the command crew, such as it was, were still strapped into their couches, though the centurions were mostly vertical, boots oriented down toward the engines and the deck.

Dunstan was hovering there too, with Rokoff just behind him, the two men noticeably separate from the other three centurions.

"What are you doing here, Dunstan?" Scalas asked quietly in Latin. This was hardly the ideal place to deal with this particular issue; every Valdekan on the command deck was watching and listening, most of them trying not to be obvious about it. But it couldn't be put aside that easily. Either honor demanded that Kranjick's orders be followed, or it did not. And Scalas was fairly sure he knew the way Dunstan was thinking.

"Kranjick is gone," Dunstan said flatly. "And I am the one whom the Brothers of Century XXXIV know. I'm the one they will follow."

"*Brother Legate* Kranjick gave orders," Scalas replied coldly.

"And does the Code not mandate that we follow the orders of the superiors in the Brotherhood appointed over us?"

"While the *Brother Legate* was alive, his orders held force," Dunstan replied, his emphasis on Kranjick's rank almost coming out as a sneer. "But now that we are no longer in a combat zone, I may appeal my unwise demotion to the Conclave on Caerfon."

"Tread very, very carefully with your next words, Dunstan," Scalas warned. His patience with the arrogant dandy was about at an end. "Appealing a demotion and ignoring it are two separate things. Or do you intend to challenge me as acting legate now? Because you *will* lose."

Dunstan's eyes flashed, but he paused and glanced sideways at the other three centurions, all of whom were glaring daggers at him. Costigan was actually cracking his knuckles under his gauntlets. Unsubtle, especially considering the Valdekans were looking on, but it got the message across. Dunstan was alone.

He shot Scalas a venomous glare. "This is not over, Centurion."

"*Acting Legate*," Soon growled.

Dunstan's mouth worked as if he wanted to spit. But he finally bit out, "*Acting Legate*."

Scalas jerked his head toward the elevator. "Get below with the rest of your century."

Still managing to appear stiffly angry, Dunstan pushed off for the elevator. No one on the command deck spoke until the doors had closed behind him.

"What was that?" Rehenek asked.

"Internal affairs," was all Scalas said.

Rehenek studied him for a moment, then shrugged and turned to Horvaset. "What is our status, Captain?"

Horvaset unfastened the upper part of her harness and levered herself half upright. "We're about three light-hours outside the system. And we'll be here for a while; we have some repairs to make."

"Did we change vector at all on the way out?" Soon asked. "Can the enemy follow us?"

Horvaset shook her head, her dark hair swishing about eerily in the zero gravity. "There was neither the time nor the opportunity. It's a miracle we made it this far without something going catastrophically wrong as it was. I think we passed within a few thousand kilometers of the gas giant."

That wouldn't *necessarily* have been fatal, not when the ship's mass was effectively negative, but it was certainly something no spacer would ever want to do.

"They could follow our vector," Horvaset continued, "but finding exactly where we went inert will be difficult. They'll have to go inert every few seconds to try to find us, and even then, they could over-shoot by light-minutes. It'll take time. Hopefully enough. I already have damage control teams at work."

"And if they go inert close enough to be within our light cone?" Scalas asked.

Horvaset raised her eyebrows. She probably hadn't imagined that a ground pounder would know about concepts like light cones—the space-time coordinates where the light from an event becomes visible to another observer. It was usually a spacer term.

"Then we'll be in trouble," she admitted. "The weapons systems weren't fully prepped before we launched, and there was some external damage. We can put up a fight, but… we might not last long."

One of the Valdekan crew called out, and Horvaset snapped her head around. Rehenek peered at the dim holo-tank sharply.

"What is it?" Scalas asked Viloshen, who seemed to have become resigned to his position as the Caractacan translator. Possibly because his unit was almost certainly dead to the last man, and he had no other position in Rehenek's tiny ad hoc resistance force yet.

"There is ship incoming," Viloshen said. "Coming fast. Some-thing about 'blue'… I do not understand."

"It's blue-shifted," Soon said quietly. "Meaning whatever it is, it's not tachyonic, but it's incoming at a good fraction of the speed of light."

That prompted another glance from Horvaset; she was learning just how well Caractacans were trained. The armored Brothers were far more than uninspired ground fighters.

"There's a starship incoming from the edge of the system," she confirmed. "No identification yet." She paused as another crewer called out a report. "We're receiving a tight-beam hail," she said, surprise in her voice.

A familiar voice came over the command deck speakers. "Starship *Pride of Valdek*, this is Captain Brecan Mor of the Caractacan Brotherhood starship *Dauntless*. What is your status?"

A sigh passed through the command deck, and Horvaset's shoulders slumped just a little bit. She touched a key in her armrest. That was when Scalas noticed that her control panel was a tablet that had been wired into the partially-disassembled armrest. Apparently the triamic controls hadn't been sufficiently conducive to human manipulation.

"*Dauntless*, this is *Pride of Valdek*," she replied. "We have sustained damage and are conducting repairs preparatory to leaving the vicinity of the system altogether."

"Acknowledged," Mor replied. "What is your combat readiness?"

"Minimal. Have you detected any Unity ships in pursuit? Our sensors took some damage." She was obviously trying to keep her tone even and cool, but Scalas could hear the trepidation in her voice. She'd already had one ship shot nearly to pieces under her by the Unity; he could only imagine her fear of it happening again.

"Negative," Mor answered. "Though that doesn't mean they aren't on their way. None have appeared within our light-cone, however. It's only by the grace of God that we detected you." He paused. "We've sent tight-beam messages to the *Vindicator* and the *Challenger*. They should join us within the next couple of hours. Conduct your repairs, Captain. We'll hold overwatch."

On the holo-tank, the *Dauntless* had gone inert barely ten thousand kilometers away, conducting her vector-matching burn. Even taking the distance into account, it was obvious that the Spear-class ship was dwarfed by the ancient triamic dreadnaught.

"We will do so, Captain," Horvaset said. "And thank you."

"We are Caractacan Brothers, Captain. We defend those in need of it. Is Brother Legate Kranjick aboard?"

Horvaset looked back at Scalas, her eyes widening a little. Scalas directed his voice toward the pickup, noting how hoarse it sounded in his own ears.

"This is Acting Legate Scalas, Captain. Brother Legate Kranjick is dead."

There was a long pause. When he spoke again, Mor's voice was distinctly subdued. "May the souls of the Faithful departed, through the mercy of God, rest in peace."

"Amen," chorused the five Caractacans.

"What are your orders, Acting Legate?" Mor asked.

"For the moment, just as you've planned," Scalas said, feeling odd about his old friend's deferential tone. "I will discuss our next steps with Commander Rehenek and Captain Horvaset, but for now, prepare to return to the Sector Keep."

"Yes, sir," Mor replied. "*Dauntless* out."

Rehenek had bowed his head at the brief prayer, though Scalas suspected that if the man had any beliefs, they were the pantheistic sort expressed by his mother and father. When he lifted his head, he looked at Horvaset.

"How can my men contribute to the repairs, Captain?" he asked.

"Very little, I'm afraid," Horvaset answered, "unless any of them are familiar with welding triamic hull plating. My crew is having difficulty enough, but it's a matter of technicality, not numbers or brute strength."

Rehenek nodded. "Show me where your damage control crews are, and I'll send working parties, with instructions to stay out of the way unless the crew chiefs have something for them to do."

"Thank you, Commander." Horvaset brought the wireframe of

the *Pride of Valdek* closer in the holo-tank, then highlighted several areas. Rehenek activated his comm and spoke rapidly into it, giving orders and instructions.

Scalas looked at his centurions. They nodded in understanding. There would be Caractacan Brothers there to help, as well. Having a task to focus on would keep them from dwelling too much on what they had lost on the planet below.

———

The repairs were coming along quickly, and there was still no sign of the Unity fleet. It was entirely possible—in fact, it was likely—that there were hundreds of the white, pyramidal ships out there looking for them, but space was vast, and the odds of finding a single ship that did not want to be found, that far out in deep space, were very long. Those odds would run out eventually—there was no hiding a starship's emissions, and there were now four ships floating in the void within a few hundred kilometers of each other—but it took time.

Scalas paused outside the compartment that Rehenek had taken up as his headquarters. They needed to discuss their next move.

He knocked, and a muffled voice from inside called out in Eastern Satevic. From the tone, Scalas gathered that Rehenek was telling him to come in, so he opened the door and pulled himself inside.

Rehenek was strapped into a chair in front of a holo pickup. He looked over his shoulder as Scalas entered, and inclined his head. "Come in, Legate. I have one more thing to do, and then we can discuss our course of action." He turned back toward the holo pickup, which glowed red. It was recording.

Rehenek spoke at length in Eastern Satevic. Scalas found that he was able to pick up a few bits of it. Not enough to tell what exactly was being said, but it was unmistakably a rallying cry and a call to arms.

When Rehenek finished, he shut off the recorder and turned to face Scalas with a faintly amused look. "You're wondering why I'm recording speeches at a time like this."

Scalas folded his arms across his breastplate. "We're about to leave your conquered home system, possibly for quite some time to come," he said dryly. "I think I can figure it out."

Rehenek laughed humorlessly and leaned back in the chair, although there was no gravity to make it anything more than an affectation. "People of Valdek, my people," he quoted in Trade Cant, "this is General-Regent Amra Rehenek. By now the invaders have doubtless told you that I am dead or captured. As you can see, that is a lie. I am alive and at large, with a core of Valdekan spacers and commandos who will form the seed of the Free Valdekan resistance. I promise you now, and let the Universe snatch the breath from my lungs if I lie, *I shall return*. Look to the skies, and do not lose hope. Someday, I will appear at the head of a fleet and an army that will scour our beloved planet's surface clean of these inhuman invaders. And I promise you, once the last Sparatan functionary on our beloved soil is dead, then we shall move on Sparat. There, I will launch a memorial to my mother and father's memory, a memorial that will float for all eternity across the lifeless debris field that will be all I leave of that accursed system. Survive, my people. Resist. And do not lose hope."

As he reached the part about destroying the Sparat system, Rehenek's voice took on a new intensity, a new fire. He might have written that speech for effect, but the words expressed an anger and a hatred that the man clearly felt in every fiber of his being.

He blinked and cleared his throat, composing himself and putting back on the detached, vaguely amused look that seemed to be his mask. "That will be put on a signal drone," he said coolly. "We'll launch it just before we leave the system. It should be able to blanket the planet with the signal for at least a day before they can destroy it."

"Hopefully enough of your people still have the ability to receive it," Scalas said.

"Enough will." Rehenek unstrapped himself from the chair. "My father was already working on contingency plans within the first day of the invasion, once it became clear how outmatched we were. There are resistance cells scattered across the planet, and all of them will be listening for that message."

"Your father seems to have been a man of great wisdom," Scalas observed. He was still feeling Rehenek out. He suspected that everything had changed, and that his own future was now inextricably caught up in what had started with the fall of Valdek. The Caractacan Brotherhood would not stand still for such an atrocity. The lines had already been drawn.

Rehenek's gaze turned somewhere far away. "He was," he said quietly. "He was a great man in many ways. Though I think that without my mother, he never would have been the leader that he was." His expression hardened again, as he took a deep breath. "But they are dead, and we have much work to do."

"Indeed," Scalas agreed. "We can reach the Avar Sector Keep in less than three days."

Rehenek shook his head. "We will go there—I can think of no better place to begin building our alliance—but I have another destination in mind first." He looked at Scalas with a glint in his eye. "I am taking the *Pride of Valdek* to Sparat."

Scalas kept his expression carefully neutral. "A suicide run is not exactly in keeping with the message of hope and resistance you just recorded, General-Regent," he said evenly.

Rehenek's laugh was a dry bark. "Trust me, Legate, I have no intention of attacking Sparat. Not yet. But I want to see it. I want to see what my father's treacherous friend has wrought. The Sparat that my father described was a rich system, but a sparsely populated one." He nodded in the general direction of the outer hull, indicating the Valdek system beyond. "The force that invaded my homeworld was far too large to have been raised in the same system my father spoke of from the days of the Tyrus Cluster campaign. I want to *see* what we're up against. What we're *really* up against."

He straightened, holding himself still with one hand on the back of the chair, his feet just above the deck. "If you must return to your Sector Keep, I understand. I am sure we can transfer you and your men to your starships in a relatively short time."

But Scalas had been thinking about it, and shook his head. "No, I think you are right. And if I really am to be a Brother Legate in the war to come, then I agree. I want to see our enemy's system, too."

Rehenek smiled wolfishly. "Then let us go see if Captain Horvaset is ready to depart, before the Unity ships back there catch up with us."

———

"This is unbelievable," Horvaset breathed. "Has anyone ever seen the like?"

Scalas and Rehenek were floating behind her acceleration couch, watching the holo-tank as the *Pride of Valdek*'s computer slowly filled in the image of the Sparat system, collecting light and radiation from farther and farther out to increase the detail.

"I have heard of a few systems that attempted it, but none that succeeded," Scalas said. "Logistics and unity of purpose have always broken down."

The Sparat system had once been a typical frontier system—a relatively agrarian "first world" with industrial platforms built on orbiting space stations and asteroids. But sometime in the last few years, it had all been industrialized. Completely. The entire system seethed with comm chatter, and hundreds of thousands of ships moved between the planets and asteroids. Not a single asteroid seemed to have been missed; every one had either been converted into an installation of some sort, or mined into oblivion. Even the gas giants had extensive stations in orbit or in the upper atmospheres.

And while the details were still fuzzy and indistinct from so far out, it all appeared to be geared toward building war materiel.

"The sheer numbers..." Horvaset whispered.

"There must be something different about this cloning technology," Rehenek observed. "Some sort of acceleration. There is no other way they could reach these numbers so quickly. My father described a system with a few hundred million people, and that was only twenty-seven years ago. To reach these numbers in such a short time…"

There was a chirp from the console, and Horvaset listened for a moment, then tapped a key. A voice blasted from the speakers. It was strident, bombastic, and unintelligible. After a moment, Scalas recognized the same language he had heard reverberating across the battlefield, directing the Unity's clone soldiers.

"That's Palawese," Rehenek said. "One of the primary dialects in Sparat. I know a little of it…" He trailed off as he listened, but Horvaset was already ahead of him, and translated.

"*…never flag, never fail. The future lies upon all our shoulders. Only through complete dedication to the cause of our Visionary Leader can the future of unity, prosperity, and progress be made real. Only through his vision can we truly reach the next step in evolution. Work well. Work hard. You are building the future for all the galaxy.*"

The voice changed. Rehenek's head snapped up, and he had to catch himself on the back of Horvaset's acceleration couch to keep from spinning backward. Scalas recognized the voice as well. That was Geretesk Vakolo.

Again Horvaset translated.

"*The first step of the plan has been wildly successful. Valdek has been brought into the embrace of the Galactic Unity, and soon will be a shining example of what a partner in our great cause can accomplish. The first major system away from Sparat has joined us. The march has begun! Soon, perhaps even within a human lifetime, the entire galaxy will be one Unity! One government, one leader, one purpose!*"

"Turn it off," Rehenek said. "I've heard enough."

An alarm sounded, and Horvaset looked up at the wider display in the holo-tank. "We've been detected," she announced. "Drive flares at forty-three light-minutes out, coming our direction."

Considering how far they were from Sparat's star, that was worrying. The Unity must have had pickets everywhere across the system. "Get us away from here, Captain," Rehenek said, pushing off for an empty acceleration couch. "I've seen enough."

The *Herald of Justice* wasn't a dreadnaught, but the *Pride of Valdek* was currently in orbit over Kaletonan IV, so the Angelos-class starship was still the biggest vessel in sight as she descended on the Avar Sector Keep's landing pads atop a tower of golden-white fire. Her drives rumbled through the ground even before she'd touched down.

The *Herald* settled, and Scalas turned away from the window overlooking the spaceport. He was standing in what had been Kranjick's inner sanctum. The printout of the missive from the *Herald* was on the desk before him. He looked around at the room, which still held his mentor's spare personal effects, let out a faint sigh, squared his shoulders, and turned toward the door.

Costigan and Cobb were waiting for him in the hallway. Costigan clapped him on the shoulder, and he returned the bruising blow just to tell his friend that he was all right. Cobb met his eyes levelly, then shook his head a little.

"They should have stood by the Brother Legate's decision," Cobb said. He smiled tightly. "And I'm not saying that because it means I won't be a centurion yet. The Brother Legate knew what he was about."

"You *should* be a centurion, Cobb," Scalas said quietly as he started for the stairs at the end of the hall. All three men were in their white tunics, sidearms at their hips. Scalas had not yet put on the red tunic of the legate; he'd had too much work to do, and somehow it hadn't felt right. Now that word had arrived from Caerfon, it was probably just as well that he hadn't.

But his senior squad sergeant shook his head again with a chuckle. "Is that still bothering you?" He stopped and faced his centurion. "I'm a good sergeant, Erekan. I know it. But I'm not ambitious. We work well together. The Brotherhood isn't like some planetary military where advancement means political power later on. I couldn't care less. Besides, which one of us was always taking the lead during our novitiate? It wasn't me."

Costigan smiled faintly. "He's got you there, Erekan."

Cobb turned toward the stairs. "Come on," he said, the conversation apparently settled in his mind. "We best not keep the Brother Legate waiting."

Scalas felt a pang at the words, though not because he thought he should be wearing the red. No, it was because for the last ten years, that title had belonged to one man. Now Kranjick was gone, and they were on their way to meet an unknown quantity.

Side by side, the three men headed for the steps.

———

By the time the sleds reached the main gates and the courtyard, the ragged remnant of the Avar Sector Legio was drawn up in formation, all in whites and blacks, the centurions and squad sergeants wearing sidearms, the regular Brothers holding their well-worn powerguns at port arms. The *Blade of the Protector* had arrived while the other five centuries had been on Valdek, so the legio didn't look *quite* as understrength as it might have otherwise, but the gaps in the ranks were still noticeable.

The lead sled came to a stop, and a short man with short, iron-gray hair got out. He was nearly as wide as he was tall, his red tunic stretched tightly across his barrel chest, the sleeves looking like they might burst around his massive arms. Brother Legate Dravus Maruks hailed from the high-gravity world of Draeyeen, and he looked it.

Maruks marched crisply up to the steps, his sidearm held stiffly in front of him to return the salutes offered by the ranks as he passed between them. He halted before the five centurions with a stamp of his heels. It looked like the impact should have shaken the ground.

Scalas took a single step forward, stiffened to attention, and saluted. "The Avar Sector Legio is assembled, Brother Legate," he announced. "I hereby relinquish command."

Maruks returned the salute gravely. "Thank you, Acting Legate." His voice was deep and gravelly, though he spoke a clipped, fast-paced Latin. "I accept command." His eyes swept the assembled centurions, and then with a single nod, he turned on his heel and faced the rest of the legio.

"Brothers!" he bellowed, his voice echoing from the walls of the courtyard. "I have come at a difficult time. A time of crisis. I mourn Brother Legate Kranjick with all of you. He was my friend, and more than that, he was my Brother. A more formidable warrior, and a better friend and mentor, could not be found in all the galaxy. I mean that." Though the speech must have been rehearsed, Maruks's voice caught slightly as he spoke. He cleared his throat and continued. "There may well be dire days ahead of us, Brothers. There will not be time for us to get used to one another before we must once more plunge unto the breach. But we are Caractacan Brothers, and we will do our duty. To God, to the Brotherhood, and to our fellow man." He lifted a meaty hand to salute the assembled Brothers. "We have much to do, and I am not much of a man for speeches. *Legio! Dismissed!*"

He turned back around, the movement as precise as if he were still on parade. "Centurions, I would speak with each of you." He turned his eyes on Scalas. "You first, Centurion Scalas. We have a great deal to discuss."

———

Maruks strode into the legate's chambers without preamble, though Scalas paused at the threshold, unsure if his new commander would insist on protocol. Kranjick never had, but he didn't know Maruks.

Maruks turned and looked over his shoulder at him. "You need not ask permission to come in here, Centurion. My door is open to all of my centurions. Day or night. Understood?" He waved toward the window. "Come, join me. We need to talk." He turned back toward the window.

Scalas followed, and stepped forward to stand next to him. He stood well over a head taller than the Brother Legate, but Maruks's sheer presence seemed to nullify the difference in height.

Maruks turned from the window and studied him. The Brother Legate's eyes were a pale green, set in a mass of crow's-feet in a face as tanned by unknown suns as Scalas's was. "If I'd had my way, Scalas," he said, "you'd be standing here wearing the red. Not because I know you, but because I knew Kranjick. If he named you his successor, that's good enough for me.

"But there are enough of the New School on the Conclave that letting a legio become the inheritance of Michael Kranjick was out of the question." He looked like he felt like spitting on the floor. "Fortunately, the Brotherhood is not so far gone that one of those fops was picked to replace such an irreplaceable man. So they sent me. Tell me: do you resent this?"

It was a blunter question than Scalas had been expecting, and it staggered him a little. "No, sir," he said. When Maruks raised a graying eyebrow, he corrected himself. "Well, perhaps a little, sir. Against my better judgment. I shall speak to Father Corinus about it."

A faint smile quirked one corner of Maruks's mouth. "I hardly think it's that bad, Centurion. You've every right to resent it. If only for the sake of Brother Legate Kranjick's memory. But the Conclave has spoken, and we have our duty. The Code is clear."

"It is, Brother Legate," Scalas agreed. He paused, and when Maruks seemed to be waiting for him to say something more, he ventured, "Sir, why would the New School want to… separate this legio from Brother Legate Kranjick's influence, even after he's dead?"

Maruks's eyes went cold, though they weren't aimed at Scalas. "Because of what he represents in the Brotherhood, Centurion," he said quietly. "I know you served under him for ten years, but knowing him… somehow I doubt you ever knew *everything* about him."

"I never knew he had been on Pontakus IX," Scalas offered.

Maruks nodded. "One of the few to survive. And also one of the oldest still-serving men in the Brotherhood. No one really knew how old he was; he never seemed to get older after a certain point. And even after that horror show, he held as strongly to the Code as anyone in the Brotherhood."

Scalas thought he understood. "And his faithfulness to the Code, as a veteran of Pontakus IX, undermines the arguments of the 'pragmatists'. If a man who survived that, and who knows how many battles since, still held to the Code, what does that make them?"

Maruks snorted. "'Pragmatists' is an overly complimentary name for them. But yes, you're right. That's precisely why they want him blotted out. Forgotten." He smiled tightly, a feral expression that didn't reach his eyes. "I fear they will be thwarted if that is their intention."

"How did they even come to such power in the Brotherhood in the first place?" Scalas asked.

The Brother Legate sighed. "The Brotherhood, as noble as it is, is still a human institution, Centurion. After almost eight hundred years, some rot is bound to set in. Younger generations might not face the same challenges that the older ones did. What recent battles have we fought that compared to Pontakus IX, until Valdek?" He paused. "It is our fault, really. Those of us with the age and experience haven't sufficiently taught the Code and its purpose. We became complacent. And with the threat before us, I fear it will only get harder."

Scalas nodded. He had no doubt of that. "What has the Conclave decided regarding this so-called 'Galactic Unity,' sir?"

"Even the most contrary of the New School could not argue with the recordings you sent," Maruks said. "Is General-Regent Rehenek still on Kaletonan IV?"

"He is back aboard the *Pride of Valdek*, in orbit. I believe he's preparing to travel to Eta Sashenaei, to appeal to their duma for help."

Maruks turned and looked out the windows. "We'll send a contingent with him. Not you; not yet. I need you here, to help me get the legio ready to go back to war. I brought replacements aboard the *Herald*. We'll have to integrate them into the wounded centuries." He looked up at the deep blue sky above the limb of Kaletonan. "I fear that the first truly galactic war in history may be at hand, Centurion," he said gravely. "And somehow I doubt that any of us will live to see the end of it."

Scalas stood next to his new commander and said nothing. There was nothing to say. The Brother was right.

Everything had changed on Valdek. And no one, not even the Brotherhood, was ready for the onslaught to come.

We hope you enjoyed it as much as we enjoyed bringing it to you. We just wanted to take a moment to encourage you to review the book. Follow this link: The Fall of Valdek to be directed to the book's Amazon product page to leave your review.

Every review helps further the author's reach and, ultimately, helps them continue writing fantastic books for us all to enjoy.

———

You can join our non-spam mailing list by visiting www.subscribepage.com/AethonReadersGroup and never miss out on future releases. You'll also receive three full books completely Free as our thanks to you.

Facebook

Instagram

Twitter

Website

Want to discuss our books with other readers and even the authors? Join our Discord server today and be a part of the Aethon community.

GET FREEFALL NOW!

"Aliens, agents, and espionage abound in this Cold War-era alternate history adventure... A wild ride!"—Dennis E. Taylor, bestselling author of We Are Legion (We Are Bob)

GET THE LUNA MISSILE CRISIS NOW!

For all our Sci-Fi books, visit our website.

www.aethonbooks.com